The Dreamer

The Dreamer

by Alexa Jacobs

Published by
Torrid Books
An imprint of Whiskey Creek Press LLC
Torridbooks.com

Cover Artist: Kris Norris
Editor: Fern Valentine
Printed in the United States of America

Print ISBN: **978-1-68299-990-5**

Acknowledgement

When I became a writer, I expected the job to be one of solitude. I imagined myself spending hours, if not days at time tapping away at the keyboard, spending much of my social life with people who don't actually exist. Boy, was I wrong. There is a community here, and like a new child in the world, there have been so many kind and guiding hands along the way.

I would like to give thanks to Catherine Chant, whose guidance helped create the backbone of this book. To Becky Martinez, whose kind and wise words were my yellow brick road. I will be forever grateful to you both. To the glorious cast of characters at the MRW, who made me feel this spot at the table was always meant to be mine. To Eliza Knight and Emily Duvall, who are both far too humble to let me say a simple coffee meeting has changed the direction of my life.

Finally, I would like to thank my personal friends who've made room for a professional me. To Mike, who gave his time, thoughts and encouragement. Thank you, old friend. To Amanda, who gave my bookworm a little bit of street cred. Tilney will be forever yours.

Dedication

For the Hubs.
Thanks for believing in this little dreamer.

Your eyes will take you far beyond the horizon.
When you climb the highest of mountains on the darkest of nights,
you will see a candle that waits for you on the other side of one day's travel.
This is as far as the eye can see.

~ The Medicine Man.

Chapter 1

A box. The dreamer examined the small dark space. Her fingers pressed on the wall in front of her, testing to see if it would give way or open. Standing, there couldn't have been more than a foot of space in front or behind her, less than that above her. Despite the solid ground under her feet, it was clear she didn't know where she was. Neither did Claire.

"Hello?" Claire said, even though she knew she would not be heard.

The woman continued to examine the space around her, unaware Claire was even there. Although people dream up weird things all the time, this had never happened before. In all her years hopping through their minds, Claire Martin had never landed herself in a box.

Are we buried? she wondered.

Claire quieted her own thoughts, a skill that had taken years to hone. Concentrating now, the emotions of the dreamer began to weave their way into Claire's system. This person seemed sad, as if they already knew finding a way out of the box was not possible. Claire felt her dreamer's emotions physically; this sadness came in the form of a dense weight holding her in place. As if the powers that be were saying, *No matter what you do, you are never leaving here.* Her hand lifted and rubbed the chocolate brown wood paneling with curiosity.

Claire admired the woman's delicate hands with oval nails covered in sleek, smooth polish. A simple silver band on her left ring finger caught Claire's eye. It was flat, but an ornate pattern carved into the silver reminded Claire of cherry tree branches. As her hand turned in exploration, the ring caught a gleam of non-existent light, flashing brilliantly against the darkness. With it, Claire felt a flush of warmth. There was love here, buried somewhere within the dark, beyond this sadness.

She's looking for a way out; good! Claire cheered silently.

With the dreamer looking all around for a means of escape, Claire got a good view of the person's body. Not having control of what dreams she landed in, or from what point of view she saw the dreams, Claire didn't always get that chance. Her only shot of identifying who she was with was to catch a reflection in a mirrored surface. Even then, she was limited to what they dreamed themselves to be. Still, she did her best to have a gander if she found opportunity.

"You're a girl; good. I like girls. Or I like being a girl. Oh, never mind. You can't even hear me," Claire rambled on to her hostess.

The box offered no useful clues. No reflective surfaces to get a glimpse of the woman's face, and no door as of yet. No up, no down, no in, no out. It would be interesting to see where they went from here.

The gentle smell of lilacs filled the air. It wasn't unheard of for Claire to be able to smell something in a dream. Most of the time it was real life bleeding into the sleeper's world. She could not count the amount of times she had been thrown out of a dream as the smell of coffee or bacon wafted in. It also could be what Claire identified as an associated smell, something the dreamer was thinking of. Associated smells were rarer in her findings, but she had enough experience with it to be able to tell the difference. These were scents tied to memories.

The smell of this pie takes me to my childhood. I imagine the warm, smooth glaze slipping down my throat. Cinnamon tickles my nose and makes my mouth water just thinking about it. I remember warm pies cooling on my grandmother's kitchen counter and how their fresh out-of-the-oven aroma filled the air. This pie is the simple contentment of a six year old me, swinging my feet under my chair at her kitchen table on a crisp fall day.

The lilacs seemed to be a mixture of real and associated. The idea was there; it felt gentle and breezy on her skin. Yet, it was so constant Claire would bet money the dreamer might have the actual scent in the room. Perhaps the woman was a florist who smelled of lilacs because she worked with hundreds of them for a wedding. Perhaps there were so many, she dreamed she was trapped by them in this silly box.

Perhaps, Claire pondered.

There was no sound as the curious dreamer fisted her hand, knocking on the wooden wall. Claire hoped for both of them somebody would hear it. She had no desire for herself or the dreamer to be here any longer than they needed to be. Experience had her anticipating it wouldn't be long. This dream was in real time, not too slow and not too fast. The surroundings were in color, and the woman had a strong grasp of detail.

Calculating dream factors Claire knew to be true, she was a vivid dreamer who was safe in a bed across town.

She was a person who falls asleep moments after she hits the pillow, giving her lots of REM to dream in. Claire loved people like this, there was no work to be done. Fast dreams that come in a flash just before one wakes up made her dizzy. Black and white dreams made her queasy. Dreams that send people from one place to another without warning gave her a headache. Regular dreams where she could exist in real time, in one place, were as close to a vacation as Claire ever got to have.

A tickle began the slow climb from the base of her stomach into her lungs.

Panic. She's starting to panic, Claire thought. *This poor soul must be dreaming she's buried alive.*

The jittery feeling Claire associated with panic began replacing the weight of sadness. It rolled into her like the thunder of a storm hitting in the middle of the night.

"Annnnnnnnd this is a nightmare, ladies and gentlemen," Claire sarcastically informed her audience of no one.

A noise caught the dreamer's attention and she closed in, pressing her ear to the wall. Somebody was on the other side, finally, and they were talking. Mumbles. She could hear the mumbles. Claire couldn't make it out, but whoever it was, they were saying one word over and over again. She could hear a faint pounding sound in the distance.

Thud, thud, thud.

As much as the dreamer was leaning up against the wall, straining to hear the sound, so was Claire. With a tight fist, the dreamer pounded on the wall in front of her. She turned around and pounded on the wall behind her. Unlike what was happening on the other side, there was no sound as her hand hit the wall. As in all dreams, Claire couldn't feel the weight of her fist coming down. She could just imagine this girl's feeling of hitting the wall as hard as she could.

As the seconds ticked away, Claire became more jittery and antsy.

The dreamer more panicked. "Find me. Help me." The words floated out into the air. It would be the only words her dreamer spoke aloud.

Knowing the voice was one she'd never heard before, Claire still identified with it in her own weird way. As she stood within this woman's mind, within this woman's body, this was her own voice, if only for a minute.

Nothing changed. The voice on the other side remained muffled, still repeating itself over and over. The pounding stopped, and Claire tried to make out the words but they were too far away. The wall in front of the dreamer remained whole and she remained trapped. Just as Claire began to roll her eyes at the monotony she was trapped in, something finally changed. The air seemed weird now, which could mean any number of things. It was a dream, so general laws of physics never applied and often were tossed out the window. Especially if the dreamer happened to have a late night snack before they went to bed. For some, food before bed seemed to be the gateway drug into a psychedelic dream world.

The dreamer stopped trying to get attention from the other side of the unyielding wall. Her attention turned to her hands as she wiggled her fingers to examine a new element she would face. The air moved, becoming wavy with the motion of her fingers breaking it into a dance. It reminded Claire of the space just above a hot grill, the way heat would rise and make the air look wavy. Just as she didn't feel the weight of her hand hit the wall, she didn't feel this either but the idea came into her mind loud and clear.

Hot.

Claire's jitters and the dreamer's panic multiplied to the brink of insanity. Claire disliked nightmares, more than most. It was like being stuck in a horror movie and experiencing all the feelings of the characters within it. Not ideal. She knew the dreamer would wake, and be fine, but she felt it every bit as much as they did. She would wake up from this, still jittery and shaky. It was her nightmare just as much as it was theirs.

Claire shot up out of bed, gasping for air. Sweat was slick on her chest under her thin sleeveless black nightgown. Her long brown hair was clinging to her neck. She took a calming breath, pulled her knees up to her chest and wrapped her own shaking hands around them.

"What a doozy," her voice rang out in her quiet bedroom.

She hoped for the poor dreamer trapped in the box that she had been thrown from the dream because the woman woke up, safe in her bed somewhere across town. She lifted her left hand and studied it. Her subtle golden skin was such a contrast from the creamy white of the dreamer's delicate complexion. Her nails were short and unpolished, very different from the sweet peach polish of the mystery woman. Because she spent most of her days on the computer, her nails never got the chance to grow. Even if they did, she soon bit them short again, a bad habit. She traced her finger over the line where the pretty silver band rested on the dreamer's hand. Her marriage must be important to her, so few people dream of the smaller details such as jewelry. She identified it as part of who she was. Or perhaps, she's been married so long she can't even imagine herself without it. Claire always tried to pick up on the good that came from the dreams which were not her own. It was a way to make the best out of what she considered to be the worst situation in the world.

Tilney pulled himself from his own sleep, and trotted over to her. Managing to get his wobbly puppy legs working enough to hop up onto the bed, he began licking her face all over. He took it upon himself to assess the situation. He was her little sweet champion of the night. His dark charcoal gray fur moved like a shadow within darkness, but his bright blue eyes shined up at her with youthful innocence.

Wrapping her arms around his neck, she whispered, "I'm fine love, I'm fine."

She hugged him before she gave him a loving shove back off the bed. Claire knew there would be no sharing space with him in six months when the Great Dane was as big as or bigger than she was. Best not to start bad habits in his babyhood.

He circled around the room a bit, settling on the floor next to Claire in the queen sized bed. They were working on boundaries. His little puppy mind had a hard time remembering them all the time.

Claire had purchased him a gigantic dog bed to grow into and put it in the corner of her bedroom, hoping just being in the room would be enough. Most nights it was, but there were some nights even that would not do. Still, her consistency was beginning to pay off. He plopped down on the floor at her first command without having to be shoved back off the bed for a second, third, or fourth time. She thought about insisting he go back to his own bed, but she found he was just picking up on her emotions. On the bad nights, she found him right under her feet as soon as she woke up. On the good nights, he slept like a baby in his own bed, snoring like a little fool. How could she punish him for loving her? Better settled, she lay back down and closed her eyes to get back to sleep.

She could only pray for dreamless sleep on nights like this. Dreamers to her were like the infant to a new mother. They were unpredictable at best, offering her full rest one night and nothing but a bleary-eyed party the next. Before sleep took her to the next dream, her thoughts turned back to the girl in the box. She thought of the dreamer and the crushing defeat the box seemed to offer.

"Just a dream," she said to the dreamer who was out there…somewhere, "it was just a dream."

Chapter 2

"I do this for a living." Claire said as she looked around her home office filled with half open boxes. "You'd think I'd have a better plan."

Tilney stood at Claire's side, sniffing a few of the boxes in front of him. Rubbing the coarse, short hair on the top of his head, Claire calculated her plan of attack.

"How do you eat an elephant?" she asked him.

Tilney lifted his long floppy ears, turning his head unsure of what she was asking from him. She smiled at his attempt to be compliant of her commands.

"One bite at a time," she answered for him.

She grabbed a box to go through, plopped it down on the new, large, white desk sitting in front of the two china cabinets that were once the extent of her entire home office. Salvaged from a thrift shop, one her father had converted into a desk for her computer and the random little things she'd need for a desk. A cheery little pencil cup, tape, stapler, and a box for the random junk she always seemed to have, but never had a place for. He'd covered the inside panel of one door with cork so she could pin her current working projects to it. The other, he added a table that could be folded away like an ironing board when she wasn't using it. The second cabinet was far simpler. He hollowed out the space for a bookcase with a gray backing stenciled with white lattice behind the books. It housed reference books she used for her work as a virtual assistant. Topics ranged from *Powerpoint for Dummies* to Emily Post's *Etiquette-Manners for a New World* and nearly every subject between them. Having an entire room to dedicate to her business was a dream come true. She had no idea how to arrange the room or where to put the cabinets. In this new space they would take on new roles, be given a new identity. Claire thought of the poetic justice in that, having felt she herself had been hollowed out to her foundation and would be repurposed in this new space much like the cabinets. And like them, she was unsure of where she fit and what her purpose would be.

At least the desk is in place, she thought happily as it sat in the middle of the room. With the china cabinets up against the wall behind her, she would be able to see out to the park below on her right, and keep an eye on Tilney in the living room to her left. This was absolutely where she planned on keeping it. Maybe.

It was a month before she found her new home in the heart of Baltimore. She spent countless days looking over ads, going on walkthroughs, and coming up empty-handed. When she found the ad for the two-bedroom apartment located in a historic building that promised unique floor plans, she wasted no time contacting the management company for an appointment. She was delighted to find the advertisement did not embellish in its promises. The thin building sat across from a beautifully flourished park, sprinkled with flowerbeds and aging shade trees. The lobby greeted her with tall ceilings and marble tile floors. The apartment itself had gleaming hardwoods and windows that spanned the walls from floor to ceiling. She hoped that here she could recreate the oasis of peace she once had, and lost.

It only took a day to bring her belongings to the apartment, she had so few that would follow her into this new life. It had been a year since she'd walked out of the home she shared with her fiancé, leaving him with all the things she didn't want to or couldn't look at ever again. In the end, she took only what she showed up with on the day they moved in together: two cabinets from her father, and her books. All five hundred and twenty-three of them, according to her mother who had been tasked with packing them up.

Her belongings had sat in her parents' garage, as Claire returned to her childhood home to regroup and heal. They told her she could stay for as long as she liked but she insisted on remaining for only as long as she needed. The year there had been a blessing, both emotionally and financially, but it was time to move on. Moving into the city would get her closer to the places she needed to run her business. The park across the street, and the dog park within it, gave Tilney the perfect spot to get out and move around. It was a win-win in Claire's mind.

She kept telling herself these things, but she knew it wasn't about Tilney or the business. It was about peace. Growing up in the suburbs, she found herself in the minds of the same people repeatedly. A variety of emotional issues stemmed from this, and desperate to get away from them, she fled to the student housing her freshman year at George Washington

University. Suddenly, her regular dreamers were no longer who she was visiting. It was there she discovered the more people around her, the more dreams she had to play with. It was there she started checking people off as she came against them in the dream world, noting everything she could to figure out what connected them to her.

With the disappearance of her hometown dreamers and the appearance of all these new dreamers she concluded two things; she found herself with the people who were emotionally wrestling with things the most, and all of her dreamers were within a certain physical distance from where she lived. There was no way, of course to map out exactly how far her radius went with any kind of science. There just seemed to be a defined circle around her wherever she was. So far, she pegged it at about twenty to thirty miles. It was here she discovered being around as many people as possible was a good thing. The addition of thousands of dreamers around her soothed her nights, and she hoped she could recreate that peace in this new apartment in Baltimore.

As much of a pain in the ass as it was, she also discovered she wasn't whole without it. Determined to escape, she announced one weekend she would be going camping, alone. With the supplies she temporarily liberated from her father's camping gear, she spent two nights on the Appalachian Trail. Not a person to be had, as she specifically chose a terribly cold weekend. They were the worst two nights of her life. Hoping for dreamless sleep, she was disappointed to get a night of what seemed to be relentless determination for a dream. She could fall asleep, but she didn't dream as most people dream. Instead, she felt as if she was standing on a precipice, looking out into endless darkness, waiting for something that never came. Rest never came because she woke feeling as if she had been on watch all night long. She needed dreamers. If she was to sleep, she needed their dreams. The experiment had done little else besides break her spirit.

As in her college days, here she would exponentially increase the amount of minds to travel in and in turn she would decrease destruction potentially caused. It was challenging to maintain any sense of normal relationships with people around her. It would be for anyone who had the ability to see what people thought of in their most unguarded moments like Claire could. She saw herself as more of an intrusion, and her dreamer the unsuspecting victim. Reasonable balance was a goal, but the world was often an unreasonable place. She tried once and failed. She didn't want to admit it, but this move to the city was another move of disheartenment. Nothing would ever be normal for her, ever.

"I was buried alive last night, I think," Claire absently told the dog who was busy fishing out his favorite blue rope from a recently unpacked basket of dog toys.

Busily searching through the boxes, she picked out the things that were the most crucial to getting Team Metis up and running. Her computer, her client files, the working parts of her desk. Already questioning placement of everything, she stayed focused on the look she wanted. *I'm a totally together person, hire me!*

"I was a girl, I like it when that happens." she chatted casually with Tilney, "I have no idea what I looked like. I was just in a box. It was weird. There was somebody on the outside I think, yelling. I couldn't figure out what he was saying. I think it was a he, it sounded like a he. Maybe it was somebody yelling in real life, maybe it's what woke her up. An angry parent banging on the door of a sleeping teenager. A lover, desperate to see the woman who keeps him from his sleep."

She giggled at the ideas coming to mind. She made up all sorts of reasons why people dreamed what they did. A small thing she found entertaining, again to make the best of the cards that were dealt to her. As she thought about the woman in the box, her bottom lip stretched out in a frown. She did truly hope there was love and comfort waiting for the dreamer when she woke from the nightmare.

Tilney did not have anything to add to the conversation, which was kind of why Claire loved him. She knew the things she told him would remain safe and sound. He was the only being she ever confessed her deepest secret to. For as long as she could remember, her dreams were not her own. Instead, she found herself experiencing the dreams of the people around her. Her role would vary, depending on the dreamer. Sometimes she was the dreamer, sometimes she was who they dreamed of. They remained unaware of her presence, and saw only the person their minds imagined, protecting her identity from them. Though she was never Claire to them, she found something about her would trigger a small hum of recognition if she happened to run into the person in real life.

"Don't I know you?" they'd inquire.

"No, I've just got one of those faces," she'd lie.

Tilney did not judge her, nor turn her in. She feared she would find herself in a mental institution, with doctors telling her the reality she knows is not real. Or worse, she'd be locked away as a testing subject for the government. It was his little secret. Well, his and Gran's. Claire's grandmother, too, possessed the same ability. According to her, it was a trait passed down through the women in their family on her side. As far back as anyone could record, generations traveled through dreams like Claire did. Somewhere along the line, they realized and noted that it only affected the first-born girl to each generation. Being a son, Claire's father, Alan, never had it, so the trait was passed to Claire. Lucky Claire. Of course, Gran refused to tell her any trade secrets, insisting it was a little different for each woman and she would have to walk her own path.

"How are you going to forge your own path if you walk down mine?" she'd pester.

"Too much information too soon can be a bad thing. I made mistakes knowing too much too soon, Claire," she'd explain.

When Claire asked her grandmother if she had ever gone to a place where there were no people around, the old woman shook head with curiosity. "No, can't say that I have. Don't know that I'd ever want to run from what I am. What was it like?" she asked.

Ugh. She was no help at all sometimes.

All Claire knew for certain was that her ability had something to do with some mumbo jumbo that happened to her great-great something or another who was one of the Lakota people living in the United States before the Europeans took over. Over the years, she'd learn things on her own and go to her grandmother for confirmation or not. This whole forging her own path thing was rather annoying. She resigned to the fact that Gran was an otherwise amazing person, so she must have her reasons. She gathered her information, one dream at a time, and logged it down in a journal so she could look at it all in the waking world and try to make some sort of sense out of it. At least she had Tilney; who was he going to tell?

"I swear, Til, if my clients only knew how completely scatterbrained I can be sometimes, Team Metis would be shut down for sure and we'd be out on our backsides. Good thing you're an excellent secret keeper." She winked at the dog.

Claire located and unwrapped a six-foot-long, large rectangular glass panel. She was careful as she scooted it along on a blanket to get as close to the wall as she could before picking it up. It was heavy, but more than that, it was priceless.

"Let's set the mood, why don't we?"

She'd already measured out where the sign would sit perfectly centered on the wall. Nails already in place, she carefully hung her company logo above a long gray bookshelf. It would serve as a reminder that she had turned a small idea into a viable business. Her parents presented it to her as a surprise on her first official day in business. To them, it was something they could offer to help her grow. To her, it was a representation of how much they loved and supported her.

Tilney sat in the doorway of the office and let out a soft, low bark. Checking the time on her phone, seeing it was near two o'clock. "Wow, the day is really getting away from me. Okay, let's go," she said to him as they walked toward the front door.

When she opened the door to her apartment, Tilney ran out and started down the hall toward the elevator.

"Tilney, wait!" she yelled as she scrambled to find his leash she knew was by the door in a pile of piles that she had yet to get to.

"Whoa, whoa. Holy crap," a man walking down the hallway said, as he saw the large dog barreling toward him with its paws and legs slipping every which way on the slick tile floor. He stood still, not sure if the dog was friendly or not.

"Stop!" Claire yelled to the dog. She smiled apologetically to the man in the hall, "Sorry, he's friendly."

"No problem," the man said, relaxing his stance as Tilney slowed down when he got closer. The man tested the waters a bit and threw out his hands to see if he could get the dog's attention and grab his collar to hold him. Tilney stopped, and sniffed all around him, and allowed the man to get a hold of his collar.

"So sorry," Claire said again as she caught up to them and hooked the leash onto Tilney's collar. "He got out the door before I got his leash on."

* * * *

The man had not yet gotten a good look at his new neighbor. Catching the commotion of movement, he knew somebody was moving into the apartment below him. *She's beautiful,* he thought.

She was on the taller side—at his own six feet, he noted there was only a small height difference between them. Her slim legs were a mile long in her light blue running shorts and her white t-shirt lightly hugged her showing off fine, smooth curves. Straight, but soft looking dark brown hair was tucked up in a bun on her head. She had a pen, or was that three pens, stuck through it, holding it up. *It's three,* he smirked as he discreetly counted. *How oddly cute.* Her eyes caught his breath, they were pale green and so clear he felt as if he could see through them. Their seafoam shade reminded him of cool mint. He cleared his throat and returned his attention to the large puppy that was happily occupied checking out the new person smells.

"He's cute," the man said, as he bent down to indulge the dog, scratching behind his long floppy ear.

"He's all knees and puppy energy. I promised him a trip to check out the dog park."

"You must be my new neighbor. I'm Max, upstairs. Directly above you, I think." He smiled and offered his hand.

* * * *

Oh, his smile. Claire was doing just fine until he smiled at her. The floor beneath her feet started to go a little bit wobbly; she ordered herself to man-up. He was wearing black dress pants, and a white button down shirt. She imagined there was a tie at some point, but with his top button unbuttoned, she guessed it had been abandoned. She imagined it shoved in his pocket or in the front pouch of the messenger bag he was carrying. Eyeing up the faint line of muscle on his arms, she instantly imagined how tight his abs might be under that shirt.

Get it together, Claire, he's just a boy.

"Claire." She smiled back and shook his hand. "And this bucket of sunshine is Tilney."

"Hi, Tilney," Max greeted the dog. "How old is he?"

"Six months. He's going to get bigger and that apartment is going to get smaller, but we'll make it work."

"Actually, Danes are good apartment dogs. Low maintenance. I did some research before I got my own dog. Of course, none of it helped because I wound up with a Golden Retriever, who is not at all a good apartment dog. He's high maintenance, but he's the one that followed me home."

"I'm guessing he's super cute, which helps," Claire offered.

"That he is," Max agreed.

"How long have you been here?" Claire wondered. She might as well get some sort of hold on the people directly around her, which would help her sort them out when she found herself in their dreams. Though she tended to zero in on the people who dealt with their issues while they dreamed, she knew those people who were within arm's reach were often chosen. She would be seeing a lot of her neighbors.

"About a year and a half," he said.

"Nice. You and your family like it?" Claire asked, intentionally trying to see if she could get him to mention a wife. Perhaps hers was the dream she had hopped into the night before.

"It's just me and Pilot. The dog, that's my dog's name. But we do like it. This building is neat, it's got a lot of history." Max looked around at their surroundings.

It was one of the things that Claire liked most about this building over some of the other ones she had looked at. It had just eight apartments, which kept those within arm's reach to a minimum. With its historic quirkiness, every apartment was different from the next. Her apartment had floor to ceiling windows that looked down on the park across the street. Max's apartment had sliding doors with a wide balcony. The rent was surprisingly affordable, mostly because it wasn't in the best neighborhood. At the moment, that didn't bother Claire. She worked from home and really didn't go out at night. If she did, it was with Tilney, and even though he was a puppy, he was still rather intimidating to strangers. That would only increase as he grew. It was also one of the few places she could afford that second bedroom for an office, so she would make do.

The hallways of each floor were as wide and tall as the main lobby. There was a grand staircase in the middle that led every floor to the entrance. The whole setting had Claire imagining it to be a former hotel. She could all but see shadows of people walking down the halls in some golden era of greatness long forgotten.

"Yeah, Tilney likes the elevator." Claire smiled at her dog who was now sitting quietly next to her. "I think because it's an old one where you can see the floors going by. Speaking of which, it's solid, right?"

"It is. In all my time here, not so much as a squeak. The powers that be actually do a pretty good job on keeping up with things. This building has a lot of pride in its historic label."

"Good to know." Claire smiled. "I've got to get this one down to the park. It's nice to meet you."

"You too," Max said. "I'm sure I'll be seeing you around."

I'm sure you will be, Claire thought to herself as she and Tilney got into the elevator. She'd be seeing him soon enough, one way or the other.

Chapter 3

The mood was light, and innocent. Claire felt wonderful as she stretched out in the sunlight, swaying side to side in a colorful hammock. Sun rays filtered their way through the green leaves of the tree she was under. She could barely make out the leaves, they were all smashed together in a big green blob. A dreamer's idea of a tree with a million leaves. With a breeze that was only imaginary, Claire felt like she could fall asleep if she wasn't asleep already.

Somewhere in the background, there were bells. No, chimes. No...something else. She listened to the rhythmic tune, and settled on it being a music box. There must be a music box playing a sweet lullaby somewhere close to her dreamer in the real world, serving as the soundtrack to her dream. She watched a little girl running around a field of endless flowers.

What is she doing? Chasing something, Claire gathered.

The girl appeared to be around the age of five, with big curls of brown hair bouncing around her little shoulders. Running around the field, she smacked her hands together in the air. She had a sparkly white dress on, with a crown on her head. Running up to the woman's side, she slowly opened her hand revealing the treasures she held so dear. Happiness flooded Claire's senses. Happiness came as the opposite of sadness. Rather than the dense weight, Claire felt like she was weightless and could easily float away if she wanted to. The woman she played for the child sat up to examine the treasure with much enthusiasm. Lightning bugs, this girl was chasing lightning bugs in the middle of the damned day. Claire couldn't see the bugs, but she saw tiny yellow lights floating around inside the protective cocoon of the child's hands. They were the idea of lightning bugs. As the woman lay back down, Claire was able to see the puffy white clouds in an endless blue sky. Such details only come from the minds of children, she thought as she swayed back and forth, watching the child. She wondered who the child saw when she looked at Claire.

Claire loved kids' dreams; they were a breath of fresh air as rules of life never applied. Their only limitation was how far a child's imagination would take them. Claire had traveled to some lively and amusing places, thanks to the children around her. She wondered where this particular little girl would take her.

"Isn't it amazing?" The child's voice filled the air.

"Yes, it is," Claire said to the girl, though the girl would not hear her.

"Yes, it is," the woman's voice echoed Claire's thought.

A small vibration, a sort of static sound echoed in Claire's mind. She smiled at the sound she always heard when the person she played in the dream said the same thing she was thinking at the same time.

Jinx, she always thought.

As the woman lovingly swept the child's hair out of her face, Claire caught a reflection in the big silver bangle bracelet on her arm. Straight brown hair, shorter than her own. It swept her neckline and fell into sharp points on either side of her face. She was wearing brown sunglasses, and her skin was golden. Not like Claire's warm honey tone, but shimmering. Whomever this child saw when she looked at Claire, she thought of them with shimmering golden skin, how cute. As she examined the face in the reflective surface on the bracelet, she felt something wet on her hands. Neither the little girl, nor the woman lying in the hammock noticed. This could only mean one thing, something was happening in Claire's world and she would be leaving this girl to dream a sweet dream all on her own.

Gone too soon, kid. This might have been fun, Claire thought as the wet feeling on her hand got stronger and stronger. *Hope to see you around.*

Claire awoke and found she was no longer alone. Doggy breath filled the air. She groaned because it was way too early after her late night of unpacking and organizing. At least she'd slept solidly through the night, she thought, as she saw the sun pouring in from her bedroom window. She scrunched her face up at Tilney who was busy hopping around the bed to wake her up. He must have decided she'd slept enough of her Saturday away, it was time to get up and get the day started.

She leaned over and looked at her clock, not even eight o'clock. *Ugh,* she thought. It was a good thing though; she needed to make the most of the hours in this day. It was her last Saturday before her business opened back up. She'd thank herself come Monday, but right now, it was the dumbest thing in the world to be getting up and out of bed this early after a long night.

"Okay, okay, okay," Claire said to him as she pulled back the covers and hopped out of bed. The image of the little girl who chased lightning bugs in the middle of the day was fading in the back of her mind. Claire wouldn't forget the dream, but it wouldn't stick to her like a bad dream would.

Showered and dressed, she grabbed a leash from a basket on the table by the front door and hooked it to Tilney's collar. She would not open the door before she got it on him and have him running off down the hallway again. She had caught a break with her neighbor, who didn't seem to mind dogs, but that might not always be the case. Tilney was the size of a small horse. It was all Claire needed to deal with an irate neighbor as he learned the dos and don'ts of his little puppy world.

"A walk for you, and a jog for me, okay?" she asked him as they headed out the door.

Down the hall, they stepped onto the elevator, closing the two cage doors behind them. Tilney sat quietly as they went down two floors to the lobby, mesmerized by the passing layers of building material. He always headed toward the elevator rather than taking the steps. She wasn't sure he would even entertain the idea of skipping the elevator ride. She'd bet he would make the afternoon of it if she let him, riding up and down watching the different layers of each floor and people pass by.

As they exited the main floor, she passed a woman helping an elderly lady scoot along in her walker.

"Hello." The woman smiled sheepishly as she tried to hurry her companion out of the way.

"Good morning." Claire smiled. "No hurry, take your time."

"You must be the new girl," the old lady said in a slower, shaky tone.

"Claire," she offered her hand. "Can we help you?"

"Oh, my granddaughter insists on these walks. Says a body in motion stays in motion. Hippies."

Claire tried to hide the amusement on her face as the younger woman rolled her eyes.

"Janice." She shook Claire's hand. "Nice to meet you. This is my grandmother, Lucy Doogan."

"Hello, Mrs. Doogan."

"That dog yours?"

"He is." She sighed. "He's the one that insists on the walks. If you ask me, I'd rather nap and read."

"Smart girl." Mrs. Doogan winked and examined the dog that was trying his best to sit still for Claire but failing miserably in his puppy excitement. "He's cute, must have a pure heart."

"Why's that?" Claire asked puzzled.

"Well, right there on his fur, of course. It shines right through."

Claire looked down at the dog, noting the tear shaped pure white fur on the center of his chest. The only change in his otherwise completely gray coat. She always looked at the patch of white like a little emblem, perhaps his shield of bravery. A pure heart, she loved the idea more than any other she ever had.

"It does look like that, doesn't it?" Claire smiled.

"It's nice to meet you," Janice offered as she continued to walk with Mrs. Doogan slowly to her apartment door.

"You, too."

As they walked out of the building and across the road to the dog park, Claire enjoyed the warm air. These were the last moments of the Indian summer, and she planned on enjoying every one of them.

Halloween decorations were sneaking onto the shelves despite it being early September. Kids were already back to school, but not quite ready to let go of summer. She loved summer. People gave themselves permission to relax more, vacation more, de-stress more. Fall was good too, moods were usually lighter and happier.

Tilney sauntered by her side until they arrived at the dog park. Claire let him off his leash and he was free to explore the world around him. His excitement to get out and explore made her smile, he was such a goofball. But he loved her with all his little puppy heart, and being able to love him back kept her sane.

He was a gift from a client. A small farm Claire worked with was able to make the jump from small town road stand to full-fledged tourist stop. Claire helped them organize and structure their new business ventures. She showed them how to market to the right people, turning their dream into a reality. She had been inspired by her first visit out to their farm on a fall day a few years ago. The pond on the center of the property was glistening, lush full trees turning beautiful shades of red, orange, and brown. Fields of corn danced in the fall air, and their small orchard was full of shiny red apples. They were a picture perfect postcard and didn't even know it. She left her card with a few suggestions, and had a message on her voice mail before she got home.

She wondered if they ever considered welcoming in groups of people. Throw a few pumpkin seeds down, buy a tractor for hay rides. They didn't have to start big, sometimes even inviting schools for field trips were profitable enough on their own. She had even looked into some grants they could get to help them make that transition to an educational hotspot. They had horses, they could add a couple of ponies for the sake of pony rides. Mr. Springfield, the farm's owner, wanted to break into the business, but always felt it was too expensive. There was the old adage—*you had to spend money to make money*—but he was just trying to keep the farm open, and food on the table.

With Claire's research, help, and connections, they started off small with the school groups she arranged. Local elementary schools would bring the kids to the farm to go on hay rides and pick pumpkins. They opened a handful of weekends in the fall to families, and eventually started offering weekday visits. Particularly if the local schools were closed.

The money started pouring in, as Claire suspected. Mr. Springfield could not have been more thankful for Claire's help. He gave her a substantial bonus over their agreed contract that holiday. The road-side stand was now a full time, prosperous functioning Maryland tourist destination.

Tilney was one of eight pups born to one of the farm's dogs, and Springfield insisted she pick one to take home. What was she going to do with a Great Dane? As she looked over the puppies, not at all entertaining the idea of taking one, she saw his little face. He was just chilling on his little blanket. His attention had been captured by a grasshopper. He didn't chase it, he didn't squash it, and he didn't eat it. He studied it, and Claire was taken by his little observing spirit. In the dream world, Claire was the ultimate observer, sitting back and witnessing other people's dreams. In the words of Claire's favorite carrot-haired, fictional character, she believed this little puppy was a kindred spirit. She immediately knew what his name would be, Tilney. Henry Tilney was one of the many fictional men she had fallen in love with over the years. He was a stand-up guy, did all the right things for the girl, and adored books and dogs. It made her giggle at how quickly she knew what her dog's name would be, even though she never ever thought about getting a dog.

Half an hour. She could give him a half hour to play, get her jog in, and get back to work. Tomorrow, she'd sleep the day away. Monday, she'd ring in a new phase of business.

Just as she was about to call Tilney back to her, Claire noticed a little girl with big brown bouncy curls. She was wearing pink shorts and a white top with ribbons of rainbow colors weaved into it. She had seen the girl a few times already; *she and her family must live nearby*. She never really paid a whole lot of attention to the child, only enough to know she was the little girl she'd dreamed of the night before. Claire examined the woman who was pushing the girl on the swing set on the hill above the dog park. A petite woman, thin and fit. She was smiling, and talking to her.

"Ah, I was Mom," Claire whispered.

Her brown hair swept her neckline, and fell into the sharp points that framed her face. She even had the brown sunglasses on, she must wear those a lot. She was just about the exact image from the dream, and Claire noted she was rather tan. Beautifully golden, as the child saw her.

It always amazed her how children could dream in such vivid detail. How they could remember something so small, yet obviously important to them. This was how a child sees her mom, warm shimmering skin and pretty brown hair. Claire felt beautiful in the dream, this little girl thinks her mom is beautiful. On a rare whim, she called for her dog, put the leash back on him and walked up to the top of the hill where the little girl was swinging.

She walked Tinley around the perimeter of the playground, letting him explore a little bit. She could hear the girl ask her mom if she could come see the dog, as Claire hoped she would. After mom checked with Claire to see if Tilney was friendly, the girl hopped off the swing to come closer.

"Hi, there," she said in her sweet little voice.

"This is Tilney," Claire offered.

"Hi, Tilney." The little girl thought nothing of rubbing her hands over Tilney's fur.

Tilney thought nothing of letting her, he seemed to love children.

Perhaps because they were often the same size or smaller than him.

"That's a big dog," the child marveled.

"He's a Great Dane," the girl's mother informed her daughter.

"He's still a puppy, just six months old," Claire added.

"Really? He's so big for a baby." The little girl's eyes widened.

"Yup. And he likes to do fun puppy stuff." Claire smiled.

"Like what?"

Just the opening Claire was hoping for, delighted with herself for weaving fate.

"He loves to chase lightning bugs." Claire's voice whispered loudly, as if she wanted it to be an exciting top secret.

"Really?" The little girl's face lit up. "I love to catch lightning bugs, but sometimes they are hard to find."

"They are," Claire agreed. "But you know, right down there by the dog park are a lot of trees. If you come back here at night, I bet you would find a lot of them. Oh, and that field right over there, tons of them. I can see them every night from my apartment."

"Wow." The child's little mind was already off, thinking about how many she could catch.

"Do you know why they light up?" Claire asked the girl.

"No."

"It's called bio-lum-in-escence," Claire enunciated. "Some people say it's how they breathe. Others say they use the light to find each other in the dark."

"Mommy said it's so they can find their soulmates," the girl added.

"That's true, too," Claire smiled at the woman from the dream.

"Mommy, can we please come back tonight? Please? Please?" The girl turned and hugged her mother, tugging on her as she pleaded.

"I'm sure we can arrange that, but only if you eat all your dinner, okay?" Mom laid down the ground rules.

"Yay!" The little girl clapped.

"Let's go, Ava, gotta get you to school," Mom informed her.

"Okay," Ava smiled. "Bye, Tilney! Bye, Tilney's Mom!"

"Buh-bye, it was nice to meet you, Ava." Claire smiled at them as she watched them walk back toward wherever it was they came from. Ava was telling her mother something with such animation, she had to let go of her hand to do it. She skipped and twirled down the walking path as they made their way out of sight.

There was a lot of love there. Spending just a few minutes inside Ava's dream, Claire could feel how much Ava loved her mama. It filled her and made her ache all at the same time. She thought of her own mother, making a mental note to call her at the end of the evening.

"Bye, Tilney's mom," Claire repeated. "Cute."

The dreams that came were not always so sweet. For the most part, Claire did her best to keep her distance from dreamers. Today was different. Today it just was a tool of information for a sweet little girl making sense of the world. Claire imagined the glass mayonnaise jar that would be sitting on Ava's bedside table at some point loaded up with a family of lightning bugs.

"Time to go, bud," she said to Tilney who was circling, still examining the grass around her. "The real world awaits us."

* * * *

"We really need to get moving on this project if we're going to get the outside structure done before the weather turns."

"It'll all get done." Max smiled as he continued to drink his coffee and ignore his business partner's panicked attitude. "We got this. Relax a little."

"I don't know how you're so calm." Aidan shook his head as he looked over the blueprints of the five-bedroom house they were in the process of designing.

"Because I know we've got this. Everything's on track, everything's been approved." Max walked over and patted his partner on the back, looking over his shoulder to the plans. "I really don't think that you can relax at the idea that there is absolutely nothing to flip out about."

"That might be true," Aidan admitted. "I guess I just don't trust when things run this smooth. Always waiting for the other shoe to drop, you know?"

"Not this time, so enjoy it. Enjoy the Type A crazy lady who did ninety-nine percent of our jobs for us before she even hired us." Max tried to ease his business partner's mind.

"She did, didn't she?" Aidan laughed looking over the copious notes their client had given them.

"Yes. Did you notice her notes are color coordinated?" He smiled as he took a seat at his own desk across from Aidan's and rolled his chair back far enough to prop his feet up on the desk and take in a bit of light from the window behind him.

"I did. I don't know if it's cute or scary," Aidan said, as he continued to measure lines and jot down numbers on the plans and check them against said color coordinated notes.

"It's cute. At least, for now," Max decided.

"Have you given any thought to yours?" Aidan asked and took a break to look at his partner.

"My color coordinated notes? No, my thoughts are all random and in more than one place. I'm afraid I might be hopeless."

"To your house, Max. Have you given any thought to settling into a more permanent spot?"

His mood immediately shifted. Max took in a deep breath and straightened, pulling back up to his desk to look over the paper in front of him. Aidan didn't often pry, but the question did manage to come up every month or so. "No, it's not in my plans. I'm still fine where I am."

"You live in a one-bedroom apartment, which last I checked had nothing in it," Aidan said frankly.

"I have Pilot," Max corrected him.

"You do. That I will give you. We worry about you, I want to make sure that you're doing okay."

"I'm fine. Assure Charlotte that I am fine." Max winked.

Aidan had been his best friend for some time, but it was Charlotte who held his heart. She had been a sister to him for as long as he cared to remember. It was Max who'd introduced them a decade ago, and they'd been happily married for eight of those years. They watched Max's life get completely turned upside down overnight. They asked no questions when he showed up on their doorstep with little more than the clothes on his back. They said nothing, as he slept on their couch trying to figure out what to do next. Aidan kept the business steady when Max completely checked out and Charlotte balanced between letting him be hollow and empty, and forcing him to move back into the world. Good cop, bad cop. Good cop, better cop. He loved them both for it.

"Then come over for dinner one of these times she invites you, and she will leave me alone! You can tell her yourself," Aidan said, relaxing substantially. He really did want to make sure Max was doing okay after what happened, but he didn't know how to handle it. Charlotte on the other hand, had a whole master plan to get Max back on his feet. They both watched him barely scoot by for so long now. The Charlotte meter was ticking.

She was always pestering Aidan with questions when he got home from work. Is Max okay? How's he doing? Is he going to stay in that apartment? Did he buy any real furniture yet? When was he going to go on a date? Has he mentioned any women? Aidan knew a lot of the answers to the questions, at least on the surface, but Charlotte always followed it with deeper questions. It was probably why she wasn't asking Max herself, she was giving him time and space. Yet, she still wanted to know so she put her best man on the job. Aidan loved her for it, but she was a pain in the ass sometimes.

"I will, I promise. And I have stuff. My apartment is good. New lady moved into the building just last week," Max informed him. *Change the subject, please.*

"Oh, yeah?" Aidan asked and then thought of a Charlotte question. "What kind of lady?"

"I don't know." Max said cautiously. "A lady kind of lady? I saw her moving in. She has a Great Dane, he got away from her and I was in the right place at the right time."

That was a lie, but Max wasn't ready to talk about it. Claire was a knockout kind of lady, and got his attention from the moment he saw her on the other end of the hall. He had seen her a few times since, but always kept a polite distance. The idea of a new woman in his life was a little bit terrifying. He wasn't ready to admit to himself that maybe it was time, yet alone talk about it with Aidan. Or Charlotte, especially Charlotte. She'd make a *thing* of it. He wasn't ready for it, or anything for that matter to be a *thing*.

"Just her and the dog?" Another Charlotte question. Aidan stood a little taller with self-pride over his discreet interrogation. He couldn't wait to tell Charlotte, she would be pleased.

"I think so, I saw an older guy with her, but he seemed very Dad-like." Max thought of the older man he saw going in and out of Claire's apartment. It was none of his business, of course, who she kept her company with, but the man looked to be old enough to be her father.

"So she's young?" Aidan asked, now completely pleased with his investigative work and doing very little to hide the amused look on his face. He really needed to get out more, this was far more fun than it should be.

"I didn't ask her age." Max looked at his friend like he was a weirdo. "She seems to be normal. Our age, I guess. Maybe a little younger." *Maybe a different subject, please.*

"Hmm," Aidan added. He wouldn't really ponder any of this information, but he knew Charlotte would eat it up. Maybe it would even get him lucky as his mind started to wander, picturing the reactions of his wife at home and his possible rewards for a job well done.

"Focus on the house, dude." Max reached over and tapped to the paper on the desk. He loved Aidan with all his heart, but he was digging a little deep today. These were Charlotte questions. Claire was a new neighbor and nothing more. He didn't realize he would have the Spanish Inquisition on his hands, or he might not have mentioned it.

He shook his head in amusement. Charlotte questions indeed, and Aidan would no doubt run home and tell Charlotte all of this information. It's what he would have done once upon a time. Going home at the end of the day, and sharing the day's happenings with the woman he loved. That was all over now. The house was gone; the woman was gone.

"Yeah, yeah. The house," Aidan agreed as he returned his attention to the drawing and teasingly repeated his partner's words. "We got this; relax a little."

Chapter 4

"This is charming, sweetheart," Linda said as she looked around her daughter's finished apartment.

"Thanks, Mom." Claire smiled as she stood in the middle of her new living room.

Claire enjoyed the vintage yet sophisticated style the apartment gave with its dark hardwood floors and white walls. She softened the living room with a large striped area rug and a soft, gray sofa that welcomed visitors with its fun patterned pillows. The end tables were flea market finds which she had painted a warm cream color. An array of nostalgic travel photos in all shapes and sizes, both in color and in black and white hung behind her sofa.

"You've done a good job, but I still do not understand why you wanted to move into this tiny apartment. You could have stayed longer, we have the room. What are you and Tilney going to do here? He's not getting any smaller. How are you supposed to run your business out of this space? You should have stayed until you could buy a house." Linda shot questions and comments at her daughter at too rapid of a speed to interrupt.

"Not if I wanted to break out on my own, you know that. I can support myself here. A house will come in time."

"Claire, honestly, you could move back in with us."

"A thirty-year-old woman and her dog living with her parents? I am so grateful for the last year, but that was more about regrouping. I've done that. I need to do this," Claire quipped.

"Would you stop nagging her?" Claire's father Alan said as he came out of her office. "Did you see how she's got everything she needs for her virtual reality in there?"

Claire smiled and shook her head at her father's impossibly cute incomprehension of the computer world. He was learning though. He had presented his new smart phone when they arrived for their visit, showing Claire how amazing the navigation app he used to find her place was. Of course, he followed that with a request to program some things into the phone for dear ol' Dad, but it was a start.

"I know it, Alan," Linda insisted, "I just don't understand the move to the city. What about Tilney? He is not an apartment dog."

"I'm a grown woman, and Tilney is fine. Actually, as it so happens, Great Danes make great apartment dogs because they don't need a lot of running around. I heard it as a fact. And I don't need to worry about him in the business hours because they are quiet by nature. Do you ever hear him bark unless there is a problem?"

"Well, no," Linda admitted.

"We will be fine. And my business is expanding, so being in the city will help." *Say it enough times, Claire, and it will be true.*

"You run a virtual assistant company, which means you can be virtually anywhere!" Linda argued.

"You're right. But this virtual assistant has to get these things done in the very real world. Being able to get to my own resources helps. Not all the magic happens on site. You've seen how many times I had to pack it all up in the car and head into the city for the day," Clair informed her.

Waving her hands in dismissal, Linda sighed and sat down on the couch. "Yeah, yeah...stop talking perfectly logical nonsense at me."

"Don't know what I was thinking; sorry, Mom." Claire smiled and kissed her mother on the top of her head.

Claire loved her parents enormously, despite the fact that she had been within their minds more than she had any other people in the world. Thankfully, her parents' dreams never revealed deep dark secrets. There were some mornings when Claire woke up, and hugged them both. They loved her, they loved each other, and it was as simple as that. When she found out about the family connection, she wondered what sort of a dreamer her father was if he was not a dream traveler. He served as a vessel from his mother to his daughter. Turns out, he was just a regular Joe. Things he watched on TV bled into his dreams, work problems, and running around with family or friends. Her mom worried a bit, dreaming was how she worked out her stress. She often dreamed of losing Claire, or one of Claire's friends and be in a desperate panic to get back to them. Claire would wake with such jitters from Linda's panic to find her child, but she always thought of it as how much she must be loved. Linda would dream of her husband rarely. Instead, she dreamed that she was trying to do something for him to be a good wife, like throw a dinner party, but the food was all wrong. Sometimes her mother would dream of a boy that Claire didn't know. He was handsome, and young. She could see him clear as day, with his trimmed black hair and dark brown eyes, so her mother's memory of him was strong. She never asked her mother who the boy was, the feeling was always love that ached a little bit. Her mother had been young and in love, and this boy was at the center of all of that. Maybe one day Claire would ask about him, as he was clearly not her father, but it wasn't something that pressed on her. It was just the teenage version of her mother, in love with a boy. It was sweet.

It was funny, she thought as she watched her parents age and interact over the years, how they dreamed of themselves younger. She supposed it was true, you are only as old as you feel. Claire's dad felt like he was in his late twenties, and her mother often saw herself as a sixteen year old girl who actually looked a lot like Claire.

"This is good. You've been very lucky with this little business of yours. It's picking up, and being in the city is going to make it so much easier to run and do things like going to Kinko's and making copies you need," Alan announced.

"Making copies? Good lord Alan, what year did you wake up in this morning?" Linda asked.

"Shush, Mom. The man's got a point. Ya know…'cause I go to Kinko's and stuff." Claire teased her mom.

"Are they even still around?" Linda asked.

"Yes, actually, but not the point," Claire put up her hands. "There are several places that I utilize for making packets and booklets for presentations. This is going to enable me to just hop down the street rather than drive an hour out of my way."

"See! Kinko's and stuff." Alan smiled triumphantly and posed his fists on his hips while puffing out his chest.

"Perfectly logical nonsense," Linda said to Tilney, who had turned his full attention to laying all over Linda and licking her to death as she sat on the couch and made her giggle. "I don't think you get enough love and attention, clearly you have emotional baggage."

She gathered Tilney up, sort of sad he was already too big for her to snuggle him up on her lap the way she did just a few months ago. She was over the moon when Claire unexpectedly came home with a puppy one afternoon because, as she saw it, dogs were just one step away from a baby. Linda's biological grandma clock had begun ticking. She planned on Claire being married by now, and preparing for her first child. Now she was back at ground zero, and had been there for the last year.

Claire hit quite the hard reset button after her failed relationship with Christopher, the stupid lying, cheating bastard. Something Linda wasn't sure Claire was over, so she hesitated to push the matter. Still, as she snuggled up with Tilney, she took the new puppy as a sign that Claire's own clock was beginning to tick again.

"That must be it. Actually, I think it's about time for him to go o-u-t," Claire spelled out the last word so Tilney wouldn't get excited and jump all over her mother trying to get to the door.

"I can take him. You mentioned a dog p-a-r-k?" Alan eyed Tilney whose ears were starting to perk up at their conversation.

"Yeah. We can all go," Claire smiled, "Mom, you want to go?"

"No, no sweetheart. I'm going to make myself a cup of tea and then look through your things so I can judge your lifestyle choices a bit more. A mother's job is never done."

"Oh lord, Mom. Okay well, have fun with that. Don't mind the suitcase full of drugs at the top of the closet."

Alan loved that his two girls had the same sense of humor. They both had wicked sharp tongues that kept him on his toes and always laughing.

Claire walked to the door and grabbed Tilney's leash. He climbed off the couch padding to the door, releasing Linda to the freedom of her cup of tea and snooping agenda.

"This is a unique building," Alan said as they walked down to the elevator. "How old is it?"

"I know very little about it. I did some research but honestly Dad, the price was right, if you know what I mean. The neighbor guy upstairs says it's well maintained."

"Already meeting the neighbors, huh? Good for you, I worry about you getting lost in those books of yours too much. Good to know they are keeping it maintained, buildings like this are pretty, but have old wiring and old pipes. It could turn into a nightmare right quick," Alan said.

"Yeah. Sometimes I feel like it was a grand old hotel in some other former life. Presidents and dignitaries would walk the halls. Famous people." Claire smiled. "We like it."

"Kind of a sketchy neighborhood though; you sure you're going to be fine here alone?" Alan asked in his rare but serious Dad voice.

"Yes, Daddy." Claire kissed him on the cheek. "I work from home, I don't go out much after dark. If I do, chances of Killer here being with me are pretty high."

Alan laughed at the idea of this goofy dog being vicious. It was far from the truth.

"Another thing I looked up when I brought Tilney home. Great Danes are known for being gentle giants, but they are fiercely loyal to their owners and don't really care for men in general. I'd give it a month or two before he puts his invisible fence around me."

"Well, that's not a bad idea," Alan admitted. "Your mother worries, you know."

"I know she does." Claire winked at him as she linked her arm in his.

They walked out of the building and crossed the street to the park full of children. No doubt their parents were trying to squeeze the last out of the warmer Saturdays to play. The dog park was even a bit fuller than normal, at least Claire thought. She had only been there a week and a half, so there wasn't enough information to have any sort of expectation.

Once inside the gate, Tilney was released to his own freedom. He galloped through the grass, sniffing, smelling and exploring. A small yellow ball of fur darted across the grass, and barked all around him. She remembered the man upstairs mentioning he had a Golden Retriever puppy. Maybe this was the Pilot that Max had mentioned. She looked around and spotted Max leaning casually up against the fence on the other side of the dog park. His jet black hair was combed back, with a few stray pieces falling into his face. He was wearing casual brown boots, jeans, and a brown pullover sweater. With the leaves dancing all around him in their shades of autumn and a puppy at his feet, he looked like he was a clothing catalog cover come to life. His light brown eyes met hers; he smiled. He hesitated a bit, eyeing the man he had seen before with Claire. The attractive man with hints of gray in his brown hair that Max wanted to label Dad. Unsure of the father or older man thing, he figured there was only one way to find out. He straightened and walked over to the pair.

"Is this Pilot?" Claire asked.

"Indeed," Max smiled. "Hi."

"Hi." Claire smiled "Dad, this is my upstairs neighbor, Max."

"Alan." He put out his hand to shake Max's. "Nice to meet you."

Dad. Max let out the imaginary breath he wouldn't even admit he was holding.

"Likewise. I saw you when Claire was moving in. Are you moving more stuff in? I can help," Max offered.

"Oh, no, but thank you." Alan said. "I just brought the last of the little doodads today. Really, I just brought her mother so she could see everything. The girls went on a bit of a shopping spree for new stuff; she wanted to see it all together."

"Oh, your Mom's here, too? That's nice." Max turned his attention to Claire.

"Yeah, she's upstairs," Claire grinned, "going through my things so she can judge my lifestyle choices."

"Ah, yes. That's what mothers are best at." Max laughed.

"A mother's job is never done," Claire quoted. "Dad, Max has that little Golden Retriever over there. His name is Pilot. That's a great name by the way, actually one of my choices when I sat down to think about it for Tilney. Mr. Rochester's Dog was named Pilot."

"Who?" Max asked.

"Oh, one of her books. She's such a book worm," Alan teased, as he threw his arm over his daughter's shoulder and patted her like a child.

"Jane Eyre," Claire smiled, "Pilot was a dog in Jane Eyre."

"But you went with Tilney?" Max asked.

"A hunk in Jane Eyre," Alan said, making exaggerated googly eyes.

"Jane Austen, Dad." Claire giggled. "Mr. Tilney was a man in a Jane Austen book. Jane Austen is a real person, Jane Eyre is a character."

"Yeah, Jane Eyre was Brontë." Max smiled.

"You actually following all these Janes?" Alan asked, genuinely surprised.

"Impressive," Claire turned her attention to Max, "you've read Jane Eyre?"

"No, but I sat through the movie once. Crazy lady in the attic, right?" he winked at Alan. Didn't want to lose his man card right at first bat.

"Close enough," Claire confirmed, "crazy lady in the attic."

"Missed the dog in the movie, but that's fun. Pilot got his name because when I decided to get myself a dog, I really didn't know what kind I wanted. I was driving home one day and I saw a road sign at this house, advertising puppies for sale. I don't know what made me stop, but I did. All the puppies were all over the place, little bouncy fur balls. And he," Max pointed to Pilot, "took to following me around. I think he liked my shoe laces. So I picked him up and asked him if he wanted to be my co-pilot. That was that. He was Pilot, and he was mine."

"Ahh, he's the one that followed you home." She remembered him saying so from their first meeting. "Cute."

"That he was," he smiled, impressed she remembered the small detail from their first meeting.

"How long have you had him?" Claire asked.

"A month, long enough to know he's a goofball."

"But a cute one," she reminded him again.

"That he is."

"Well, it was nice to see you again Max." Claire said and then turned to her father. "I'm going to go check on Mom. I fear she may be reorganizing my files. Nobody wants that."

"That she might be," Alan admitted. "Go, I'll bring Tilney back up in a bit. Let the pup run and play with his friend a bit longer."

Claire kissed her dad on the cheek and returned to the apartment building across the street. On her way there, a little girl ran up to her and excitedly told her something. Max watched as the girl with big bouncy brown curls waved her hands all around telling Claire something of much importance. Claire smiled and gave the child a high five, and nodded politely to the little girl's mom before they continued on their way. As they passed the dog park, the little girl stopped for a second to say hello to Tilney and pet him, which Tilney did not mind letting her do.

"Alright Ava, let's get to the playground. We've only got an hour before Daddy gets home and we have to go. We'll see Tilney another day, I am sure." The woman smiled at the two men who were standing with

Tilney and Pilot.

Alan and Max continued to watch the dogs play. The contrast between their sizes was quite hilarious as Pilot was weaving in and out of Tilney's long legs. Max was a little worried Tilney would mistake Pilot for a small toy or a ball, but they seemed to be fine.

"Well, seems like Tilney's making friends everywhere," Alan noted.

"Guess so," Max said as he watched the little girl and her mother head up the hill after their run-in with Claire. "Claire seems very sweet. I've run into her a few times in the hallway."

"Oh, she is," Alan boasted. "She's a bit shy, I do worry about her in the city all by herself."

"It's a good building. Quiet. I've been here about a year and a half. The building is older so the apartments are bigger. We've only got eight units. Claire's got a very friendly nature, she'll fit right in with everyone. Does she have any friends here in the city?"

"I don't think so, though I admit I couldn't even say for sure. She went to a big college, but she was focused on her education there. We've always had to push her to be social. Yet, when she is, people treat her like they've known her for years and she speaks to them with such ease. She's the most extroverted introvert there ever was. Even strangers will chat with her. She's a good listener, in world full of talkers, I think."

Max played out the scene he'd just seen in his mind again. Claire bending down to be face to face with the little girl to have an excited conversation. Whatever the little girl was saying, it was important to her. Claire made it seem like it was important to Claire, too. "I could see that," he noted.

"I think this will be a good move for her. She needs people in her life. Real ones. She's become far too much of a bookworm over the last couple of years. But, she always was my little academic nut."

"Oh, yeah?" Max couldn't help but wonder what information he could get on his attractive new neighbor. He cursed himself a little bit for giving into the weakness.

"Straight As. Scholarship to college. She worked with some big corporate deals, but never settled into anything she loved."

"No?"

"Nope. She always liked the jobs, but maybe sometimes not the people. In any case, she's got a drive for perfection. She couldn't find the perfect job, so she created it."

Realizing he had no idea what she did for a living, Max asked, "What does she do?"

"She runs her own company. Right from home, too. Team Metis. She's a virtual assistant. I don't really know what all that means, but from what I see, she pretty much runs other people's businesses."

"Oh, yeah, virtual assistants." Max smiled. "That's a thing. She could be doing small things like managing appointments right on up to things like running other people's businesses for them. She could actually be doing exactly that."

"Do you have a virtual assistant?" Alan asked, kind of thankful Max knew what he was talking about. He didn't want to call his daughter a secretary. He had done that once, and caught holy hell for it. The girl had a degree from George Washington University; she was not a secretary. If anything, she was a CEO.

"No. I'm an architect, I design houses. I work with a partner who may or may not think we could use somebody like that, depending on the day."

"Nice. Well, if you do need one, you won't have to go too far." Alan smiled. "It was nice to meet you, Max. I'm going to get Tilney together and see what my girls are up to."

"Nice to meet you," Max shook his hand again.

Alan and Tilney stepped off the sidewalk to cross the street, but stopped short when a car came around the corner and didn't stop at the crosswalk. The car drove on, unaware that anyone was trying to cross.

"Hmm, don't even think she saw us, buddy."

Chapter 5

The middle. It felt like Claire was interrupting this dreamer in the middle of the dream. When the dream flooded her mind, she had no idea where she was or what she was looking at.

"Back up," she told her dreamer, "I need you to back up."

As if her voice could be heard, the dreamer complied by taking two steps backward down a set of stairs. Being able to focus more on the image in front of her, Claire realized it was a door. Her hand touched it and ran down the antique white wood to the gold brass handle and tried turning it. It didn't budge. She turned around on the step she was standing on and looked down the flight leading into an unfinished space that held random things.

We're in a basement, okay....

Inching down the steps, she noticed the contents of the room were blurry. People don't remember every detail of everything, so objects quite often appeared this way to her. Claire usually got the idea when the dreamer wasn't thinking too hard on the finer details. There were no windows, just gray cement walls. She noticed a light, mint-green bike up against the back wall. Unlike the other items, this was not blurry. Her dreamer knew this bike well, it was a cute beach cruiser bike with a tan seat and wicker basket. The dreamer skimmed the handle bars and found the silver bike bell. She pushed it, but no sound came. Claire didn't expect it to, this was not her dream after all.

As the dreamer glided her hand lovingly over the bike, Claire caught a break. She was able to see an obscure reflection in the shiny handlebar surface. She could see her own reflection, or her dreamer's as it was; a woman with long red hair.

The smell of lilac was in the air, a scent she had smelled just a few weeks before. The weird dream, with the girl in the box.

Ooh, am I back again? Claire pondered as the familiar soft scent permeated her senses.

Claire felt the fingers on her right hand wiggle. Her dreamer looked down at them, and just like before, the air was full of clear wavy lines.

Yup, same girl. It has to be.

Claire guessed being locked in a basement was an accommodations upgrade from the box. As she twirled her fingers and watched the waves of what she believed to be heat dance through the air. She felt the mood settle into her stomach. The only way Claire could ever describe it was having a metallic taste in her mouth. Fear. This woman was scared, and now she was scared, too.

She felt the need to leave this place, as quickly as she could. The dreamer took her back to the stairs and started up them two steps at a time. She grabbed the gold brass handle of the door, turning with all of her effort. Again, it did not move. She took her fist and pounded on the door.

"Hello?" The static echo filled the air as the dreamer spoke the words Claire was yelling in her mind. Seems like this time, Claire and the dreamer were on the same page.

She placed her ear on the door to find out if she could hear anything, and much like before she heard a muffled voice. One word, over and over. Just like before, she could not understand it.

What the hell is that? She would really like to know.

Claire felt the dreamer's panic as her body started its jittery hum. The dreamer turned back to the basement again and what she saw sent Claire's jitters off the charts. Fire. She wasn't sure when it started, but everything was engulfed. It was an angry fire, with the edges licking at the steps she was standing on.

"Help!" The dreamer's voice screamed into the air as she continued to pound on the door. "Help me!"

Shit, Claire thought. *What's with you?*

She could feel the desperation to get the door open, but she wasn't sure if it was the dreamer's or her own. The fight or flight feeling was deep within them both. The fire wasn't going to hurt her, she knew that. It looked hot, it looked hopeless, but for her at least, it was harmless. She would wake up with no burns to be had…eventually.

Until then, she'd go through the motions. Her heart was pounding, and sweat poured off of her neck and back. She knew this was her own body reacting. In reality, she was laying in her bed, her heart pounding and sweating through her nightgown.

Claire wondered what in the world was going on in this girl's life to have two dreams now of being trapped. And now the heat had become fire.

As the dreamer pounded, Claire saw the silver wedding band on her finger, once again full of detail.

Different place, same problem? Maybe.

Claire was a little surprised to find herself with the same dreamer again so quickly, but if the girl was stress dreaming, she'd be more of a target.

The sound in the air was screaming, she could hear the screaming. Broken sounds, scattered sounds. Somebody was screaming. Was it her? The static swam through the air as the mixture of the dreamer's voice and her own thoughts mixed together.

The dreamer sat on the steps, and Claire felt the air get heavy. It was hard for her to breathe, maybe even hard for the dreamer to breathe if she was imagining the air so thick. She focused her attention on the bike she somehow saw through the flames. For a moment, it sat pristine. It was as if seeing it calmed her. Claire and the dreamer watched as the flames crawled up over the tire wheels, and caught the wicker basket into a ball of fire.

"You have got to get out of here," she whispered to the dreamer.

"I'm alone. I will die alone." The dreamer's words came out of her mouth.

Chills ran through Claire.

Rather than stand up and trying to fight, she remained sitting. She curled up into a ball, and covered her head with her hands.

Claire switched focus to try to find the dreamer's emotions. Deep within, as if the dreamer wanted it shoved as far back as it could. She felt the subtle pangs of heartbreak. Maybe she was heartbroken but was trying not to be. This was all too much; it was consuming her.

Claire had come close to dying many times in dreams, as one does. Falling from something and waking up at the last minute. This was different. Death was looming, it was in the air with the heat that she could not feel. With the fire that she could not stop. This girl was going to die in her own dream. As she closed her eyes and let the flames come, the heartbreak finally broke free and consumed her.

Claire ached for her.

* * * *

"Knock knock," Max said as he quizzically walked past Claire's open front door and stepped inside the apartment.

"Hello?" Claire's voice floated out of the kitchen as Tilney came down the hallway to greet their guest.

"I'm sorry, I knocked. There was a package," he said, as he tried to locate where her voice was coming from.

"Kitchen," she yelled over the music streaming from her docking station before turning it down. "Hi. Sorry, I didn't hear you knock."

"Hi. I didn't knock. Did you know your door was open?"

"Unlocked?" she asked.

"No, open. As in wide open," he informed her.

Claire turned and gave the innocent looking pup a smug look. Already familiar with her expression, he lowered his head with a guilty whimper.

"Somebody has learned how to open doors," she said. "we've already had a chat. I guess I'm going to have to be better about remembering to chain the lock. Sorry."

He had never been in this apartment, as he didn't know the people who lived there before Claire. It was a slightly different layout than his. Same long hallway, with bathroom and washer dryer closet on the way to the main space. The kitchen and living room the long hall led to were smaller than his, but she did have that second bedroom.

"You had a package at the door." He shook the box in his hand. "Guess the delivery man didn't want to be the unsuspecting victim walking into the apartment with the door wide open."

"Like you just did?" she needled.

"It's true, if this was a horror movie, I would have been the first dead. My whole life tossed away because I was the dumbass that went in there."

Her face brightened with a smile and laughter, a nice soft contrast to the business tone the crisp white blouse and sleek black skirt she was wearing gave off.

"Thank you, it's very thoughtful of you to put your life on the line for new business cards." She paused from chopping herbs. Looking at her wet hands, she was going to make a mess if she touched the box. "Uh, would you mind taking that into my office there and setting it on the desk?"

"Sure." He smiled and walked across her living room.

Impressed with the office, he looked around as he put the box on her desk. It was feminine, but professional. Sleek and slim-line, as he imagined it would be. She had brochures sitting out on a low bookshelf with rows of books on marketing, sales and team leadership. He liked the way she re-purposed the china cabinets behind her desk. More books, more clinical in nature and baskets with supplies sitting organized on the shelves. A ton of books neatly lined by subject in the other cabinet. It gave the professional space some style. Along the long wall, she had two more bookcases, with what looked to be several classics. They ranged from Alice in Wonderland to the latest edition of Harry Potter. He smiled at the silver framed black and white photo of a smiling Claire and her parents. He had yet to see her mother at the apartment building, but her father he recognized. Their cheesy grins on a hot summer day at the Grand Canyon made him happy, but also made him ache in a place he'd tucked away long ago.

As he turned to leave, in front of her desk on the wall he noticed her company sign.

"Nice office," he said as he walked back into the kitchen. "That's where all your virtual magic happens, huh?"

"It is," she said, as she slid the finely chopped greens into a bowl of yellow liquid.

"What are you making?"

"Herbs. This is the last of my little window garden I had a while back. Chop them up, put them in butter, put that into ice cube trays and freeze. You now have a yummy little base for pans when you cook." Claire showed him as she finished up and stuck the tray into the freezer.

"Huh, learn something new every day."

She was very cute as she worked her way around the kitchen with a yellow apron over her work clothes. The skirt hugged her long legs and curved up and over her in a flattering way. The hair Max had become accustomed to seeing up in some sort of a bun, was down and had a slight curl to the ends. Her green eyes shimmered with soft makeup. He only had run into causal Claire in the halls and at the park, this must be work Claire.

"So, what does Team Metis mean?"

"Well, Metis comes from Greek Mythology. She was one of the Titans, first wife of Zeus. She was the Goddess of wisdom, prudence and deep thought. With my business being what it is, I thought she'd make a fine symbol."

Max's eyebrows went up and he cleared his throat and focused his attention back on her rather than her rear end in that skirt.

"Huh, learn something new every day." He focused as he repeated himself. "I'll let you get back to work."

"You're fine for a while if you want to sit. I've got a meeting in a bit, but really I'm just biding my time. I needed a break from looking at scheduling, so I wandered out here for a few minutes. Stay. My brain is fuzzy today," she admitted.

Over the few weeks that Claire had been in the building, she and Max had crossed paths several times. Between the dogs and the fact that they both worked in and out of the house at all sorts of odd hours, they found themselves running into each other. Max found Claire to be a sweet girl, but her father was right when he said she was on the shy side. He had not seen any indicators of a single girl life. No late nights, no parties, no girlfriends in and out. If he didn't cross paths with her often enough to know she was smart, funny, and friendly he would have passed her off for a hermit. Or a crazy cat lady.

She became the perfect neighbor, and was beginning to become the perfect friend. She never pried into his life too much. He actually liked that about her. He really wasn't in a place where he wanted people asking too many questions. He wasn't ready for the questions about his future, and he sure as hell didn't want to answer any about his past. Claire was happy to chat about whatever with him, in the here and now. They could talk about anything, and get completely lost in the moment. With every day that passed, he found himself making more and more excuses to run into her in the hallway.

Claire enjoyed his casual way, his ease. He never pushed for information, he never dug too deep. The biggest things she currently appreciated about him was that he had been within a small distance from her, but she had yet to dream of him. She had no idea why and did not care. Maybe he was just one of those sorts who rarely dreamed, like her dad. Maybe his life was so chill, he didn't pop up on her Stress-o-meter. It allowed her to relax around him more and more. She remained cautious, knowing that in the end the other shoe always dropped. For now, it was a wonderful surprise. She was actually making a friend.

"Rough night?" Max asked.

"Didn't sleep well. Nightmares," Claire said honestly.

"Sorry," Max offered. "That's the worst."

"Want some coffee? I made a fresh pot, it will be the only way I get through this day," Claire offered as she poured the fresh black drink into a mug, adding a good bit of cream and a way too unhealthy heaping spoonful of sugar.

"Nah, I'm good, thanks," he said. "I'm going to let myself be good and tired, just go to bed early tonight."

"Now that is a good plan."

"Yeah, I fear I couldn't handle that regiment of sugar and caffeine you've got going on there," he teased.

"The sugar rush brings me down from the caffeine high. It's a highly calculated formula," she smirked daringly as she took a sip. "Come, sit for a minute in the living room. Can I ask you a question?"

Trouble. This only leads to trouble, he reminded himself.

"Sure."

"I haven't met everyone in the building yet," Claire said thinking about the mystery redhead from her dream who stuck in the back of her mind all day. "Do you know everybody?"

"Pretty much," His eyebrows came together as he ordered the residents of the building in his head. "You want the lowdown on everyone?"

"I think I do," Claire confirmed.

"Okay, well, on the first floor we have Mrs. Doogan," he began.

"I've seen her at her door sometimes. How old is she?"

"Old. I have no idea, she's got to be in her nineties," Max said.

"Wow. Wonder how long she's been here." Claire couldn't imagine a person in their nineties still living all on their own. Her own grandparents had moved to an assisted living retirement community over a decade ago. She saw how even though they were active, they still needed a lot of help.

"I think she has been here since the building was actually built." he smiled. "She cracks me up because when you talk to her, you can see that she still feels like she's a young single girl in the city."

"I've noticed that. Was she a young single girl in the city?" Claire was curious.

"I think so, in nineteen-forty something. I can't even imagine. I think she was married; her husband passed a few years back. I've heard he was a Navy Vet. Before my time here, but I've seen her dressed up on the war hero days. She's still a proud wife."

Claire's mind drifted to a dream she recently had. She was a skinny little thing in a light blue tea-length dress, and she danced with a young sailor who was so handsome it was a shame he was only a dream. The music was blaring; it nearly gave her a headache. Big band swing music, and there was smoke hanging in the air. Fun and nothing but trouble were the feelings she got. Claire felt like a silly little fool when she woke up, like she had been drinking and partying all night long right along with her dreamer. It was awesome. Claire thought about the dream logistics, and wondered if the old woman saw herself in dreams. It was the only way Claire ever got to take the role of the dreamer if there were other people in the dreams, too. A complicated web of information with circles and arrows flashed through Claire's mind—a page in her dream journal when she was trying to figure out why she was sometimes the dreamer and sometimes just another person in the dream. Just thinking about how long it took her to figure that out made her cross-eyed. She still wasn't sure she had it right.

"It's amazing how young you can feel on the inside." She smiled, hoping that it was in fact Mrs. Doogan's dream. "I'm surprised she's living on her own."

"She's not. The unit next to her is her granddaughter. That way she has her freedom, but not really."

"Oh, I didn't realize she lives here, too. That's a fun arrangement then. Um…Janice, right?" Claire asked.

"Right." Max confirmed "She's nice. From what I've been told, the family pays her to take care of Mrs. Doogan. I think Mrs. Doogan has two kids, but they're both really old because she's really old. So now it's fallen on the grandkids to take care of everyone and Janice picked her. Janice is near retirement so she was looking to work less, and they were looking to spend less on elderly care. I'm sure it's not fun most days, but they actually seem to have a good little routine going on there. Mrs. Doogan's a real firecracker; I can only imagine what she was like in her younger days."

"I'm sure." Claire masked her amusement. She knew exactly what kind of firecracker Mrs. Doogan was, or at least the kind of fire cracker that she saw herself as, if those were her dreams Claire was dancing in.

"She pinched my butt once," Max confessed.

"Really?" Claire worked hard not to snort her coffee.

"Yup. She and Janice just giggled themselves silly as I hurried to get away from them."

"At least she has that." Claire smiled. "Fun for both of them."

"As long as it's not at my expense, thank-you-very-much. Let's see, who's next? Oh, then we have you. You've met Harvey and Rida down the hall?"

"Yup," she confirmed. "Nice folks."

"Me, upstairs. Jack down the hall from me."

"Oh, yes, flirty Jack," Claire said with a smile that made her stomach hurt. She had popped in on the mind of Jack just once and it was a wild ride. The man liked women, and he liked them naked and bouncy.

"Ah, you've met Jack." His head bobbed in agreement with her assessment.

"That I have." Claire scrunched up her face in minimal distaste. She'd run into him twice in the laundry room and though he was pleasant to her, he kept staring at her. As if he knew she was with him in the dream, and it made her feel violated. It wasn't his fault of course, and she tried to remember that, but he did have a flirty nature and was very inquisitive with his conversation. He was exactly the sort of person she did her best to stay away from. People like that tended to grab onto that little small connection they have with her and create nothing but chaos.

"He will tell you our floor is the bachelor floor, where the party is happening," Max said. "Feel free to ignore him. I swear he is actually harmless and a nice guy once you get around the whole single-and-ready-to-mingle thing."

"Noted." Claire's eyebrow lifted as she tried to sound objectionable. Hopefully, he was right about Jack being harmless.

"On the second floor there's a younger couple. I don't know them too well; they keep to themselves. Or maybe they're always gone. Brian and Brittany. I want to say they travel a lot. And then you've got Taylor who you know." Max said referring to the building's superintendent.

"Yeah, I do know Taylor. He's a nice guy. I don't know if I've seen Brian and Brittany though. What do they look like?" Claire asked, sitting on the edge of her mental seat, hoping that Brittany was the mystery redhead from her two dreams.

"I think they're in their late twenties. Brian's got brown hair and glasses, Brittany has long wavy brown hair. You'll know them when you see them, they've got that just married way about them that kind of makes you want to puke a little."

"Oh," she said, masking her disappointment that Brittany was a girl in her twenties with long wavy brown hair. Guess the mystery woman lived somewhere within Claire's imaginary bubble, which didn't do Claire any good.

She and Max chatted for a few more minutes about how things were going with her business and then he let her get back to it. She cleaned up the kitchen from lunch, and began checking emails, but her mind wasn't focused on her work. She pushed her chair back from the desk and stood at the large bay window.

Looking out over the park, seeing the lives of people happening, she found herself looking for someone specific. She scanned over the tiny people, focusing in on the women, looking for her fair-skinned ginger mystery. It was funny to her how she moved to the city to get away from the dreamers in the real world, yet here she was looking for one for the second time inside a month. First the little girl at the park, and now the mystery woman.

"Who are you?" she asked her mystery dreamer. "Where are you? What is happening to you?"

Chapter 6

Music was pouring out of the speakers on the computer Claire had been typing away on all morning long. The transition made from the suburbs to the city had been seamless for the most part, as she hoped it would be. It was important to Claire that none of her clients felt her absence. Five years into building this dream, she was finally on her own. Business was good, and she wanted to keep it that way.

She'd had various jobs through her teen years, but she never stayed anywhere long. There was always some dream she found herself in, and it would inevitably change the way she looked at those around her. Claire never knew what to do, or if she should say anything when it came to learning information about a person through their dreams. If she found something off, she couldn't prove it. There was no real world evidence of any wrong acts, yet she knew they happened. Or, more accurately, she knew people were thinking about them happening. She couldn't start shaking her finger at somebody, only to go silent when they ask, how do you know? What was she going to do, really? Accuse people of unconscious crimes that may or may not have been committed yet? Shouting that dreaming about their teeth falling out is a symbol for the fear of losing something or a change that they didn't want? These were for movie plotlines, not for real life.

She found herself retreating more and more from the real world. She got her degree in business, and took shelter with a temporary agency. At least then, she was never anywhere too long. It seemed like the perfect plan, except when her drive had her going to big wigs and making suggestions on how to improve work flow. Or when she was able to introduce a way of doing things they had never thought of. She never stayed anywhere long enough to see her plans out. A few of the corporations offered her full time positions after pulling her resume and seeing that she was well educated in business and marketing, surprised she took such a small role in her career. She always thanked them for the compliments, telling them she was trying her hand at a few things before she settled into one. The best boss for the job is the one who knows what it's like in the mailroom, she'd note. It was a truth that Claire believed in, it just wasn't her truth. Her truth was an office that was a lot like high school—too much drama and not enough space.

As it so happened, one of her co-workers at the temp agency suggested perhaps she would be successful if she branched off on her own. Jane knew how requested Claire was, and saw how hard she worked.

One afternoon in an email chat Jane told her she would bet money Claire could do her job in her sleep. *Funny choice of words there, Jane.* Still, it got Claire thinking. She might not be able to do her job in her sleep, but she might be able to do it from home. As it was, ninety-nine percent of her work was done on a computer, why did she actually have to be in an office, around people she didn't want to be around? Just like that, Team Metis was born.

Her fiancé didn't understand why she wasn't going after more prestigious positions, but supported her because it meant she'd have more time to be a doting wife when he settled into his high demand career. She kept costs as low as she could, creating an entire business out of two old china cabinets that sat in their off-campus living room. She took on one project at a time, and with each project she lowered her availability to the temp agency.

As technology grew, working from home became easier and easier. She could log onto anyone's server and work on her computer as if she was sitting right there in the office. Her contact list grew, and the services she offered grew with it. With this last client signed up, Claire was working a full work week and no longer had to depend on the temp agency. Couldn't ask for anything more than that. Team Metis was one-hundred percent booked.

In need of a break from the current data entry she had been doing, she backed up from the computer and closed her eyes. An image of the woman with red hair came to her mind, her all- too-familiar friend now. Remaining faceless, she floated silently in Claire's imagination, having yet to provide a reflective surface to reveal what she looked like in any sort of finer detail. She was only able to see her body clearly, and the long red hair. This woman must have had a strong sense of self because most people didn't dream of themselves so vividly. Usually they were a little fuzzy. Her finger traced where the silver band laid. It had been more than a week since she had dreamed of the faceless mystery, and it was a very strong possibility that Claire would never see her again. She was doing her best to shake it all off, and move on. It was two dreams, and they were terrible, but it was by no means real, nor was it the end of the world. Whoever this woman was, she was living her life, and didn't owe Claire a damn thing. In fact, she didn't even know Claire existed, yet here Claire sat, still thinking about her.

"I have got to get a life," she admitted to herself as she spun herself around in her office chair watching the blur of colors go around.

A small chime from her phone rang out; she stopped the chair and stretched herself out, grabbing it off her desk to read the incoming text: *Not going to make it home any time soon, any chance you are around to let Pilot out?*

Claire smiled, and tapped back a response. *I may not want to return him.*

She laughed at Max's immediate reply: *Dude woke me up at 3:30 this morning, really, he's all yours. There is a spare key to my apartment in the laundry room, attached to the back of the middle dryer of the row.*

"Really?" her face scrunched up in confusion and surprise as she said the word she typed out loud.

My schedule sometimes does this. Never wanted to be stuck, don't know who's around, so I put a key there in case of emergency because who's going to look there?

"This is true," again she said as she typed.

I can take him and T for a playdate, they will love it.

Thank you, I owe you one! I plan to be home about nine tonight. Maybe earlier, but nine for sure.

Claire set the phone down, wheeled her chair back up to her desk and finished up the data entry she had been doing with a renewed reason to get her workday done. She flew through the remainder of the data, singing along to her selected all nineties station, allowing herself a little bit of a smile at the idea of a playdate with Max. A playdate for the dogs, she meant. It was just him asking her to watch his dog, he wouldn't even be there. Yet, she still liked the idea of being in his world, and having a reason to see him at some point.

Friendship continued to feel so easy with him, and natural. To date, her mind remained clear of him. No dreams, and that was her ticket to freedom. She knew little to nothing about him, and loved it. There was a chance it would all end tomorrow if she dreamed he had a slight shoe fetish like flirty Jack did, but with every passing day, she grew more confident Max was going to somehow magically slip through the cracks.

Again, she compared Max to her father. The man slept like the dead, and it was amazing. She smiled at the idea of Max sleeping like the dead, and she even was so bold as to allow herself to think about what he might wear to bed. She didn't know why, but he struck her as the type to wear soft lounge pants and no shirt. It wasn't a bad image. Ok, fine. Maybe she had a small crush on him. It was harmless, as she had no intention of acting on it.

She opened up a new tab, staring at Google and wondering where to start with the most pressing matter of her day.

Red head. Baltimore, Maryland.

She found a couple of links to a design company and one link to an escort company.

"Please lady, don't be a hooker," she said as she hovered over the link to the escort service before returning to Google.

Ginger haired people, Maryland.

This search garnered a few friendlier sites, offering up which States were the more Redhead-friendly, but also remained firmly in the dating sties with preferences. This woman was married, so that would be of no use.

Claire opened up an email tab and sent a note to Jane.

Hey lady,

If I were to be looking for somebody but don't really know them, where would I look? For a client…

She sat a little straighter as she devised her cover lie before she hit send.

He saw her from across the room and got all hot about her.

A little chat bubble popped up a few minutes later.

Did you take on that Madam?

Claire laughed at Jane's reply. Jane always cut to the chase, and Claire loved her for it.

No. Guy and I got to talking and he said he recently saw a beautiful redhead across the room but she got away before he could find out more. It was all very sweet. She's got long red hair, on the wavy side. Slim figure. She lives here in the city.

Claire waited, secretly hoping that Jane would reply back with the woman's name and number somehow.

How old is she?

A fact that Claire didn't know. Even if she could have seen the woman's face clearly, who knew if it was her true self.

Not a clue, didn't ask. He has very little to go on, told him hopefully he would see her again, and get more info.

Jane replied immediately.

This guy, he seems legit?

Claire smiled.

Yes. I wouldn't be asking if otherwise.

Ten minutes later, Jane did have a name and number for her.

Brad Rich, Loch investigations. (PI, one of my clients) Sending you his contact info now.

Claire's phone chimed with the information and she finalized their conversation.

Thanks, love.

She turned the music off, saved all her files, and shut everything down for the day. It was getting to be dinner time, and she didn't really have a plan yet. Between college, living with Christopher and then back home with her parents, she rarely ate alone. This being on her own thing would be an adjustment for sure. Truth be told, she never outgrew the takeout leftovers and surprise casserole dishes that would show up in her freezer when her mother came for a visit. With the week solidly at home, on her own, and concentrating on work, she knew there was no more of either on hand. She grabbed her purse, keys, and Tilney's leash.

At the sound of his leash being picked up, he met her at the door.

"You've got a playdate, kiddo," she informed him as she hooked the leash to his collar. "Want to play with Pilot?"

Tilney barked and scratched at the door at the mention of his buddy's name.

"I'll take that as a yes." Claire smiled.

As the two walked down the hall and got into the elevator, she pressed the down button to go into the laundry room to find Max's spare key. Her stomach growled at her, dinner would need to be dealt with soon.

"We'll stop at the little Thai place right outside the park. Okay? Okay. Good chat." She smirked to the dog.

Claire walked into the laundry room, located the middle dryer in the row of three dryers and stuck her hand behind it. Sure enough, she felt a small black box that was clinging to the dryer. She pulled it off and stuck it in her purse.

"A little weird, but who am I to judge? Let's go get Pilot."

* * * *

"Thanks for seeing me," Max settled onto the small brown leather sofa sitting next to a little table with a box of tissues on it.

"No problem, happy you called." Dr. Morgan smiled as she reviewed his file. She sat comfortably in her chair. The chair that, of course, sat across from the small brown sofa, that of course, sat next to the little table with the box of tissues. "I haven't seen you in a while; what brings you by?"

"Did I ever tell you this office is a little bit cliché?" he asked as he rubbed his fingers along the top of the tissue box. *Maybe this is a mistake, he didn't know what he was thinking, calling to see if she had an opening.*

"That it is." She smiled without apology. "But it provides what you need in a safe environment. Sometimes clichés are comforting."

Remembering what it took for him to walk into her office for that first visit, she wasn't wrong. The weekly visits that followed, laying himself out on that exact sofa and being offered one of those tissues as his emotions got the better of him was easier than he thought it would be. He was honest after a lifetime of lies because he felt like he was somehow in a safe little bubble for a time out from life. Sometimes clichés were comforting.

"I'm having a hard time sleeping," he admitted. "I guess I just need some advice on that. Or help."

"Why do you think that is?" The doctor started writing words that he would never see in her file.

"I don't know," he said. "I'm doing well. I moved last year, I got a dog. It's kind of all of the sudden."

"That's great to hear, really," she smiled, and for a second Max saw a fair-haired forty something-year-old pretty woman dressed nicely in a crisp cream blouse and trim brown dress pants. That was the problem, really. He was noticing women again, really noticing them. He was starting to live life, and it was throwing him into a panic. The passing glances hadn't bothered him; he was a man after all. He appreciated the female form, but now his attentions were becoming more focused. He didn't want to quite admit it yet, but he found himself thinking of Claire more than he would like to. She made it so easy for him to drop his guard, but his attraction to her had begun disarming his usual defenses. He wasn't ready to be close to anyone again.

"Yeah, but I think I'm just feeling...I feel bad that I'm trying so hard to move on from a past that I don't really want to forget. I don't want to leave it there, for everything to be forgotten. I don't know how to explain it." He laid his head in his hands in frustration.

"That's okay, Max. What you're feeling is completely normal, and you are explaining it right. Your wife is gone, but you don't want to close the door. If you do, you're walking away forever."

"Very much," Max confirmed.

"You have to find the balance here. It's been a year and a half; it's time you let go a little. You might even find yourself falling in love and getting married again."

"No," Max said quickly. "Married? No. I'm done with marriage."

"It's okay, Max. You don't have to think about that right now. You have to just think about letting go a little bit. Not everything has to happen all at once," Dr. Morgan assured him.

"How?"

"By realizing that you don't have to let go of everything in order to move on. Carry the good, let go of the bad. Your wife loved you. Are you telling me you doubt that love?"

The guilt pressed into him. "I wasn't truthful with her. I didn't want her seeing the monster, you know? I didn't trust she wouldn't run from it. I lost her because of it."

"The guilt you feel is understandable, it really is. But it's not necessary. You have got to try to understand that. I'm glad that you're doing well, but I'm here if you want to come back more often."

"Maybe." Max really didn't want to put himself back into therapy.

"I'll send you out with a month supply of sleeping pills. You clearly need rest. Maybe that will be enough time for you to think about things with a clear head."

An hour later, as he sat in his car, he remained unsure of how to move forward. Proud of himself that he didn't break down and reach over to the little table with the box of tissues on it, but a little ashamed his past was very much still a part of his present as he looked at the sleeping pill prescription in his hand. He was a flawed human being, and that weighed heavy on his heart.

As he drove through what once was his neighborhood, he took in the scenery. His whole life now unrecognizable from what it was when he was there last, he was a completely different person. Yet here, life remained untouched from his past; nothing had changed.

Pangs of recognition hit him as he drove the same roads he had taken every day to get into the heart of the city where his office was located. He slowed down as he drove by the elementary school, long quiet from its busy day. He knew that school like the back of his hand, and nearly every single person who worked there. He could see the children in his mind, playing on the playground that sat to the side of the entrance of the building. He could hear their voices, blended into general happy kid sounds. It was a good thing he moved away, he thought, because no matter how hard he tried, he wasn't going to be able to escape his past. Not here anyway, it was around every turn.

The doctor was right, this was a moment of truth. There was a new apartment and a new life that depended on him. Would he be strong enough? He didn't know, but he had to try. Feeling like he needed to rip off a Band-Aid, he picked up his phone and punched in Aidan's number. He closed his eyes and clunked his head on the headrest of his car as the phone rang. He hoped it didn't ring long, it wasn't going to take much for him to change his mind and hang up.

"What happened? Does the bathtub not fit? I told that woman—"

"Slow down, slow down," Max interrupted his business partner's rant, "everything is fine."

"Everything is fine?"

"I think so," Max admitted. "So far, so good. Last I checked, people answer the phone with hello and not demanding rants."

"Oh, well, then...hello." Aidan's voice lowered and settled.

"Hi. How are you? Are you good? Are you stressed? You seem

stressed," Max said to lighten the mood.

"What's up?" Aidan wondered why Max would be calling so late in the evening if there wasn't a problem.

"I'll come to dinner."

There was a moment of silence on the phone. Aidan grabbed his wife's shoulder to grab her attention.

"Tonight?" Aidan looked at his wife in panic as she was putting the last clean dish away from the meal they just finished.

"No, it's late enough. I've got to get home, I've got a dog sitter. I mean, in general. I'll come to dinner. Tell Charlotte to expect a yes the next time she invites me."

"Oh," Aidan said as he slumped in relief, giving Charlotte a thumbs up, and returned to putting the dish away himself, "everything okay? I mean, with you?"

"Yes, it's just time, man."

"Well, that's my boy!" his voice said in victory as he winked at his wife, "I'll tell Charlotte. When's good for you?"

"Whenever is good for you; we have the same job, dude."

"True. Alright, I'll let you know in the morning," Aidan continued and said his goodbyes. This would be fantastic because then Charlotte could just pester him with questions herself, and leave Aidan out of it.

Max quietly knocked on Claire's door when he returned home. It wasn't too late yet, but he wondered what time she settled for the night. He heard nothing, not even the dogs barking. Curious, he pulled his phone out of his pocket and punched in her number. He looked at the handle and wondered if he should try it. *No*, he thought. But then he did, like an idiot.

"Hello?" her soft voice quietly answered.

"Hey," he adjusted his own voice to match hers, as people do for no real reason "I'm standing outside your door. I knocked, but you didn't answer. I'm home."

"Did you try the door?" she asked sweetly.

"Actually..." Now shameful to admit it, he said, "yes."

"Don't be that guy! Don't go in there! It's a trap!" she teased.

"It is oddly quiet out here. It's too late for you to be out, I was a little worried so I checked the door. You could have been the unsuspecting victim, too, ya know."

"Good save."

"Thanks." He could hear the smile in her voice.

"I'm actually in your apartment."

"You are?" Max's light brown eyes looked up to the ceiling to the floor where his own apartment was.

Claire noticed his hesitation and felt guilty with her choice to feel free to invade his space without his permission. Seems she was doing it anyway, without the help of the dream world. She smacked herself in the head at her own stupid realization. "I'm sorry, I hope you don't mind."

"Oh, you're fine," he assured her, "I was just confused. I'll see you in a minute."

She was at the door when he walked out of the elevator. He couldn't help but take in the sight of her, waiting for him. Her long slim legs were tucked into big, fuzzy pink socks. Her hair had a little bit of a gold shine to it from the hall lights, it was down, sweeping just below the neckline of her shirt and dancing slightly around her curves. When he got close to her, he noticed she had matching flecks of gold in her eyes. Florescent lights were oddly very flattering on her.

"I'm sorry," she whispered as she let him into his own apartment.

"It's okay. Everything okay?" he asked, as he put down his messenger bag by the closet door.

"Oh yeah. They wore each other out," she pointed to the two sleeping dogs cuddled up on the floor together. It was quite the cute scene because Pilot looked like he was Tilney's stuffed animal, all small and tucked under Tilney's legs.

"Good, thank you so much. I had a…" he hesitated, "um, an appointment come through at the last minute. Poor planning on my part, I just didn't think it was going to happen."

"Anytime. He ate, that's kind of why we're here. I forgot to ask you about his diet, and well, I want him to be comfortable. So when we got back from our playdate outside, I just brought us all here so he would be with his own food and his own stuff."

"Oh, that's very thoughtful." Max hadn't even thought about mentioning food or his favorite toy. He was so preoccupied with Doctor Morgan calling him after he put in a request and telling him she had a last minute opening. Claire was so thoughtful and caring, he was sure Pilot had been in very good hands.

"I took them to the pond a couple miles down. They had a ball. He's got a lot more energy than Tilney does, but it was fun." Claire smiled as she started to gather her purse and the book she brought with her.

"Good book?" he asked as he turned his head to read the cover.

"Yeah," she said as she showed him, "it's about this woman who comes back to her childhood town after her husband is killed in the line of duty and she finds herself in the company of the town loner who happens to be an old high school friend, and they fall in love. Trashy romance novels are a guilty pleasure."

"We all have our vices," he smiled, "You want to leave sleeping beauty over there?"

"Tilney," she raised her voice a bit and the dog magically pulled himself from sleep, untangled from Pilot who stirred only slightly, and trotted over to her.

"That's cool. Is he a light sleeper?" Max asked curiously.

"No, I am. He just keeps me company when I'm up." She smiled and patted the dog's head. "Good night, Max."

"I owe you one," he insisted.

He watched her and Tilney walk down the hall together toward the elevator. Tilney bumped into her with his long, tired puppy legs. She sweetly nudged him back making Max focus on her backside. A sweet little sway she had, he shook his head at his gutter thoughts and locked up for the night. She was the first real friend he had made, and this was how he was repaying her?

"So, you do anything fun while I was gone?" He whispered as he scooped Pilot up and carried him into the bedroom, laying him down on the bottom of the bed where he always wound up anyway.

He returned to the living room and picked up a few things. He looked at the messenger bag on the floor and knew what he was going to have to do. He did need a good night sleep, he did need a clear mind. He retrieved the prescription bottle, went into the kitchen and swallowed one of the pills with a glass of water. It went down with a bit of an emotional sting, but he knew it was for the best, at least for a little while. One step at a time.

As he got in bed, and gently patted Pilot who had scooted up closer to him, he found himself thinking of the girl downstairs.

"Sweet dreams, Claire," he whispered into the dark.

Chapter 7

Swirls of colors, blues and grays. Claire's instinct was to wave her hand through the air to see what it was, but she didn't really have a hand to wave. She didn't have a body at all; she was just there. She felt like nothing, floating around in nothing. *Huh,* she thought, *this is different.* There was no sound, no movement other than the swirls. She thought this might be what it felt like to be in a Picasso painting. The dream didn't last long, just a few muddled minutes before she woke up on her own for her day. Weird was the feeling; her dreamer just felt weird.

Claire turned her head, peeked one eye open, grabbed her phone and checked it for the time.

"Ugh, seven-thirty. I don't need to be up at seven-thirty on a Saturday." She put her phone back down and rolled back over to snuggle with the warm blankets and soft pillows on her bed.

Tilney trotted in from wherever it was he had been, apparently up for a while. He circled around the bed with the scrolled brushed silver headboard, trying to find his owner who was snuggled deeply in the middle of all the blankets. He climbed up in the bed, and laid down next to her, licking her face.

"Doggy breath!" she yelled as she shoved her hand in his face and moved her head out of the way. "You've got such doggy breath, my love."

Tilney nudged her as he hopped back out of the bed and circled in front of her bedroom door.

"I don't need to be up at seven thirty, but you are like flipping clockwork." She threw the covers off herself and sat up. "Can you wait until I take a shower?"

Tilney barked in response and trotted quickly to the door.

"No," she said to herself as she grabbed a pair of gray sweatpants out of her dresser drawer.

She located a gray t-shirt in her closet and pulled it over her head. Good enough for a quick walk, she mused. Walking through her dark apartment to the bathroom, she flipped the unforgiving lights on and looked in the mirror.

"Our next place is going to have an en suite," she raised her voice to

Tilney who was sitting by the front door waiting for her.

She patted her cheeks and pulled at the barely noticeable crows-feet on the edges of her eyes. She looked at her hair, which was in its sleepy bird's nest state on the back of her neck. After a normal work week back in her routine, she was looking forward to having an entire weekend for relaxation. Another hour of sleep would have been nice, but duty called.

"I'm a beauty queen," she said as she heard Tilney bark for her attention a little louder from the hall. "I know, I'm coming, I'm coming."

She grabbed her brush and ran it through her hair, straightening out the bird's nest. Pulling it back in a bun was her only option at the moment, she twisted and wrapped it up, securing it with a long white hair stick adorned with pink flowers on the end.

Much to Tilney's relief, they made their way out of the apartment. The crisp fall air smacked Claire in the face and she zipped up the hoodie she smartly grabbed on their way out the door.

"Winter," she said as she gave him a painful look, "I didn't think about what winter is going to look like with a dog. Any chance we can potty train you?"

Tilney answered her by pulling her down the sidewalk in front of the building to a grouping of trees.

"Guess not," rolling her eyes at him and smiling "Too bad I already love you, or back to the farm you'd go."

"What farm?" A man's voice came up behind her as the sound of jogging feet slowed to a stop.

Claire turned to see Max coming toward them. He was wearing a long black jogging suit under a gray sweatshirt and blue shorts. His hair was tucked under a blue and white baseball cap sporting the familiar lion silhouette of Pennsylvania State University.

"Good morning." He smiled.

She noticed he hadn't shaved, and by the looks of it for a few days. Chills ran up her body and she fought the shiver sent through her. She had gotten used to the way she felt when he came around, passing it off as nothing more than a small crush. Today reminded her she was in fact, very attracted to him. She was ignoring it. There would be no way she could casually date a neighbor, and at the moment, casual was all she wanted.

"Good morning," she returned as she pointed to his face, "you're all scruffy."

He smiled and lowered his head to the ground for a second at her mention of his physical appearance.

"Winter. Winter's coming in, by March, I'll look like a mountain man."

She studied his face for a second trying to imagine him with a full beard. She was never one who had strong opinions on facial hair, but she liked the idea of it on him. Just before the fantasy took her over completely, reality crept in. Specifically, the reality of how attractive she was. Hoodie, gray t-shirt, sweatpants, no make-up, and her dirty hair up in a bun. *Fan-flipping-tastic*, she cursed herself. *I'm a beauty queen.*

"Uh," *say something Claire*, "Tilney. The farm that Tilney was born on."

"And why are we returning him?" Max asked as he reached down to pet Tilney. "What did you do, buddy?"

"Oh, nothing. I just didn't think about having to get up early and walk him in the cold weather that's just going to get colder. I didn't think out my ownership responsibilities."

"Yep, yep. Dogs, man. What are you gonna do?" Max smiled. "What kind of farm?"

"Um, one of the local farms. Springfield farm."

Max smiled softly as he remembered his wife dragging him from time to time for apples and pumpkins. "I know that place. Used to be more of a road side thing and then they got into the country-living tourist thing."

Claire stood a little taller, and smiled with pride.

"Yeah, them. They've been clients of mine since I started, and when things for them really started to pick up, and they turned that corner from roadside stand to country-living tourist attraction, I guess they were looking for a way to thank me."

"Wow, if that was you, good job." He remarked, "It was a full house the couple of times I've been. So, they gave you Tilney?"

"Among other things. Mr. Springfield is a very good man, very considerate. Horseback riding lessons, which I don't get to often enough. Pumpkins every season, I've got a free hay ride ticket for life."

"Man, all the good stuff. I'm so jealous." His dimples made a small appearance under the growing facial hair. She would miss seeing those, she noticed they only made an appearance when he was totally amused by something and they were ridiculously adorable on him.

"Last time I was there, one of their dogs had puppies and Springfield got all mushy on me. Told me to take a puppy home to love, and when I saw Tilney, I just kind of fell in love on the spot."

Max imagined Claire scooping up a baby version of Tilney, snuggling up to him the way he's seen her do now from time to time. She kept things very light and friendly with people, but when it came to Tilney, he could see the love pour out of her.

He wondered if she knew how pretty she was. Even standing here in front of him in nothing more than sweatpants and a hoodie and her hair kind of a mess, she was somehow flawless. Her features were sharp with high cheekbone and a square jaw. Her makeup was always so subtle, he was never sure if she was actually wearing any at all. He found himself distracted by the line of her collarbone dipping down into her jacket.

"Nice," he pulled his mind out of the gutter, "There are worse places you could send him."

"I'm taking my grandparents out there today to get some fall decorations and pumpkins. He's coming along, it'll be fun."

"Shame on them for using their own granddaughter for her connections to get themselves a free hay ride," he winked.

"And pumpkins. They will get free pumpkins too."

"Despicable," he continued, and then thought about the simple act of getting a pumpkin. The year before there was nothing. No Halloween, no Thanksgiving, no Christmas. His life had come so undone, he didn't know how to even celebrate a simple holiday. The act of buying a pumpkin seemed so paralyzing all of a sudden. "Uh, actually…."

"Would you like to go?"

The invitation surprised her as much as it did him.

"Can't today," he recovered smoothly, "but if you happen to see a pumpkin you think I may like…"

"I'll see what I can do."

* * * *

The ride out to the farm was an adventure in itself. Claire's grandparents were in their late eighties, but on days like this they acted more like two small children. That included the consideration of naps and snacks. Claire's grandfather said this was the true key to happiness when you're under three or over eighty-three. They sold the bigger house that Claire remembered from her childhood, and moved into a small retirement assisted living home. She loved visiting with them, and seeing them be two active little social bees. Her Gran loved being around people and was always involved in something. It gave Claire the only bit of hope that sometimes got her through the night. Gran found balance in her older age; Claire was hopeful she would too.

They pulled up to the busy farm, already brimming with families and children searching for their perfect fall accoutrements. Claire hopped out of the driver's side of the red Jeep Grand Cherokee and opened the back gate, freeing Tilney. She returned to open the back door to help her grandmother out of her seat. Her grandfather was still fit as a fiddle, climbing out without assistance. Tilney casually stood by his side as if to offer a hand in case the man needed it.

Claire introduced them to Mr. Springfield and his wife, who were all too kind, boasting about Claire to her grandparents. People like them reminded Claire she did, in fact, love her job.

"Do you have time to see a few photos of how your granddaughter helped us grow to this?" Mrs. Springfield asked the trio.

"We have all the time in the world today," Claire's grandfather Charlie offered. "Whatever Claire wants."

"I'm not five anymore, Pop. You don't have to indulge me so much."

Claire waived her hands in the air in defeat. "We would love to see pictures. Don't tell anyone, but you guys are my favorite clients. Not only because of Tilney, but you guys were my first client on my own. I'm proud I could help you do such a wonderful job here."

"Thank you," Mrs. Springfield said as she pulled a green leather bound photo album from behind the counter, opened it, and spun the book around on the counter for her guests to see.

The photos in the beginning of the book were of the Springfield' farm when they purchased it, their grins youthful and hopeful. A few pages in, there were some smaller projects they tackled on the farm at various stages. Restoring barns, planting fields and flower gardens. Claire recognized a few of them in their infant stages, now in full bloom wth fall colors.

"Oh, these are some of the field trips, right?" Claire asked, pointing to a grouping of photos that featured groups of sweaty, happy children.

"Yes, that's where you told us to start. Such a simple thing, but you opened such big doors."

"You. You opened those doors. I just showed you where they were," Claire corrected.

She brushed her hand over the photos of children and their teachers smiling with pride.

"I love this; thank you for sharing it with us," Claire said as she closed the book and pushed it back across the counter to its owner.

"That's our Claire, always thinking about the bigger picture," her grandmother smiled.

"What are your plans for today?" Mrs. Springfield asked.

"Pumpkins, hay ride. I think Pop wants to ride on a pony. Right, Pop?" Claire teased.

"That's right." He winked. "Now, that would be something to see. You can charge admission!"

Mrs. Springfield smiled at the old man. "Can we offer you a golf cart? We don't offer them to the general public, but you're family, dear."

"Oh, that's so kind. I think, if you don't mind we will take you up on that offer. These two would wear me out otherwise."

"Sure thing. Just give me about five minutes."

"What do you want to do first, Gran?" Claire asked her grandmother once they settled into the cart that one of the farm hands drove up to the main entrance for them.

"Oh, let's just start at the end and work our way back. We got all day, we'll do it all." Gran smiled as she watched the kids running around the cart, down to the play areas the farm had set up.

"Amazing." Claire smirked. "You two really do know the key to staying young."

"I told you, snacks and naps. That's all you need. Right, boy? We're going to wear you out today," her grandfather said as he patted Tilney who was sitting on the seat next to him.

"My eighty-five-year-old grandfather is going to wear out a seven month old puppy?"

"He will!" Gran insisted.

The Dreamer

"Oh, I know he will. Like I said, you guys have figured it out. I like snacks, I like naps. Can I be part of your club?"

"Well, love, that's entirely up to you now. But, all good things come in due time." Gran patted her granddaughter's knee as they drove down the cobblestone path through the farm.

"I hope so. If we start at the end, I do believe that would be a hay ride and picking pumpkins. We can pick some, and have them boxed. We can leave them on the golf cart when we go to see other things."

"Oh, sweetheart. You and your analytical brain, you always have to have a plan and a place for everything." Gran smiled.

"Don't know where she gets that from at all, Adelaide," Pop's voice chimed in from the backseat.

"Oh, hush now, Charlie. You've benefited from my weirdness for sixty-five years." Adelaide brushed off her husband's comment with a wave of her hand.

Charlie grabbed her hand, still so soft in his mind, leaning forward as he swept her long white hair back so he could whisper in her ear, "Sixty-five years isn't enough, I want sixty-five more." He kissed her hand.

They were amazing, they really were. Claire's father told her many times about growing up in a house filled with love. His parents never shielded from showing their affection for each other in public. They thought it was important for Alan to see what love looked like, how a couple should treat each other. She thought of a story Gran told her about when Alan was very little. Every time he walked by, he patted Adelaide's behind because it was something his father did every time he walked by her. Charlie had to stop doing it for a few years, which cracked them up.

How it happened had always been a mystery for Claire. She knew from a very young age that Adelaide had the same ability she did. Adelaide spent a lifetime dreaming inside the minds of the people around her, yet she was able to have a life herself. She found love, she was able to stay in love. She got married and had a child. She was one of the most outgoing, social people Claire ever met. She was always dragging Charlie to things, and he was happy to go, as long as he could be with her.

Over the years, Claire went to her grandmother for guidance and support, and to get answers to questions. Adelaide had been kind, and comforting. She answered what she wanted to, and told Claire that some lessons were better learned on her own. They compared a few notes and marveled over some differences. She was always there, and for Claire, having that was more than enough.

Claire also knew Adelaide never told Charlie. Adelaide suspected he knew, she told Claire once. She said it so sweetly, the man knew her heart and soul, inside and out. How could he not know? That's what stuck with Claire whenever she thought about finding somebody for the long run, Adelaide never said the words out loud. As far as Claire knew, it remains true to this day.

Could she keep secrets from a man she loved, for a lifetime? She never thought about telling Christopher when they dated, only to think about it when he proposed marriage. They didn't get far enough into their engagement for her to worry about when would be the right time to tell somebody she could see inside their mind.

Claire also knew her father didn't know. When Adelaide realized Claire's time had come, she pulled Claire aside, and told her not to tell anyone. Not even her Mommy and Daddy. As Claire grew older and asked more direct questions, she was told her father had never been clued in on his mother's ability. Adelaide lived with a secret in her heart, but how was it not holding her back from life? Adelaide and Charlie bought a big house in a small town, raised Alan, and stayed there until the house became too much to take care of. Now in the retirement village, Adelaide must dream about all her friends. Yet, she had them. It was a mystery.

"First stop, hay ride!" Claire said, as she pulled the golf cart to the side of the barn where the tractors sat in wait for guests.

The trio dropped Tilney off with one of the farm employees who was happy to take him to the private neighboring area where all the farm dogs were happily playing and wandering around. Tilney's mother was there, and Claire had been careful to bring him back often enough for them to recognize each other and enjoy a very familiar relationship. She knew they would be happy to see each other.

She enjoyed the afternoon with her grandparents, and was pleased with their selection of picked pumpkins and gourdes. Her grandmother purchased some fresh stalks of hay for her front porch and fall-colored mums for her planters. Claire got all the treasures situated just right at her grandparents' house before she sat down with Adelaide for a cup of tea.

"Honestly, Gran. I don't know how you do it." Claire marveled as she poured the hot tea into their two cups.

"Do what?" Adelaide asked as she waved to her younger, sixty-year-old friend who was enjoying an afternoon powerwalk through the retirement village.

"That!" Claire waved her hands in the air. "You have friends. You have a life. How do you deal with all of it after spending all night inside these people's minds?"

"Well, dear," Adelaide began. She always tried to be a truth teller, but knew Claire wasn't ready for all of it just yet. She chose her words carefully. "It's no disability for me, as you see it. It can take your life away from you if you let it. You either choose to live with it, and power through, or you choose to let it consume you."

"I wish I was as strong as you are," Claire admitted.

"You are, child, you are!" Adelaide looked Claire right in the eyes. "You're just not sure of it yet, but I am."

"Thank you, Gran."

Charlie pushed the slider open, and walked out on the deck with a blanket. He wrapped it around his wife, and kissed her on the top of her head. Rounding the table, he met Claire with the same sweet offer of affection.

"You girls have fun, I'm going to take a nap. Tilney's got the right idea," he said, pointing to the sleeping dog in the middle of the living room floor.

"Enjoy, Pop. I'll probably be gone when you wake up. I love you, today was fun." Claire smiled.

"It was. I like seeing all those kids running around. Makes me feel young and spry," he boasted.

The women watched Charlie disappear back into the bedroom of the small rancher house.

"I think we wore him out; he's getting old, you know," Adelaide quipped.

"So you still haven't told him?"

"Told him what?"

"Gran, I ask you every time I see you. Will your answer ever be different?"

"When you've been married as long as we have, you don't have to. They just know. He knows, he's always known. But no, I've never told him," Adelaide admitted.

"And he loved you anyway?" Claire asked.

"That he did," Adelaide said with confidence, "and he loves me still. We've been over this. What's on your mind today, kiddo?"

"How did you get past it? Does he not dream? Don't you feel like you're invading his privacy on an absolutely insane level?"

Again, Adelaide chose her words carefully. She loved her granddaughter and lying to her was not on the agenda.

"I can tell you that I love that man with everything I am. I didn't care what I found in him, because I wanted to know him, inside and out. Good, bad, and everything in between. No dreams were ever going to change the fact that he is a good man and he is my man."

"True," Claire admitted. "Still, you had a life with him, you've had a child."

"Yes, because I deserve those things. I wanted those things. No disability prevents you from living, you prevent you from living. Are you living, Claire?"

"I think so. I'm trying. Being in the city helps, lots of people to pick from." Claire enjoyed talking on this level of honesty.

"Have you been able to make friends? I worry about you since you work at home all day long. If it weren't for Tilney there, I think you'd never leave the house." Adelaide shivered as she wrapped her hands around the warm tea. Getting older was no joke, she was cold all the time.

"I get out. I have friends, Tilney has friends."

"Friends, Claire? Or just people that you happen to see because you take your dog out at the same time they do?"

Boy, Adelaide was sharp as a tack. She never missed a beat.

"I have friends, Gran," Claire assured her. She did have friends, most of whom didn't live within a thirty mile radius of her. "In fact, I've been able to enjoy a little bit of a friendship with the man upstairs from me."

"Oh, a man?" Adelaide's ears perked up. "You haven't mentioned a man in a really long time."

"It hasn't been that long. I've been on a few dates here and there, but I'm not looking for anything serious. I don't think I can do serious in the grand scheme of things."

"Claire," Adelaide scolded.

"I know, I know. I just...I don't want to get hurt again. I had to overcome so much with Christopher. I gave him five good years, and I thought maybe I could do it. When we lived in the city it was perfect because there were enough dreamers that kept him out of my mind all the time. It was when we moved for his job that reality hit."

"I did not like Christopher." A solid fact from day one.

"I know, you said as much. How long do you think it would have taken me to figure out he was having an affair without putting together clues from his dreams?"

"You saw his true self. His true, stupid. lying, cheating bastard of a self." Adelaide had all but coined the term so well over the last year that nobody in the family could think of his name without her voice and those words following in their minds. *Christopher, the stupid, lying, cheating bastard.*

"Gran, you're terrible." Claire gawked.

"I'm glad you saw it. I'm glad you left him. You be glad, too! Didn't I tell you it would serve you well to pay attention to the little things?"

"I guess," Claire conceded. "I guess I just thought I could make it work, knowing that the more calm and settled the person is, the less likely I am to dream of them. You know, expect things now and again, but not all the time."

"Good plan," Adelaide agreed, "and I told you that, then. It wasn't your plan that was the problem. It was the man."

She wasn't sure she would have ever found out. Christopher had been so careful. He just landed his first big job at a local law firm and was putting in close to eighty-hour work weeks and traveling to see clients all over the place. Claire was so proud of him, and supported his decisions. She had been in his mind countless times, but nothing stuck out as harmful. Honestly, she was hopeful she'd start finding herself in dreams of a wedding. He was home just a few nights a week, and that gave her a good balance.

Where she did find herself was in dreams where he was being chased down as if he had done something. She found herself in dreams where he was trying to protect somebody, and after several months, she caught a reflection of a woman in one of those dreams. She never saw the woman before, but that all changed at an office party. She recognized the leggy blonde from his dreams almost immediately. And then the unspoken flirtation all but sang from them, once Claire knew she was looking for it. Little things, glances and standing a little too close. All things Claire would never have noticed if she hadn't been looking for what he wasn't telling her about.

It had gone on for more than a year, he told her, when she cornered him about it. The truth had crushed her, and she knew he would have been able to continue on without her ever being the wiser. The night she left him, part of her not only swore off him, but a serious relationship with any man.

"And this man upstairs, he's just a friend? I think it's time you looked for something more," Adelaide prodded gently. "There's been enough time for your heart to heal."

"Don't jump to conclusions," Claire warned her grandmother. "He's got a dog, Pilot. Tilney and he play together some times. So far, knock on wood, I haven't come across Max on the other side."

"Maybe he's a calmer, more settled person. Or somebody who doesn't dream a lot, like Alan." Adelaide pondered.

"That's what I was thinking." Claire smiled. "It's allowed me to get to know him. He's a nice guy, and I think I'm making a real friend. I just am too scared to be definitive."

"Enjoy your life, Claire," Adelaide said seriously. "This is the only one you get, and you have got to make the best of it. You've got to let yourself fall in love with somebody. Somebody who isn't a stupid, lying, cheating bastard."

"What if there are things I can't get past? Maybe not an affair, but what if there is something else? Everyone has something," Claire began.

"Then you have not found the one who is worth getting past it all," Adelaide firmly interrupted. "You have no idea what your future holds. Go claim it."

"You did," Claire said, as she motioned to the blanket wrapped around her grandmother's shoulders.

"You're damn right I did," Adelaide agreed. "And you will too, my sweet girl; you just have to allow yourself the opportunity. Take this Max person, is he cute?"

Claire blushed before she could even answer, Adelaide had her answer without waiting for the words.

"Let yourself live child; don't let the dreams get in your way."

Chapter 8

The drive back into the suburban town outside Baltimore was fraught with déjà vu. Though Max had traveled back only once or twice in the last year, the commute was forever burned into his muscle memory. Autumn colors in the prime of their life danced on the trees that lined the familiar rural streets. An early evening sun washed their leaves in an orange glow, setting the muted earth tones into a beautiful blaze of color. As his car zipped down the road with fallen leaves scattering in its wake, Max remembered the first time he'd made this drive with his wife.

"Fields. I want to run around in fields one day," Rebecca had said to him as she gazed out of the passenger's side window. She looked content as they passed the rolling green hills that welcomed them into the suburbs.

They had been dating six months, and Charlotte was dying to meet the new girl in his life. Max was cautious when it came to introducing people to Charlotte. They would fall under as much scrutiny as they would with his own mother, maybe even more.

Aidan had met Rebecca several times in passing at the office when she and Max would meet there before going out. Aidan thought she was sweet, and knew his wife would like her. Seeing his business partner get jittery over a girl was fun. Max became a little obsessed with keeping the office clean in case she stopped by. He was dressing nicer, and when she did stop by, he proudly showed off their latest designs. Now that it was serious, it was time to meet his family. It was time to meet Charlotte.

"With all that fresh air? Don't you get enough of that at school?" he teased her, patting her leg.

"I hope they like me. Do you think Charlotte will like me?" Rebecca asked as she twirled the simple gold chain at her neck.

"I think she will love you," Max assured her. This dinner was the last check mark before things would change. Rebecca had already met his mother, and now she would meet Charlotte. These two women were the only family he cared to know. Charlotte already knew they were meeting because Max was thinking of his future. He didn't need her approval but he did want her blessing.

He knew Charlotte would love Rebecca. Charlotte was a born

mother with no children yet, and Rebecca spent her time encouraging the imaginations of twenty-three five and six year olds every day. Rebecca was sweet and patient, creative, and saw the good in everything and everybody. Charlotte would be a fool not to fall in love with her. He fell in love with her himself even before they met, when he was sitting at a table in a coffee shop watching her fret over which reward sticker a six-year-old little boy might like best on his paper.

He was grabbing a quick breakfast that morning, but just as he was packing up the designs he was looking over, she caught his eye. His attention wavered between the cute glasses balanced on the end of her nose and under the table where he could see her knee bouncing with energy. He wound up sitting at a table across from her for a solid ten minutes past the last sip of his own coffee, just watching.

She was completely engrossed in whatever it was she was working on and the scene of her was nothing short of adorable. He wondered how often she stuck her pencil in her mouth to chew on, and then quietly removed it, reminding herself to stop the habit. He had seen her repeat the task at least three times since she arrived. Papers were spread all over her table and after studying each one, she would occasionally mark something with her green marker or place a sticker on it. As she leaned over and reached into her bag, she accidentally knocked over her coffee cup, spilling its contents all over the papers.

That was the moment he became her hero. At least that's what she told him when he jumped up out of his seat and hurried over to her with a pile of napkins in hand. Together, they blotted the papers and contained the spill. As he picked each one up to wipe clean and sit on a different table to dry, he noticed they were the works of small children.

"Are you a teacher?" he asked, as he smiled and transferred the papers to the new table.

"Kindergarten." She smiled. "Thank you so much for your help. I can't believe how clumsy I can be."

"Happens to the best of us. Hope nothing is ruined."

"No, I think we got to everything on time." She studied the papers now laying side by side on a new table. Some of them had small stains but thankfully most of the coffee had pooled between the papers or off onto the floor. "You're the hero of room two-oh-six today."

"Well, thank you." He smiled at her as they gave the papers a final check. "I don't remember even writing so much as my name in Kindergarten."

"We're working on sight words, silent *es*. They were to write and draw the words the *e* turned into. Tub into a tube," she pointed to one child's large writing with a picture of what he assumed was a toothpaste tube, "that sort of thing."

"Complicated," he mused.

"What's your name, hero?" she asked.

"Max."

"Thank you, Max."

"Teachers are heroes, I'm just a guy with napkins. Here you go, Missus…?" He may as well put a name to the face he would no doubt be calling himself an idiot over at some point later that evening.

"Lang. Ms. Lang to them." She pointed to the papers, but blushed a little, lowering her head and tucking her hair behind her ear, "Rebecca to you."

He cleared his throat in effort to speak. Just the way she said her name made him forget his own. *Don't be an idiot, Max.* He reminded himself.

She went home with her slightly stained, graded papers and he went home with her phone number. Their first conversations were as easy as that first meeting at the coffee shop. She lived in an apartment in the city with her college roommate, but had interest in getting out to the suburbs now that she secured the job at Jefferson Elementary School.

She'd wanted to be a teacher most of her life, having a love for children early on. She taught every grade before she settled on Kindergarten, and she settled on Kindergarten because she believed it was the magic year where children were still hopeful people pleasers, yearning for the desire to understand the world and not at all touched by jaded reality. He loved learning all of this about her, and especially loved the days where she craved adult attention and prattled on about nonsense when he called.

He met her for coffee again where they put a ridiculously large stack of napkins on the table when they sat down, just in case. They met for dinner, which eventually led to breakfast, which eventually led them to being joined at the hip. When they returned home from this dinner with Aidan and Charlotte, he would be asking her to move in with him.

They bought an old Victorian house just inside the school district that Rebecca fell in love with the minute she laid eyes on it. It was nearly a hundred years old and there were more things wrong with it than right. Max saw the house with his architect's eye. A never ending list of foundation fixes, wall replacements, window repairs, and he didn't even want to think about how many hours it would take him to track down pieces that would fit the old house.

It would be a project that could potentially take them years to complete. Rebecca looked at it with a teacher's eye. She only saw what could possibly be if somebody would take the time to help it get there. A circular wraparound porch where she could sit with family and rock on rocking chairs. A room with wall-to-wall, built-in book shelves that held ten thousand books. A warm fire crackling as she snuggled up on a deep sofa on a cold night to read one of those books.

Max had no idea if he could make any of these things possible, but he would give anything to try. When he saw her face as they opened the back door to the porch leading out onto the expansive back yard, he knew. This was her home. It was his job to build, as it was her job to dream.

"A field, my love," he bowed to her in grand gesture, waving his hand toward the back yard.

Little did he know how quickly that dream would turn into the nightmare it did.

Remembering the moment now, he looked over to the empty seat in his car and ached at its unyielding loneliness.

* * * *

"Have any trouble getting in?" Charlotte asked as she took Max's jacket and hung it in the hall closet.

"Nah," Max said, "the usual traffic, nothing major. Did I beat Aidan back?"

"No, man. Been home for an hour at least," Aidan said as he walked out of the kitchen. "Glad you could make it."

"He's a deadbeat, ya know. Insisted on having a long lunch with a client and then taking the rest of the day off," Max teased as he swooped Charlotte up in a hug and kissed her on the cheek. It had, all of a sudden, been way too long since he had seen her last. "When are you going to cut him loose and marry me?"

"You had years with me before he came along. You snooze you lose, buddy. Besides, you would never survive a vegetarian household," Charlotte offered.

"This is true," Max agreed, "I do love a good steak. But, for a good woman…."

So did Aidan, Max knew. Aidan always offered to take clients out to lunch when they needed to, usually to his favorite steakhouse. Aidan always thought that as long as it was every once in a while, what Charlotte didn't know wouldn't kill her. Charlotte knew of course, but what Aidan didn't know wouldn't kill him.

"Yeah, yeah, yeah." Aidan grabbed his wife from Max and threw his arm around her as the trio walked into the dining room where Charlotte had everything ready and waiting.

"This looks really great, Charlotte, thank you for having me."

The look on her face was passively chastising. She'd make any mother of a son who forgot to come home or call proud. "It's been far too long, Max."

It was the first time since he'd moved off their couch and into his apartment that he had been over. Of course it had been Charlotte he ran to when his world fell apart; she was the one person he could be himself with. Her place would always be a safe place for him. Yet, once he was able to walk on his own two feet again, it was the last place that he wanted to be. Charlotte and Aidan were wonderful, but Rebecca was here, and that hurt.

"How's your apartment? I haven't been invited over to see it yet." Another passive castigation.

"There's nothing to see. He's got a couch, a table, a bed…" Aidan never knew if he should take Max's side or Charlotte's on these sorts of matters. He did his best to bring rational thought to both parties.

"I have what I need," Max interrupted, and aimed an invitation to Charlotte. "And you are welcome to come over anytime you'd like. You know that, so don't play that card with me."

"How's the puppy thing going?" she asked as she started dishing out the meal. She'd made a spinach lasagna with garlic bread as she remembered it was a favorite of Max's.

"Pilot's great. He's crazy, and gets into everything. Nothing is sacred. He has to pee every five minutes."

"Oh, so you got married again," Aidan teased, looking at Charlotte.

"Watch it, Mister. These are the hands that feed you." She reminded him.

"Why didn't you bring him?" Aidan asked. "I'm sure he's dying to get out of the house by now."

"Oh yes," Charlotte added, thinking of a poor puppy in a crate all day long. "Please tell me he's not locked up in some cage."

"He's not." Max assured her "He has a crate, where we keep the door open most of the time. He's got a piddle pad he's pretty good about getting to, though that's still a work in progress."

"You should get a dog walker." Charlotte offered. "I'm sure you could pay some kid ten bucks to walk him after school every day."

"Well, actually, I've got a new neighbor. She has a dog, and she works from home. I don't ask all the time, but on the occasion, she swings by my place and grabs Pilot when she takes her dog out."

"Oh, that's nice." Charlotte smiled.

"Claire, right?" Aidan prodded.

"Yes," Max gave him the *shut up in front of your wife* look.

"Hmm…" Charlotte caught the warning glare between the men and just mentally filed it. If Max didn't want to talk about it, she wasn't going to push him…yet.

"What are you doing for Thanksgiving?" Charlotte changed the subject, much to Max's relief.

He wasn't sure if the subject change was better, or worse. Halloween was just around the corner, which he had enough trouble with, and that wasn't even a real holiday. Claire picked up a pumpkin and a couple of gourdes for him on her trip to the farm with her grandparents. She asked him if he was going to carve it, and his natural reaction would have been to say yes. He was actually a pretty skilled pumpkin carver, if he did say so himself.

Every year, he and Rebecca would pick out patterns from magazines or books and they would open some wine and carve away. He would roast pumpkin seeds with Old Bay, Baltimore's favorite spice. No, the pumpkin would stay intact, he told her. He filed it under the very reasonable excuse that because he was gone all day, and it was technically food, he was afraid Pilot would try to eat it. It wasn't a whole lie, Pilot very well may have eaten it, but it wasn't the whole truth either.

"Going to go visit my Mom," he confirmed.

"Have you spoken to the Langs?" she gently asked.

"No. I don't think they want to see me."

"Oh, Max," Charlotte began.

"We're having a nice night. Let's not go there."

"I love you, Max. You know that, right?" Charlotte grabbed his hand and gave it a good squeeze.

"All the good, and the bad. You're a saint." He lifted her hand and kissed it.

"Charlotte, I think you'd like the house we're working on now," Aidan offered to lighten the mood.

"Oh, yeah? Why's that?" She agreed, time for a subject change.

"The closet is the size of a guest bedroom. I think she's going to have everything custom built with shelves when we're done."

"Oh, that does sound nice." Her mind began to wander at the idea of a wall full of shoes and all of her clothing neatly in a row on wooden hangers.

"Big bay window above a Jacuzzi tub," Max added.

"Oh, one day." Charlotte poked her finger into Aidan's shoulder, "One day."

Max and Aidan cleared the table and washed the dishes. Though it had been a year and a half since Max had been there for a meal, he quietly fell into the habit from every evening when he was staying with them. She'd cook, they'd clean up.

"We're thinking about buying a house," Aidan whispered as they washed, dried, and put away the pots and pans.

"That's great man, where?"

"Couple miles from here, by Ultimate Health Center," Aidan said, referring to the local fitness gym.

"Do you have one in mind already?"

"No, we just started looking." Aidan said. "We weren't supposed to be in this house this long. Two bedrooms, no basement. This was never the house for kids."

It was a small house. Charlotte did her magic and made it feel like the coziest little cottage there ever was, but the fact was, it was nine hundred square foot shoebox. They bought it right after they got married, which was weeks after they graduated college. Charlotte filled the very small yard with a garden bursting with colorful flowers, and she made the big stone fireplace the focal point of the living room. They had a galley kitchen, but the house did offer a sweet little dining room off to the side, where a round table for six nearly filled the space.

"Kids?" Max asked, very cautiously.

Over the years, Charlotte miscarried two children. Only a handful of friends knew, Max among them.

"We found out a while back but she wanted to hear the heartbeat before she said anything to anyone," Aidan said, with a very painfully equal dose of caution.

"That's great, man." Max put the lasagna dish he was drying down and wrapped his arm around Aidan who was trying so hard not to give himself permission to be happy and hopeful.

"How's it all going?" Max asked.

"Good so far." Aidan cranked his neck out of the hallway to make sure Charlotte was still out of earshot. "She's never made it this far before."

"I'm so sorry." What in the world do you say, Max wondered. Even with Charlotte, the subject was rarely broached. His instinct was to fix it for her, but he knew he couldn't. He also knew he needed to step aside for Aidan. A brother and a husband both had their places in her heart. Aidan never tried to stand in the way of Max's friendship with her, and Max was certainly not going to stand in the way of Aidan's rightful place as her husband.

"It's part of life. Human bodies aren't perfect. But she's actually thrown up a few times."

"That's good?"

"Yeah, that's good." Aidan confirmed. "I think she's going to wait until we know it's going to stick before we buy a house. I told her we can buy one whenever we want. We're ready. We've been ready for a few years now. I just think she can't stand the idea of having a big house to fill with no kids to fill it."

"I understand the feeling."

"Well, I think we're going to start looking. For real. Let her tell you all of this of course, but I wanted to tell you now."

Charlotte returned to the men in the kitchen after cleaning up the dining room a bit, and grabbed dessert plates for the chocolate cake she'd made. Her chocolate peanut butter cake was truly sinful; Max had been hoping she made it. Charlotte sat on the counter and the guys stood as they ate, opting for the casual space in the kitchen to hang out. Max knew her at nearly every stage of life as he studied her frame. She was wearing leggings and a loose fitting top, what she often referred to as her holiday clothing, which were kept to accommodate a few extra pounds over the winter. She must have gained a few extra pounds already and pulled those clothes out. He wiped away the grin on his face before she caught it.

"Did Aidan tell you we're having a party?" Charlotte asked.

"Nope, it didn't come up."

"Yeah, I'm just in the mood for a party."

"Am I invited?"

"Of course, silly." She lovingly kicked his side with her foot. "Costumes required, before you ask."

"When?"

"Next Saturday." Charlotte returned her attention to her own husband, daring him to stop her from finishing her next demand. "And I think maybe you should have a date."

"Uhh…," Aidan began, but quickly got the stare of death.

"I have a friend who is single, and cute. I was thinking maybe you could—"

"Sorry, man," Aidan offered Max. "I can only hold her back for so long."

"I don't need a date. I'm a party all by myself." Max smiled at Charlotte.

"I know, but she's cute. And I thought maybe you'd want to get out there a little bit. You've just been work, work, work," Charlotte argued.

"I have a life, thank you very much."

"Come on, Max, please?" Charlotte hopped off the counter and leaned against Max's shoulder, pouting her lip and looking exactly like she did when she was fifteen and asking him to drive her somewhere.

She was pregnant. He looked over at Aidan and could see the desire for hope so clearly on his face. How was he going to break her heart?

"How about I bring a date. My own date?" he asked.

"Are you seeing somebody?" Charlotte backed up and her tone became serious.

"If I bring a date, will you leave me be?"

"A girl date?" Charlotte asked.

"Yes, a girl date," he scoffed.

"A girl who's not your cousin, or your Aunt, or your—"

"A girl date, of no blood relation."

"Okay, but if your girl date does not materialize, promise me you'll meet my friend." Charlotte batted her eyes at him.

"Fine." Max kissed her on the top of her head. "I gotta get back into the city. Thank you for having me over."

"Not so long until next time," Charlotte said, as she hugged him and whispered, "I miss my friend Max. I want him back when this baby gets here."

"Baby?" he would play the innocent card here.

"I know he told you as soon as I turned my back. I let him have these little things, makes him feel powerful."

"I love you." He smiled and pressed his hand to the tiniest of baby bump, "and I'm here no matter what."

"I know," she said. "Now go. Be safe."

* * * *

Max lay in his bed, with Pilot snoring away next to him. A date. He was going to a Halloween party, and he was going to bring a date. All of the sudden, dinner seemed to be turning in his stomach. Charlotte meant well and he couldn't deny her anything at the moment. He hoped for her sake, she wouldn't have any complications this go around; she'd make an amazing mother. A life planned, a life lost. He would give her the world if she asked. It was interesting to him that the idea of giving her the world seemed easier than finding a date.

"It's not the end of the world; I'm sure she's cute," he told the sleeping dog.

"I can get my own date," he argued with himself, "because you know, I do it all the time."

It had been just about a decade since he last asked someone out on a date. He didn't even know where to begin to look. Telling Charlotte he would bring a date was just what came out of his mouth as every part of him panicked at the idea of being set up.

As he was closing his eyes in sleep, his phone made a soft chime. He reached for it in the dark and looked at the incoming text: *Hey, I'm sorry to ask, but I have to be out all day tomorrow. Could you possibly take on the beast when you get home from work?*

Max straightened up in bed, and smiled.

No problem. I'll be home around three. That okay?

Her reply took a few minutes. He wondered what she would be up to that would leave her gone all day.

Yes! Thank you. Big work event, all hands on deck deal. I have to be on site. Tilney will have plenty of food and water. His leash is by the door in the basket. He likes the red ball with the yellow star lately. Watch him with the grass, he's been eating too much of it. I should be home around nine, but you certainly don't have to keep him entertained that whole time. A walk will do, then he can continue being my little freeloader.

Max smiled as he typed, her way of chatter was so cute. Tilney was a dog, he did dog stuff. He could already picture the sheet of paper he will no doubt find on her kitchen counter detailing Tilney's ever changing doggy preferences of the week. Max would take it all into account of course, but at the end of the day Tilney was a dog. He did dog stuff.

Oh, I had big plans, Mom. Nine p.m. is really going to put a cramp in our style. We're men, we need to party!

Her reply was immediate this time.

Nine p.m. on the dot, Mister. I don't need my boy hanging out with the riff-raff that comes out at ten. Bad influences, the lot of them.

"Yes, Mom," he said aloud as he typed the words.

Thank you, Max. Seriously. Tilney's comfortable around you, please let me know if he doesn't behave himself.

He was a sweet dog. Pilot will be excited for the playdate. And it wasn't like Claire hadn't saved his backside a few times when he called her, stuck in a meeting or in traffic.

No problem, least I can do.

His phone chimed once more several minutes later.

See you tomorrow. I owe you one.

No, she really didn't, but that was Claire. He set his phone down and the image of her came into his mind. She had the prettiest smile, there was something about it that was so genuine. Everything was easy around her, she was the easiest person in the world to talk to. There was just something about her, he remembered her father telling him. People could just talk to her. It was true, she wanted nothing from him. Just to be there, to hang out and have fun. She was awesome.

He grabbed his phone before he lost his nerve.

You still up?

His phone chimed just a few seconds later.

Nope. Sound asleep in my bed, and this is all a dream.

She was funny; he loved that.

I think I may have thought of something. How do you feel about…

He took a deep breath in, knowing it was now or never. And really, maybe it would be okay. Claire was so sweet, and kind, and fun. Maybe a friend like that would be exactly what he needed to dip his toe into the water. He squeezed one eye shut, and typed the last two words out slowly as if each tap of his finger was painful.

Halloween Parties?

Chapter 9

It's not a date. It's just two friends going to a party. Claire stared into the blank space above her computer screen and lightly tapped her fingers on the keyboard in a rhythmic motion as her mind wandered. The invitation Max presented her with the evening before rolled through her thoughts for what seemed to be the millionth time. She picked up her phone from its docking station on her desk, pulled up the text exchange, and re-read it.

How do you feel about Halloween parties?

She didn't feel about them, having never been to one. Through her high school years there were party invitations but she never desired to socialize with the people she dreamed about the most. In fact, by the time her four years were up, Claire successfully blended so well within the background noise, most people couldn't identify her by name. *Yes, she goes to my school. She was at that party, wasn't she? Maybe not. I don't know, I can't remember her name. But I know her, everybody knows her. Don't they?*

They didn't know her because she didn't let them know her. They just thought they did, because on some weird, cosmic level she couldn't even begin to understand, they recognized her from their dreams.

I can neither confirm nor deny that I like them. She finally replied to Max's question about Halloween parties.

My friends are having one, and they've invited me. Only…

Only what, she wondered, and waited several seconds before the rest of the text came in.

They want to set me up with a girl who will be there. I'm sure she's a perfectly nice girl, I'm just not a fan of blind dates. I have to go, best friend obligations and all, so I was hoping if I show up with my own date, I can escape the love connection.

Claire remembered sitting up in bed at that point to give him her full attention.

And you want me to find you a date? Um, that's not in Team Metis' current dossier, though I might be able to recommend a lovely older woman who has several young ladies on file that specialize in…..this sort of thing.

His reply was immediate.

No! One blind date for another? No, thank you. I was hoping maybe you could go with me. Save me, be my non-wing woman. Wait, you know a Madame?

A wicked smirk flashed across her face against the glow of her phone, she did indeed know a Madame. She politely turned down a request from Veronica, a proprietor who had been given her name as a suggestion for a schedule coordinator. She wanted Claire to keep track of her girls, their dates, and maybe do a little cross reference filing on...preferences. Over drinks, Claire admitted to Veronica she was intrigued, but for now would kindly pass on the opportunity. Still, she kept the woman's contact information on file because Claire was in the business of making things happen. If there ever came a time where she'd have to fill a banquet room with beautiful guests, she knew exactly who'd she call.

Sorry, I don't discuss my clients ;)

As expected, there were several seconds of stunned silence before his response.

I don't know—I....um...yeah. Okay. Anyway, feel free to say no. I just thought it would be fun and you'd be saving me by being my "date." It's Saturday night, costumes required, unfortunately.

Claire looked at the last words between them, cursing herself for the indulgence. Data entry, she was supposed to be doing data entry today. Instead, she was re-reading the exchange...again.

Okay, I'll go.

"I'm clearly not going to get anything done," she said to herself as she put the phone back down on its charger. "Maybe a little break."

She opened a new tab on her screen and pulled up a popular costume and party supply website. She hadn't a clue what she could be. Max told her he would most likely pull something from his closet and make the best of it. As she scanned the online collection of costumes she quickly realized her options were limited. She could be one half of a couple's costume, which obviously was out. That left goth, or sexy, or sexy goth. Occasionally, very inappropriate sexy children's cartoon characters. *What is wrong with people?* Rolling her eyes, she closed the tab in defeat. Maybe Max's idea of pulling something from his closet might not be a bad idea after all.

She could be Metis, she smiled at the idea of shameless self-promotion. Goddess of wisdom and deep thought. The goddess you'd have to be careful around as she was also brilliantly cunning. She could easily enough make a toga, or pick one up at a local shop. The online store had several options to choose from, but all involved barely there fabric draped across a spray-tanned model. Way to make a first impression on his friends, dress like a slut. No. She could be any number of fun fictional characters from one of her books. Her mind drifted to a few years ago when everyone and their brother was a sparkly vampire. That would be the last thing she wanted. A Jane Austen character would be a strong front-runner if she had not already named her dog Tilney, there was a fine line between fangirl fun and fanatical obsession. Witty? Maybe. It would be easy enough to fashion a black silk nightgown with double entendres. A Freudian slip. And we're back to being a slut. No.

Hearing her stomach growl, she pushed away from her desk and headed into the kitchen to make herself some lunch. Maybe something would inspire her as she put together a turkey sandwich. She added some apple slices, and took her plate on a rare self-allowance out to the living room to watch a little TV. Tilney curled up on the floor in front of her as she checked her DVR to see what she had recorded and selected her show. As she watched the blue box spin around on her TV, Halloween inspiration hit her.

* * * *

Max had no flipping clue what he was going to be. It was nerve wracking enough to be going to a party in his old neighborhood where he knew he'd make a few people uncomfortable, but ultimately they wouldn't say anything. Especially if he had Claire by his side, she'd be his shield and wouldn't even know it. He hoped the invitation he extended to her came off as a polite invitation. He found her to be attractive, a knock out, truth be told. But she was Claire, his sweet and fun neighbor. Claire, one of the easiest friendships he'd made in a very long time. Claire, who knew nothing of his past and never dug trying to find it. She was freedom, and tonight, she'd be protection.

He ran a razor over his face, shaving off the small beard he had been growing. He hadn't really wanted to shave, particularly because Claire mentioned a few times the scruffy look was cute on him, but it would aid with the easy costume he finally settled on.

"Let's go get my costume together," he said to Pilot who was playing with a squeaky toy on the white tile bathroom floor.

Max walked into his bedroom and opened his closet. He ran his hands over the selection of wardrobe, locating the plaid patterned, red shirt he was looking for. He pulled dark blue pants from the stack of denim, a black belt and hauled out the heavy tan boots he wore when he went to visit construction sites for one of his projects.

"Uncanny, if I do say so myself," he said, after trying it all on together and viewing it in a mirror. He turned from side to side in self-adoration of his simple, but genius idea.

Pilot looked at him with a curious little face, and quickly dismissed him to return his attention to the toy in his mouth.

He showed up on Claire's doorstep exactly on time. He knocked, and ignored the unexpected little flutter of nervousness in his stomach. All of a sudden, he felt much like the fourteen-year-old version of himself did, when he stood outside Jenny Scott's house just before his first real date.

"Hi." Claire smiled when she opened the door.

She looked beautiful, and a little weird. The sleeveless olive green dress she was wearing was cinched above her waist with a large black belt, and there seemed to be a gun holster attached to it. Black leggings and knee-high boots were almost lost on him, as the main distraction was her hair. She somehow managed to get the stick straight hair he knew she had into a mass of tight curls all over her head.

"You look…nice," he said, as he was trying to figure out who it was that she was supposed to be.

"Thank you," she said, as she grabbed a small bright blue purse with a dark blue square pattern on it. "You shaved."

"For the cause," he admitted, "it will be back in a couple of weeks. You ready?"

"All set. Are you ready, tiger?" she teased him.

They walked together to his gray sedan parked in the apartment parking lot, and he opened the door for her before he got into the car himself. The drive out of the city was very quiet, as most people were coming into the city for Saturday night fun. Add Halloween to the mix, and some areas were brimming with weirdness.

"I'm pretty sure I just saw a gigantic man with a beard dressed up as a My Little Pony," she said, pointing out the window to the sidewalk full of people walking towards a number of night clubs in the area.

"Halloween in the city."

"Crazy-town. I do kind of love it, though," she admitted. "So, this is your business partner?"

"Yes, Aidan."

"And his wife," she paused to remember the name, "Charlotte?"

"Yup. They live just outside the city, small house in the burbs." Max confirmed the few things he told Claire about them already.

"They have kids?" Claire asked.

"They're…headed that way."

"How did you two meet and become business partners?"

"College," Max began, "we both got jobs with the same architect firm as part of an internship program. They liked how we worked as a team, so they put us on a project together fulltime. We did that a few years, and then branched off on our own about six years ago."

"And that's going well?" She knew nothing beyond what he told her, which was never really much. She made a mental note to at least look up his company so she could familiarize herself with what he did for a living.

"Yeah. We started off just doing additions. Then, before we knew it, we were redesigning and restructuring. Eventually, it became we're pretty much building places from scratch. We do okay."

"Aidan commutes in?" she asked. "I can't imagine that drive every day."

"It's not too bad if you leave early enough, but living in the city right in the heart of everything is nice. I like it."

"I hope they like me," she said out of the blue as she shifted in her seat.

Rebecca's words echoed in his mind. The pain in his chest jabbed at him hard and unexpectedly, he did his best to shake it off. His teeth gritted together, and his jaw tightened.

"Even though there's really no pressure, because it's not like you're bringing home a girl to mom, but still…" she added. "You're doing me a huge favor, thank you."

"What if she's stunning? What if when you walk into the room, your eyes meet and you're instantly captivated?" she asked, as she clutched over her heart with one hand and laid the other on her forehead.

"Ah…you're a drama queen. I've been trying to figure out your costume." he smiled.

"No, never." She smiled. "You don't have any idea who I am, do you?"

"Honestly, no. But your hair is cute like that."

"Thank you, only took seventeen bottles of hairspray to get it this way. I'm quite sure I am singlehandedly responsible for another layer of the Ozone being gone."

They arrived at the party, which was just getting into full swing. Charlotte greeted them at the door in a black witch dress. Her black hair had been straightened, and her whole face was covered in green makeup.

"You must be Claire," Charlotte beamed at her, and received a cocked, frustrated eyebrow from Max. She ignored him.

The two settled in with the other party guests, all who were dressed in costumes which varied in complexity. She counted three vampires and a couple of cute cops with their prisoner dates in tow.

Over the last couple of weeks, her dreams had been unpredictable and random, which was exactly what she had hoped for. She did find herself within the dreams of her neighbors the most—casualties of war, she thought of them. Admittedly, she loved Mrs. Doogan. The woman was well into her nineties, Claire suspected, but always dreamed of herself at maybe twenty-three. Always wearing combat boots, Claire had no idea why. Jack was a handful when he popped up. Brittany dreamed she was in a foreign country, and after finally meeting them and hearing of their travels, Claire supposed maybe the girl sometimes forgot where she was. She smiled at Max; she hadn't seen him once. It was awesome. A few faces rang small bells, as if they were customers in her high traffic retail store. *Maybe the mystery redhead will be here*, she thought as she scanned the faces.

"Apparently, the tooth fairy over there," Max's voice interrupted her thoughts as he noticed her scanning the crowd.

Claire looked over at the blonde girl standing in the corner of the room with the white sparkly wig, short, white tank top and skirt, and white high-heeled Mary Janes. Her skin was light, but warm against the bright white costume, and her makeup had sparkles ever so lightly scattered to catch the light. She looked perfect, Claire sighed. She was instantly jealous, and she had no idea what to do with the feeling.

"Oh, Max," she said honestly, "she's really pretty. Maybe being set up won't be a bad thing. I could make myself scarce."

"No chance, doll, you're stuck with me tonight." He smiled.

"Want me to go chat you up?"

"You'd be my wing woman?"

"Why not?" she batted her eyes at him. "I could totally make that happen."

"No, but thank you for your sweet offer."

Max introduced her to the folks who came over and said hello. She noticed that Max kept things light, and most people came by to say a quick, but oddly awkward hello, and then went back to the group that they came with. Max seemed to float on the outer social edge, which was exactly where she was comfortable. As the evening went on, she caught a few glances her way, a few whispers. Max didn't seem to notice at all, and she didn't know him well enough to ask. She toyed with the idea of cornering him about it, but always stopped short when she remembered having a hard time growing up when she was still trying to figure out the rules of the game, and being weird around her friends. When they questioned her, all she wanted to do was hide. Or be invisible, which was a joke because that was the problem. She was an invisible guest in the dream world, and would give anything in the world not to be.

"Having a good time?" the scarecrow joined them and asked.

"Yes, I'm glad Max brought me along. I'm Claire. You must be Aidan."

"What gave me away?" he asked.

"The costume. I met Elphaba," Claire pointed out Charlotte who was refilling snack bowls, "which makes you Fiyero. Book or play?"

"Both?" Aidan said after a moment of reflection, "I like a good book, but I think Charlotte just got lost when she saw it on stage. I think I watched her actually fall in love."

"Tell me you don't feel eighty feet tall when you hear Defying Gravity."

"I like her." Aidan smiled at Max. "And by the way, awesome

costume."

"Thank you."

"You know who she is?" Max chimed in curiously.

"You don't?" Aidan asked.

"She won't tell me."

"Spoilers." Aidan winked at Claire.

Charlotte joined them soon after she checked on everyone. She chatted effortlessly with Claire, which made Max happy. Claire mentioned how cute she thought the house was, particularly with all the decorations and that launched Charlotte into the list of selling points for the house she had been working on in hopes of getting it on the market before too long.

"Well, sir, I do believe this date is going quite well," Claire said to Max when they were alone again.

"You do?"

"Yes, all the boxes were checked so far." She smiled.

"And what boxes are those?" he was curious.

"You picked me up, no flowers."

Max made a scared face. Should he have gotten flowers?

"I find them to be a little hokey on the first date. I think flowers are wonderful, when they mean something. Sunflowers on a plate to remind you of an afternoon you once spent, that sort of thing. Flowers on a first date mean nothing more than the guy wants to be a show off."

"So no flowers, good?" He wasn't all too sure he was following.

"Exactly, wait until they mean something. You opened the door for me. Good job to your Mama for teaching you manners."

"Noted."

"You've introduced me to people you know, you remember my name." She teased, "and you paid little to no attention to the tooth fairy over there."

Max turned his head to see the small woman happily cozied up to a thin framed guy in a football uniform. He had seen him a couple times before in years past, *a co-worker of Charlotte's,* he thought. *She must have had a back-up set up for this girl.*

"Well, it's hard to pay attention to anyone else in the—"

"Annnnnd no cheesy lines," she spoke loudly over him so that he would not finish his statement.

"Noted." He did not finish the cheesy line. "Did you have a good time?"

"I did, thank you for getting me out. It's been a long time since I've done anything like this."

"Well, you two, be careful getting back into the city. You know you're welcome to stay," Charlotte said as innocently as she could pretend to be when she offered her goodbyes.

Max knew exactly what she was thinking; they had one pull out bed. One. He shook his head at her.

"We had a lovely time, thank you," Claire said, as she put the little blue purse over her head and let Max put her coat around her.

"That's an awesome costume by the way, well played with the purse." Charlotte said.

"Thank you." Claire smiled at Max, as if to say *See! Told ya so.*

"Is your hair naturally curly?" Charlotte asked.

"No. Straight as an arrow. Took me hours," Claire didn't mind admitting.

"Well, it was well worth it." Charlotte smiled as she kissed Max goodbye and gave Claire a hug.

"You know who she is?"

"Yes. Do you?" Charlotte smiled.

"No. She won't tell me. She's been getting compliments all night. I'm starting to think I'm missing something big."

"Spoilers." Charlotte winked.

"What the hell does that mean?" Max asked as they headed back out to the car to go home.

* * * *

The ride home was chatty. Max filled Claire in on several of the people who had been at the party. Who was who, how they were connected to each other.

"So you used to live near them?" she asked, gently dipping her toes in the water.

"Yeah."

"Keep in touch with any of them?" she wondered, as it seemed that none of them had seen him since he moved to the city.

"Hard with work and all." It was, that wasn't a lie.

"Yeah, being an adult does get in the way."

"How about you, got any close friends that you're dying to drag out to the city or go back home for?"

Claire all of the sudden didn't want to talk about it anymore.

"As you said, hard with work and all. I keep up on social media, that's enough for now."

Can we talk about something else? Please?

"I don't do social media. What is the point?"

"To keep in touch with people that you're too busy to keep in touch with. Like the tooth fairy girl." Claire smiled innocently. There you have it, perfect subject change.

"I'm sure she's fine. She went home with the football player."

"I don't know, I think the Brawny Man would have been the better bet. Mr. Football fumbled a few times in his play," Claire noted as she remembered him checking her out once or twice while the tooth fairy wasn't looking.

"You know who I am?" He was surprised, she hadn't mentioned it once all evening.

"Of course. I don't live under a rock like some people," she said smugly.

He walked her to her door, where he begged her to tell him who she was. She finally relented, and told him the tale of a girl named Melody Pond. In an odd way, Claire had a bit in common with the wild-haired heroine. Never in the right time or the right place. Always at a disconnect with her own life.

"And we come to the goodbye part of the evening. Does he walk her to the door? Does he hug her? Should he lean in for a kiss? What if she goes for the cheek and he slips her the tongue?" Claire sweetly listed all the possibilities as she leaned up against her door in the quiet hall.

It was well past midnight. Max had arranged for Pilot to spend the night with Jack and Claire had dropped Tilney off at her parents' house, though it was late, neither of them were in a hurry for the evening to end.

"What if he goes for the cheek and she slips him the tongue?" Max defended man-kind.

"Really? When does that ever happen?" Claire asked.

"True," Max agreed.

"Well, Ms. Martin, here you are at your door safe and sound." He straightened himself up and stood tall over her. Her face lifted to his, and she smiled.

She was naturally beautiful, in the most effortless way.

"You have beautiful eyes. I like how the light reflects the gold in them." The words came out of nowhere.

Claire's heart started to thump a little harder. Of all the things he could have said, that was the last thing she expected. Somehow the cheesy line wasn't so cheesy coming from him.

"Watch it, Mr. Duncan, you're teetering on cheesy," she warned.

"This is the part where, I, Max would take my date's hand," he said, as he attempted to bring the little bit serious back to silly where it needed to be.

"Is that so? And as your date, I would stand straight," she said, as she straightened back up from leaning against her door.

"And I'd take a step closer, and bid you a good evening," he said as he kissed her hand.

Claire found herself lost for several seconds. His dimple was hinting at the sides of his mouth as he smiled, she could once again see it on his freshly shaved face. His jet black hair was just disheveled in the cutest way after their evening out. She lifted her hand and pushed the stray hair that always seemed to fall out of his face.

"You got some smooth moves there, buddy. I think when you're ready, tooth fairies will be lined up around the block."

Her gentle touch gave him chills down his back. *God, in another life, Claire.* In another life he'd take a step closer to her. They stood in the hall with the unforgiving lights casting down on them, yet they didn't notice. He could reach out and touch her, but he remained where he was. The burn in his chest would have to be ignored.

"You're not so bad yourself," he admitted.

"Spoilers," she said gently.

He closed the distance between them, leaning his head on hers, and laughed.

"I guess I have a show to watch," he said, backing up to a safe distance away.

"Goodnight, Max," she whispered before she let herself into her apartment. Once she closed the door, she quietly leaned up against it and slid to the floor. *Oh, boy.*

Max had the exact same thought as he let himself into his own apartment. This could certainly be trouble. She was a friend, nothing more. She was Claire. He depended on her to be Claire, but no doubt there was a moment there. He may have been rusty, but he wasn't dead.

He let himself into his dark, silent apartment, opting to pick up Pilot in the morning since they had returned so late. He passed the kitchen without stopping for water. He passed the bathroom without opening the medicine cabinet. He shed the costume, tossed it into his hamper and fell onto his bed.

As the thoughts of her swirled around, exhaustion hit him. He never got back up, he feel asleep right in the middle of the bed, on top of the covers. There was a moment where he wasn't the Max who had come to live here a year and a half ago with a small box of the life he was torn from. For the first time in a long time, he was just Max.

Chapter 10

It was a nice day, not a cloud in the sky. Following her dreamer's movements, Claire looked around, noticing the subtle colors. Everything seemed to have a natural palate, including the sky, which was blue, muted with tan, as if it were merely a fading picture. She walked with the dreamer down the middle of what looked to be a basic, non-descript Main Street, USA. There were stores, benches, and signs as any town would have. Although Claire couldn't read the signs because they were blurry.

Ok, where we are isn't important to you, popped into Claire's thoughts.

Claire was used to the muted sounds most dreams have. Like other elements; it was more of an idea than the actual thing. That phone is ringing, but there would be no ring unless it was ringing in the dreamer's real world and they were on the brink of awaking.

This place was different though, the idea was silent. If it were a real place in a real time, Claire knew not even the hiss of wind would make a sound. As far as Claire could see, there were no other people around. She felt her hand grip the suitcase her dreamer was carrying as they walked. Her dreamer never looked down at the luggage, but Claire knew what it was because the dreamer knew what it was. She also knew it had been hers for as long as she could remember.

These were the strange things that connected her to a person she'd never met.

Her eyes remained on the road ahead of her, which went on endlessly, as if the dreamer saw no end to Main Street, or as if it was on continuous loop. In what seemed to be miles away and never getting closer was a field of green. She could see a small red square tucked on top of one of the rolling hills. *A house? No. A barn, maybe.*

As she walked, Claire noticed none of the store fronts, despite their pristine conditions, had anything in the windows; just windows that seemed to be void of detail—black.

Makings of a nightmare, Claire thought to herself. *Come on, be a nice dream.*

This girl was looking around, in every direction now. It all looked the same. She continued to walk down the silent, endless street with the barn that never got closer. Claire felt like there might have been trees around, but her dreamer wasn't thinking about it hard enough for them to actually be there. This girl was just putting one foot in front of the other and walking, walking, walking.

Where we going, love?

Claire felt the weight drop into the pit of her stomach, the feeling she got when a dreamer couldn't find their way.

"We're lost?" she asked the dreamer, even though they couldn't hear her.

We're waiting for somebody, she concluded. *They aren't here.*

As she passed by, yet another black window in yet another generic store front with pretty flowers in front of it, Claire caught an unexpected break. The dreamer turned, and faced herself in the window.

Well, hey there, you.

The woman was beautiful, petite, several inches shorter than Claire's long lean frame. She looked young, just barely thirty. Pangs of recognition shot through Claire's mind. She studied the face, wondering if it would be anyone she recognized. It was a face she knew, a face she has always known. A face she could trace every line of, and remember for the rest of her life. She wished the dreamer's own recognition would stop crowding her thoughts so she could concentrate.

"Have I seen you before? This would be so much easier if I didn't feel like I've known you forever." The fact she wasn't heard never stopped her from conversations.

The dreamer was wearing a wraparound yellow dress that framed her body perfectly, stopping just above her knees. She lifted her hand to the window and touched the reflection, and Claire caught the shine from the simple wedding band on her hand. For a moment, Claire gained control of the situation with the burst of recognition. She had seen this woman before. She waited for the scent of lilac to gently flow through the air, but it never came. Still she was excited to finally see.

There she was, and for the first time, Claire was treated to vivid detail. The redheaded mystery woman. Her hair with its long, soft waves was really beautiful. Her eyes sparkled with every known shade, hue and color of brown. Even though it was not her own, Claire enjoyed admiring the dreamer's reflection, momentarily imagining herself as the dreamer—red hair instead of brown, brown eyes instead of green. An overwhelming feeling of longing washed over her as she gazed at the reflection.

Reign it in, Claire, it's nice to see her again, but get a grip, she scolded herself over how excited she was to see the mystery dreamer again. Never in her life had she been so attached to one dreamer; it made no sense. She dreamed the dreams of a thousand souls, but this one stood out. She felt connected with this woman in a way she could not comprehend, as if the world was a better place when they were together.

Oh, I wish I knew who you are in real life. I feel like we need to be friends. "You left me here."

As the words came from the reflection, out of her mouth, Claire felt an icy chill run down her back. She wasn't expecting the dreamer to say anything, much less something on the rather creepy side. However, this girl liked to bring on the death. Claire could almost guarantee a truck was going to come out of nowhere and run them over. As she stared at the woman in the reflection, a wave of guilt flushed over her. She wasn't sure if it was hers or the dreamer's.

Claire had never been so uncomfortable in all her life, and for as much as she was hoping she would get a glance at this woman, she now could not wait for her reflection to stop looking deep into her soul. It was almost as if she was accusing herself for being stuck here, on this endlessly dreary main street.

The dreamer slowly let her hand down, turned back to the road and continued to walk. With every step, Claire felt the ball in her stomach.

I don't know where we are either, but I vote let's get out the hell out of Dodge, lady.

As she was walking, she noticed the fabric of her dress was fading. It was becoming invisible. The dreamer did not stop to see what was happening to herself, she just continued to walk into the endlessness that was Main Street. Claire felt the disconnect sink deep within her. She'd never experienced anything like it before. Her fingers got itchy to grab and hold onto the woman whose body she currently inhabited. She wanted to hold her before she disappeared completely.

You're fading away, Claire thought sadly, *why are you fading away?*

* * * *

Team Metis for the win. It had been a successful week, and her weekends were finally hers again. The music was streaming through the kitchen docking station as Claire was writing the last few items on her grocery list, and personal to-do list. It was a silly thing, writing her lists in her notebook, but it was a habit she just could not break. Claire organized online calendars, color coded schedules, had mass marketing on an automatic drip for her clients, but when it came to her own personal list making, nothing quite did it like a good old spiral notebook and a freshly sharpened pencil.

After her non-date with Max, Claire threw herself into work. She was by nature a workaholic, but things with Max had been a little off since the night of the Halloween party, and she chose to hide rather than deal with it. They had seen each other, the conversations had been as easy as they ever had been, but there was a little bit of lingering at the end. As if he wanted to say something more, but didn't. As if she wanted to say something, but didn't. Her relationship with him continued to be an anomaly that pleased her to no end, which left her in quite the mental state of confusion.

"I think...I'm distracted by the cute puppy." She offered to Tilney who was quietly chewing on a bone next to her on the couch. Tilney grumbled with objection to the idea that Pilot was cuter than he.

"Relax." She patted her lap and his big bony puppy body climbed on her to lick her face. "You're still my guy, even though in a month you will be bigger than me."

The knock at the door had Tilney crushing his paws into her stomach as he jumped from her lap to meet their guest.

"Jesus Christ, dog. I might need those ovaries one day," she said as she rubbed her stomach and side, following him to the door. She looked through the peephole and saw four faces making googly eyes at her. Her parents were on the other side of her door, and they brought along her grandparents too.

"What are you guys doing here?" Claire smiled at the surprise of seeing the four of them standing there with grins on their faces. Her grandfather had a shiny red triangular cardboard hat, tipped ever so slightly on his head.

"Happy birthday!" They all yelled in unison.

"Oh, good lord. It's finally happened. Am I being initiated into some sort of weird club? Do I have to get a tattoo of my AARP number?"

"Oh, hush you," her mother said as they shuffled into her apartment with all sorts of supplies Claire couldn't see until she opened the door. "Don't even talk to me until you have your first hot flash."

"What's all this?" Claire asked, taking a brown paper shopping bag from her grandfather and peeked inside.

"Break out the good China, baby girl; we're having a party," he informed her.

Claire looked at Tilney who was happily checking out the new toy Linda brought just for him.

"Oh, I see how it is. This one bribes you with a new toy and it's all grandma, grandma, grandma. Mom, seriously? A new toy every time you see him?"

"Well, if I had any grandchildren...." A not so subtle hint sang from her lips.

"Okay, okay." Claire gave up, and turned to Tilney adding, "Traitor."

"Well, when you said you were just going to have a quiet weekend at home, we thought you meant you'd have a quiet weekend at home with all of us."

"Thirty-one is no cause for celebration."

"Any age is cause for celebration," her grandfather reminded her.

Her father, Alan, kissed her on the cheek after dumping all the party goodies they'd brought. "It's your birthday." He grabbed her hands and pulled her close, twirling her in a dance.

"I've got sunshine...." He began singing, badly.

Claire lowered her head to his shoulder, and just shook her head in embarrassment. She giggled as he continued to sing, and dip her in the living room. Her parents always made her birthday special, every year. They woke her up at the crack of dawn to sing her happy birthday, and to tell her that her grandparents would be calling shortly. She would tell them, every year that her grandparents already called, at the actual crack of dawn. It was the one time she allowed their complete indulgences. No matter how silly or obnoxious their plans were for the day, it was a day Claire felt their complete, unconditional love. She told them that after several long weeks of moving, setting up her new life, and getting business back on track at her new location, she just wanted a quiet weekend at home. Silly girl to think she'd get it.

"So what's the plan, Gran?"

"We're taking you to the harbor. Get us some good crab, everything."

"Yum!"

"Sounds fun. Mom, what if I wasn't home?" Claire inquired as she unpacked the party goodies from the bag onto the kitchen counter.

"Oh, we knew you were home. I have my spies in this world," Linda winked at her daughter.

"Are we going to that joint with the girls in hot pants?" Alan asked as he handed his wife a roll of crepe paper.

"It's not your birthday, love," Linda scolded. "We're having a nice lunch and then coming back here for some pie."

Claire smiled as she watched Adelaide carefully pull a homemade birthday pie from one of the bags. Lemon Meringue, Claire's favorite. Adelaide baked every single birthday cake, and pie as it later turned out to be, Claire had ever wished over. Claire watched Charlie kiss his wife on the cheek as he folded up the bag. They really were the two most perfect people in the world.

"Well, if we are going to go out, I need to walk Tilney. I'll be back in about ten minutes."

"Gives us just enough time to decorate," Charlie said as he patted his hands on her cheeks and pinched them.

Claire hooked Tilney to his leash and headed down to the park for a quick lap and bathroom break. As soon as they got to the dog park, she spotted Max playing with Pilot.

"Hey!" he yelled to her as they entered the park.

Her heart began to pound and she scolded herself for it. A grown woman, with a crush. *Get over yourself, Claire,* she thought. In the week that passed, Max kept his friendly demeanor just that, friendly. She clearly made up the moment standing at her door to be much more than what it actually was.

"Hi," she said, "beautiful weather today."

"Yes." He smiled. Was she really starting with the weather? Man, this friendship was going downhill fast. She had been dodging and avoiding him ever so politely all week. He got the message loud and clear, she wasn't interested. Not that he was interested. Or rather, not that he wanted to be interested. "Have any fun plans this weekend?"

"Going out to lunch in a bit. Then nothing really, just peace and quiet." Claire smiled, not mentioning it was her birthday.

"Sometimes that's a gift in itself," he mused.

Just as she was about to respond Tilney made a run for the ball Pilot was playing with before Claire could get him off the leash and he pulled her like a rag doll. She plowed right into Max, losing the grip of Tilney's leash, letting him fly freely to the ball. Her hands went up to stop herself and they gripped Max's navy blue hoodie for stability.

"You okay?" he said after wrapping his hands around her to steady her.

She looked up at him, momentarily letting herself sink completely into the warmth of being in his arms. She had never been this close to him. His soft cologne invaded her senses. Despite the cool breeze of November, he was warm to the touch.

"Yeah," she whispered, looking up to meet his gaze.

Rather than letting go, his hands held tight around her waist keeping her pressed against him. The sound of the people in the park faded and all Claire could hear was her own heartbeat pounding in her ears. When she bit her bottom lip, lost in the thoughts running through her mind, a streak of desire ran up Max's spine. There would be no hiding from this moment for either of them. As if it was the plan all along, he lowered his head to hers and found her soft mouth waiting for his touch.

The kiss was soft, and slow. Claire felt as if she was finally breathing for the first time in a week. Leaning into him, she lifted her hands and wrapped them around his neck. He kept her steady where she was, feeding his own desire. There was nothing else here in his mind, just her. With a gentle reluctance, he pulled back but didn't let her go.

"Uh…beautiful weather we're having," he whispered as he tried to make sense of the muddled mess his mind just became.

"You just—I just—we just." And it felt so good, Claire couldn't find the words.

"I did. You did. We did," Max agreed.

His grip around her loosened and she straightened herself up, shaking her head for clarity. The world came back into focus as she watched him casually slip out from between her and the fence he had been leaning on to walk over to where the dogs were playing. He grabbed the leash on Tilney's collar and unhooked it, bringing it back to her.

"I'd say punish him, but..." his smile was uncontrollable.

"Sorry." *Don't be embarrassed Claire, you are a grown ass woman.*

"Claire. I—" He'd kissed her. And she'd sure as hell kissed him back.

His hand took her chin and lifted it up so he could look her in the eye. He was going to say something, really, he was. He just didn't know what. He lowered his head and kissed her once more, deeper. The taste of her was intoxicating, and it completely flooded his system—a system that had been emptied far too long ago. He felt his heart flutter a bit as the kiss kick-started it out of its suspended state.

He had done nothing but think of Claire since the night of the Halloween party. He knew he would have to let his feelings sort themselves out, but he hadn't calculated what he would do if he all of the sudden found her in his arms.

The sound of her name had her pushing herself quickly out of his arms like a guilty teenager. He looked in the direction the voice was coming from and saw four older people waving from the apartment building across the street. He instantly stepped back to give her the space she wanted.

"I have to go," she said to him as she gathered Tilney to get him back inside.

Watching her grab the dog's leash, tugging him along as she scurried back to the waiting group as quickly as she could allowed Max to feel what laid under the desire. Anger. Lies had led him to this apartment to the city, and here he was about to drag this perfectly sweet girl into his tangled web. It was the last thing he wanted.

"Did you see that?" Linda whispered to her mother-in-law as they watched Claire jog across the street, her faced flushed, surely not from walking the dog.

"I sure did," Adelaide confirmed.

Chapter 11

It was an enjoyable family lunch, even though Claire kept catching the nods and winks between the other two women at the table. They had seen the kiss, she was sure of it. She rolled her eyes and excused herself from her father and grandfather to the ladies' room, knowing the other ladies would follow her in.

"So, was that your fella?" Adelaide grilled Claire once inside the ladies' room.

"Who's that?" Claire played innocent.

"We saw you at the park, sweetheart." Linda proclaimed.

Claire felt the warm flush rush over her body, her face betraying her in a smile as she tried to shake it off.

"Did Dad see?"

"No. Gran and I were ahead of them. Caught the tail end of what looked to be quite a good kiss."

"Is that the fella from your building?" Adelaide continued to prod.

"Oh, your father told me he met some man in your building. And Gran knows who he is? Where's the love, Claire?" Linda threw up her hands with exaggerated accusation.

"Nothing to tell, Mom. I told Gran when we went pumpkin picking that I've made a new friend." She threw her hands up in defense. "A friend. Dad met him when I moved in. This is not a thing I was hiding."

"I didn't realize making a new friend entailed passionate embraces," Linda observed. "I'll be sure to include that the next time—"

"I don't know what that was," Claire stopped her mother. She really didn't know what that was. A much unexpected moment, yet somehow not unexpected. His lips were so soft and his touch so gentle, as if they had all the time in the world and kissed a million times before. His embrace was somehow already familiar to her, comforting to her. It unnerved her to no end. "But he is just a friend."

"Are you going to date him?" Linda whispered.

"No," Claire insisted firmly. She would not let herself, not with him. She'd begun to care about him too much. They had a good thing, and she didn't want to screw it up. "We're friends. He is very handsome. I think we both just lost our heads for a minute. Tilney got away from me and it made me plow into Max. It wasn't on our agenda to kiss. It just happened."

"I accidentally ran into Dr. Thomas when I was coming from my check-up last week. I didn't kiss him," Adelaide quipped.

Claire shook her head, "Hot Dr. Thomas? You should have kissed him."

"Claire, you have to get out there at some point," Linda said. "What do we know about this boy?"

"Nothing," Claire said loudly and then quieted herself down. She gave her grandmother a glance, because Adelaide would be the one to understand the words that she wasn't saying. "I haven't really looked into him. He's just a neighbor I happen to get along with."

"Claire, in today's world that's not—" Linda didn't get to finish her sentence.

"I want some pie. Go pay the bill before I die of starvation," Adelaide said loudly, and that was that. When Adelaide said march, you marched.

Linda shook her head at her mother-in-law, she was right in the middle of a sentence. Sometimes she wasn't sure if it was hearing loss or Adelaide getting to the age where she just didn't give a damn anymore about what other people were doing.

"Let your daughter live the way she wants to live, dear, it's tough I know," Adelaide said as she looked at Claire in the reflection of the bathroom mirror. The girl had been wanting to spill her guts, but not to her mother, and Adelaide knew it. There was nothing wrong with her hearing or her attitude. "Claire can help me in here, go get the check, dear."

"Yes, Ma'am," Linda quipped.

Once she was out the door, Adelaide turned to her granddaughter and gave her an all knowing look. "Spill it."

"It's nothing," Claire began, and washed her hands to give herself something to do, even though she had just washed them. "It's just...have you ever looked for a dreamer?"

"In a dream?"

"No, in real life."

"What? Why would you want to do that?"

"I've had these dreams, three of them now. At first I was just curious because this girl was a little weird. I don't know why I can't shake it, her dreams aren't all that unusual."

"She's not somebody you know?" Adelaide asked, knowing the strongest of connections happen with people she knew in the waking world.

"No, at least not that I know of. I was hoping she was a neighbor in my building but I've met them all. I guess she lives nearby. I don't know that much about her. I just feel like I need to find her, just to see. If I've had three dreams with the same girl, she must be stressing over something. I'm worried she may be in an abusive relationship or something. She keeps dreaming that she's trapped."

"Claire, that's dangerous," Adelaide warned.

"Gran," Claire pulled towels from the little basket on the counter, offering a few to her grandmother.

"I'm serious, Claire. Fooling with people in the real world because of what you find in dreams is not a good idea."

"I know, I just…"

"Just nothing, Claire. If this girl is a stranger, keep her that way. If she's in danger, let her work that out. It's not your job to find these people if they aren't naturally in your life."

"Alright, alright. Forget I asked. Jeeze!" Claire was surprised that Adelaide was so closed minded to the idea. She had always been so open to everything, or any idea that Claire threw at her. This seemed to be an unexpected wall.

"Let's go get that pie."

"Yes, Ma'am." Claire repeated her own mother's words with very much the same frustrated attitude.

They had their pie, with their silly cardboard hats. Linda lit three candles, one for every decade. She said when a woman reached a certain age, she only aged by the decade. So Claire was thirty, again. Fine with Claire. She opened gifts, and gave hugs and kisses goodbye. She tucked the leftover pie in the refrigerator, and pulled down the streamers and balloons because she wasn't sure if Tilney would try to eat them while she wasn't looking.

He would most likely sleep through the night, she thought as she checked in on him, and found him sound asleep in his bed. Rather not take any chances, as he had been fascinated with the crepe paper and balloons all night.

It was just past ten when she settled herself on her sofa with a blanket and pillow to watch a movie. Her phone lightly chimed.

Hi.

Claire waited for the rest of the text to come in, but that's all that it said. Just hi.

Hi, Max. What's up?

Casual. Casual was good. *Totally not thinking about today when you kissed me.*

The next bubble of text popped up.

What are you doing?

Okay, he's being weird. She didn't want weird.

Getting ready to watch a movie.

She waited for his reply, perhaps a request to rescue Pilot. Hopefully something funny to get them back to normal.

What movie?

Oh, she really should lie. Really, truly, she should not tell him what movie she was about to watch. She'd never live it down.

Porn? She thought *No.* The truth shall set you free. Maybe the joke he would surely come up with would be the key to that normal they needed.

Princess Bride. What are you doing?

She waited for him to make a snarky reply.

Standing outside your door. Been here about ten minutes, I can't seem to go upstairs. I can't seem to knock. It's a problem.

Well, not snarky. Claire blew out a steady breath of air, as the butterflies threatened to take it away. Before she could overanalyze her actions, she quickly typed and hit send before she could stop herself.

You can come in, watch the movie with me. If you want to.

His three-word reply had the butterflies breaking free and her falling over on the couch to scream into a pillow. He reduced her to a teenage girl.

As you wish.

Claire quickly jumped up, straightening up the blanket and pillow and gave the room a look over to make sure it was tidy. She shook her head at herself because she just finished cleaning up from the birthday events; it was tidy. She ran into the bathroom and threw back some mouth wash, gargling as she ran a brush through her hair. As good as it was going to get on no notice, she thought, and she opened the door to him standing in the hall.

"Hi."

"Hi." As they stood in the doorway of her apartment, the awkward silence crept in. Should he hug her? Kiss her? High five her? As a result, he just walked past her into the living room.

"I don't want to interrupt your movie," he said as he sat on the couch.

"It's okay, I don't mind." She went to the kitchen, pulled the water pitcher out of the refrigerator and poured him a glass before joining him on the couch.

"Haven't seen this movie in years," he recalled "is it on TV?"

"No. DVD. Kind of an annual tradition this time of year," she admitted. It was her favorite movie, had been since she was a little girl. She indulged herself by watching it on her birthday just before bed every year for at least the last decade. She could not help but allow herself, if only on her birthday, to somehow want love to defy all odds as it had for Buttercup.

They sat together like awkward teenagers for thirty minutes while Claire had internal arguments with herself. Here she was, with a gorgeous man sitting not two feet from her, her fingers itching to touch him, and her eyes were focused on the man looking for the six fingered man who killed his father.

"This is stupid," she finally said aloud.

"What?" Max asked, turning his attention to her. He resorted to sitting on his hands to keep them to himself.

Without warning, he found her in his lap and the taste of her kiss assaulting him. She could no longer breathe without his touch. The heat of his mouth on hers tantalized every inch and her body tingled in response. When his arms wrapped around her, his fingers dug into her sides and a breathless moan escaped them both. Hunger. Need. Now.

"Claire," he barely got her name out, the world was tumbling already.

"I need this," she whispered into his ear as she trailed kisses down his neck. "I can't take it anymore."

The desire that had been simmering slammed into him. As she wrapped her arms around his neck, he scooped his arms under her lifting her as he stood. He needed her naked and under him. He was in her bedroom within four quick strides. He was a man in a frenzy, soaking up the freedom of the sun after a lifetime of darkness. As he lifted her shirt and pulled it over her head, he filled his mouth with the peaks of her breasts. Her hips grinded into the bed beneath her in response to feeling his tongue circling.

"Out, out, out," she demanded as he trailed down and sank his teeth into her side.

"What?" *Did she say something?* His mind tried to focus on her words.

There was a noise in the corner of the room, an objectionable grunt followed by the sound of a jingling collar.

"Oh," he devilishly grinned as he watched the dog trot out into the living room.

"Lock the door," she panted in a whisper. "Now."

He broke himself from her only to do what he was told. When he returned, he found her in the middle of the bed on her knees with her hair cascading over her breasts. There were no words between them as she slowly unbuttoned his pants and slid her hand under his waistline until she found him, hard and aching. At her touch, he lifted her again, throwing them both onto the bed.

He gripped the button on her jeans and ripped them down as her hands lifted and gripped the rails on the headboard behind her. His mouth trailed around the inside of her thighs, she spiraled when his hand found her, nearly going over the edge that very second.

He climbed back up to her mouth, with his beautifully callused fingers just a little rough on her soft skin trailing along. He heard his name as a frantic plea in the exact moment he drove into her. There was no control now as her hips arched to take more. He buried himself into every part that she let him. She held nothing back, giving him the parts of herself she gave to no one. As her body tightened around him, she let his control take her. The release of pleasure was unlike anything she ever experienced, and as it slammed through her, she pulled him from his last grasp of restraint. He let it take him and tumbled over the edge with her.

It was minutes before either of them moved. Hours? Days? Laying together was a lifetime spent apart from the rest of the world. Where were they before this? There was nothing after this, just here and now. Her eyes were still closed when she felt the trail of his finger tracing her hip. Everything felt like liquid. She turned to him, laying her head on the pillow when they were face to face. Shadows of the room danced over their naked bodies.

"You can stay, if you want," she whispered.

It was the line she hadn't crossed since Christopher. She poured so much hope into him that when it shattered, there was nothing left. She would never let anyone see that part of her, not now or ever. She called the shots, she had control, and she would never open herself like that again. As Max lay with her, she felt as if the rules she worked so hard to define in the minimal dating life that was the last year did not exist. When she was with him, she was not a dream traveler. She was just Claire.

I want to be just Claire, forever.

"I do." He kissed her nose, bringing her back from her thoughts. "Can I get a glass of water?"

"Yes. But get a new glass, I'm sure the ones in the living room are warm by now. I keep the fancy stuff in the fridge, help yourself." She smiled.

As he walked out of her bedroom, completely naked, she smiled at the sight of his butt. His body was amazing. Hard and toned everywhere. Jogging did a body good. She willed herself to stand up, instantly regretting it when the chill of the air hit her body.

"Nope," she said and climbed back into the warm bed, making sense out of the sheets and pillows that had been tossed and twisted under their naked bodies.

"So," he smiled as he climbed back under the covers, and grabbed her hips to pull her closer. "It's your birthday?"

The pie! A few slices left with the plastic lid on top declaring in colorful marker Happy Birthday, Claire!!

"It is," she admitted.

"Why didn't you tell me?" Max asked. "Is that why your parents and grandparents were here?"

"Yes. I just...I didn't know what was going on with you and me. It's just a day, really." She found herself feeling foolish that it was, in fact, her birthday.

"Well, at least I am dressed for the occasion."

She giggled, "That you are. We both are."

"Seriously, Claire, happy birthday."

"Thank you," she lifted her head and let the warm feeling of his touch spread through her.

His face scrunched up in embarrassment.

"Um, how old are you?"

"Thirty one," she confirmed.

"I'm sorry I didn't know that." It was an odd truth. When he gave it a second, he realized he knew so little about her. Yet, laying with her here, he felt like he had known her his whole life. He knew every inch of her, inside and out. Somehow that was true even before their movie was interrupted.

"We'll discover things about each other at the right time, no need to rush." Her odd truth, the one she would fiercely hold to.

He said nothing as his fingers brushed her cheek. He stopped just as his lips found hers again, just before he made love to her again. His words whispered against her lips.

"Right here, right now. It's all I need."

Chapter 12

The space around her filled with blue smoke. It was thick, and swirling around her legs as if she was walking through clouds. Claire paced back and forth in a single line and the smoke broke up, dancing around her before it settled back down onto the ground. Everything around her was black; she was surrounded by darkness. She went on a cruise with her parents once, and spent a few minutes on the balcony of their suite looking out onto the water. There were no stars to be seen, the moon was hiding, and the blue of the ocean matched the blue of the sky resulting in the odd illusion Claire was standing in perfect nothingness. Everything around her, as far as she could see, was just, nothing. This dream reminded her of standing on that balcony.

As she paced back and forth, Claire realized she wasn't a person. She could feel the power in her legs, all four of them. *A cat? No, bigger,* she thought. She concentrated on the feeling her dreamer was giving to her, and her heart sunk deep as those feelings became clear. A light broke her concentration, piercing the endless darkness and breaking up the thick layer of blue smoke around her feet. It was there she saw the boy, who was painfully small. She was sure he wasn't that small in reality, he was just imagining himself to be tiny, so he was. He stood no more than two feet tall, with his brown hair disheveled, in what must have been his favorite Spiderman pajamas because Claire could see them clearly. He knew them well.

No, no, no, no, no, no, no. The single word screamed within Claire's own mind. She was now dripping with fear. He was dripping with fear. He stood in the doorway of light, gripping his tattered bear's hand that was dangling from his own. He pulled the bear up, and shielded himself with it. The slick taste of metal filled Claire's mouth, and she was overcome by the wildest mix of fear and hunger. This poor child was imagining his hunter was hungry for him. The taste of him teased her, as Claire found her body pacing back and forth faster. She was hunting him. The steps the animal took quickened, she realized it was only awaiting its target.

As her body broke free from its pace and Claire could do nothing but watch as the boy got closer, she noticed his eyes grew big with fear. His fear filled her to the brink of madness. He was a child, and had conjured up the scariest thing in the world. Maybe she was a lion, or a jaguar. It was something he'd seen on TV, heard about at school, or perhaps was nothing more than a shape an innocent household object made on the wall when the lights were out in his room. She felt huge, again through his imagination. He was tiny; she was huge. Though she knew monsters were not real, she was unable to escape the feeling they were. In this moment, in this space, his monster was real. Claire was trapped within the monster, unable to comfort the boy.

"My sweet boy, I am so sorry." They were words he would not hear, but she still said them as she raced toward him. *Please wake up, please wake up in your mother's loving arms.* Deep within her own mind, Claire heard an odd sound. It was soft, but persistent. It did not match the boy's dream, and moments before she reached him, he faded away.

"Claire," the voice whispered.

Claire jolted out of the little boy's nightmare, her arms flailing wildly trying to escape whatever they were trapped in. She could now hear the words she was saying to the boy.

"So sorry, so sorry, no, no, no," she helplessly mumbled, waking Max in her process.

"Claire, shhh…" Max's voice remained gentle as he continued to try to hold her still and get her to stop waving her arms in escape attempts. He wrapped his arms around her, and cleared her hair out of her face.

The world finally made sense again and Claire realized she was in her own bed, but it took her a beat to remember she wasn't alone. It was Max, he was holding her tight. He was bringing her back.

"You were having a nightmare. Are you okay?" he whispered.

Her heart was racing from the fear the boy poured into her, her breath still jagged. She felt Max's arms around her, his warm body pressing up against hers as he pulled her closer to him. Though Christopher had not been her only lover, he was, until tonight the only man who spent the night. This was why. Traveling into worlds unknown, and doing God knows what when she got there. She had no desire to have an audience. As the warmth of him wrapped around her, slowing her breath and heartbeat, she sank into a comfort she had never known. His gentle touch a far better welcome than the sometimes groan and shove she'd get from Christopher.

"Just hold me a minute." It was all that she could say.

He wasn't going anywhere. He could feel her shaking. "What was the dream?"

Claire thought about it for a second, she wanted so desperately to be able to tell him the truth. "There was a little boy, I was trying to save him from a monster but the closer I got, the closer the monster got."

"Did you know the boy?"

"No, I just wanted to save him."

"That's very sweet. I'm sure if he was real, you would have. Thankfully, you don't have to, it was just a dream." He spoke the last few words, echoing what she usually said herself when she woke from bad dreams.

The large thump had both of them jumping. A few seconds passed, and scratching at the door along with barking rang in the air.

"Tilney," she said and she started to get out of bed.

"I'll get him," Max whispered and kissed her lips softly.

Max stood from her bed, still naked with the shadows of her darkened room dancing around him, he opened the door. Tilney raced in and leaped into the bed to rescue Claire, as it had been his job for the last several months.

"I'm okay, baby." She sat up with the sheets wrapped around her and comforted him.

"He must have heard you," Max said as he began to walk back to her, but stopped cold when he heard Tilney's low warning growl.

"Uh, I think stay there a minute," Claire offered. Tilney was not sure of the source of Claire's distress, and he made it pretty clear that Max wasn't going to be moving from where he was standing.

"It's okay, baby," Claire repeated as she reached over and turned on the soft light of the lamp on her bedside table.

The light filled the room and Max could see Claire sit up against her pillow with the sheets wrapped around her naked body. Her hair was a tousled mess, but the contrast of her skin against the dark blue sheets made her look so soft. He couldn't help but remember the feel of running his hands all over her, the softness of it under his fingertips. His body began to react to his imagination, he quietly cupped himself to not disturb her.

"See, it's just Max. He's harmless." Claire smiled while Tilney settled himself next to her on the bed. She rubbed his now impossibly long body, he really grew into quite the giant over the last few weeks. "I love you, thank you for checking on me. I'm okay. I'm going to just go get some water. You want anything?"

"I'm good, thanks."

Claire took Tilney back out into the living room where he curled back up in the giant dog bed that was getting smaller and smaller by the day compared to his growth spurts. She grabbed a glass of water from the kitchen and gulped down the chilling liquid while still standing in front of the refrigerator. Max was right, she didn't really have to save the boy. He was fine, in his bed. Most likely he has already woken up and in his mother's loving arms.

As she returned the pitcher of water to the refrigerator, she closed the door and her eyes fell on a picture she had seen a thousand times a day. A four by six photo of Tilney and her standing in front of Springfield Farm on the day she officially adopted him. It wasn't her grin, or the sweet tininess of Tilney that caught her eye, it was what was in the background.

"Holy shit," she whispered, snatching the photo off the refrigerator door. She hurried across the living room to the office and flipped the light on casting a bright glow against the darkness.

"Everything okay?" Max called out from her bedroom.

"Yes," she called. "I um...just remembered something. Have to write it down or I'll forget it."

"I hear old age will do that to a person. You are over thirty now."

"You're not funny," she cracked back. "Whoever tells you that you're funny is a liar."

She waited impatiently for her computer turn on and logged into her recent emails. She didn't even bother sitting as she scrolled down to the recent email she had received from Mrs. Springfield.

Claire,

So Wonderful to see you today! I hope your grandparents enjoyed their visit, it was very sweet of you to bring them. I hope I get to see them again sometime. Anyway, getting that photo album out made me realize that I hadn't shared these with you before. I picked out just a few pictures, the ones that make me think of you and how we wouldn't be here if it weren't for your monster marketing skills. Stick them in your own scrapbook, be proud of yourself, kiddo!

Claire scrolled through the attached photos as she had once before, seeing a few with the open field and red barn in the background. The red barn from the photo of her and Tilney; the red barn from the dream she had with her mystery girl.

"I have seen you!" she mumbled to herself.

Her hand stilled when she got to the photo she wanted. A crisp fall afternoon day, Mr. Springfield sitting so handsome on a shiny red tractor with a long trailer behind it holding bales of hay. The small group of children with their smiling teacher and parent chaperones. Excitement swam through her veins at the idea she may be able to locate this girl.

She opened a new email box and found the contact information Jane sent her for Brad Rich. She attached the photo, along with a message.

Mr. Rich,

My friend Jane Whitmore referred me to you. I am looking to track down this woman for a client. Not sure if Jane mentioned it, sort of an attraction at first sight thing. All on the up and up, he's a good guy. This photo was taken at Springfield farm about three years ago. The woman with the red hair in the center of the adults is the woman I am looking for. I don't know if she's a teacher or a parent. Jane says if anyone can find her, you can. Please give me a call tomorrow if you are interested in taking on the case, and your fee.

Thank you.

Her grandmother's words of warning popped into her mind. She wasn't going to interfere too much, what harm could come of it? She just wanted to see the woman, with her own eyes. Maybe if she saw that the woman was fine and nothing was off, she could finally shake free of the need to help her.

"All right with the world again?" Max asked as she turned out the lights and climbed back into bed with him.

"Yes. Sorry about that. The nightmare reminded me of something, believe it or not. But I needed a minute anyway. I'm still such a sucker for this sort of stuff. Horror movies, nightmares, being scared of the dark. No matter how old we get, we still sometimes find ourselves running from the boogie man," Claire said thoughtfully.

"I could never sleep with my closet door open," Max admitted to make Claire feel better. "I kind of still can't. Don't tell anybody."

It did make her feel better, it made her smile.

"Fuzzy socks," she offered, "I have to have my feet covered. Socks."

"And fuzzy socks are the best ones?" he asked, as his bare feet found hers and rubbed them.

"Boogie men can't handle them." She smiled. "They are allergic to the fuzz."

"Well, you don't have the fuzzy socks." He said as his legs wrapped around hers, and his arms wrapped around her waist and he began to run his hands up and down her back.

Her skin tingled at his touch, she nearly moaned.

"Will I do?" he asked.

"I believe the question is—" She lifted her head and wrapped her hands in his hair as he began a slow assault trailing down her neck. "What will you do?"

He rolled her under him, and filled all of the space around her. Unlike the urgency that they had earlier in the evening, he seemed to be in no hurry. The warmth of the bed, the soft feeling of his skin over the hard muscles in his back as she ran her own hands over them, everything overtook her. His lips found hers, and his kiss continued fuel the mad, slow climb of passion in her body.

"Max," her voice whispered as she felt him fill her, gently and slowly.

Chapter 13

"You look lovely today, sweetheart."

"Thank you, Gran." Claire smiled as she walked with her grandmother into the restaurant of Adelaide's choice. They had a monthly standing date for lunch, which Claire enjoyed immensely. She knew time could be fleeting. Her other set of grandparents, Linda's parents, were already gone. Linda's father had died of a heart attack at the age of fifty, when Claire was just a baby, and her mother died of cancer when Claire was a teenager.

Adelaide chose a French restaurant this month, feeling in the mood for soups, breads and cheeses. The autumn air had settled into Maryland, the beautiful foliage was turning to their darkest shades and falling off the trees. The smell of cinnamon and spices welcomed you at nearly every store and food vendor. Thanksgiving was on everyone's mind. Claire was happy to break out the first of her fall wardrobe of knee-high, brown leather boots, black leggings, and a long cream sweater that swooped lower in the back. Having very few friends and few hobbies, Claire did allow herself to be spoiled with a fashionable wardrobe.

"New sweater?" Adelaide asked, as they were seated at a table near a large stone fireplace that had a small fire already going to ward off the afternoon chill.

"Picked it up on Saturday, as a matter of fact," Claire confirmed. "How's Pop today?"

"Oh, good. He's been on a nature channel kick. He still wants to hunt, and most of the time it doesn't bother him. He really only gets fussy about it this time of year."

"Sorry, Gran. I know Dad would take him if he wants to go," Claire said as she looked over the menu.

"I know he would. It's not that, I think he's just missing being young. We're lucky, we've got our health, relatively speaking. At the same time, that makes it harder because it's frustrating when you just can't do something simply because you're old."

"So he watches the Nature Channel."

It really must be hard, getting old. Claire had a better understanding than most about how older people didn't see themselves as old. She thought about the dream that she had when she was just a young thing, dancing with the most handsome sailor in the world. It was how she felt, young and free. It was the feeling that she got whenever she ran into Mrs. Doogan and her granddaughter in the halls. Mrs. Doogan shuffled herself so slowly in her walker, all her movements thought out. Her mind though, was still so young and free.

"That he does. All those hunting shows and fishing shows," Adelaide continued, and then found her attention to the people being seated at a table nearby. "Oh, my."

"What's wrong?" Claire asked, following her grandmother's gaze to the people being seated just a few tables over.

"That's Cathy's daughter," Adelaide whispered.

"And her grandson?"

"No," Adelaide's eyebrows went up, "that's Cathy, her daughter, and her daughter's new boyfriend."

Claire looked at the pair who sat with Adelaide's friend Cathy. The daughter had curly blonde hair, and way too much makeup on. This would be the dead giveaway that she was a cougar trying to pass for a cub. It was well done, Claire thought the woman probably got a lot of compliments for her youthful look. She was wearing a white blouse tucked into tight white pants with a gold chain belt. The man who was pulling her chair out for her couldn't have been much older than Claire herself. He was wearing a black leather jacket and jeans.

"Well, well," Claire smiled. "Good for Cathy's daughter. She's got what, twenty years on him?"

"Eighteen. She got divorced from her husband last year, and this guy popped up a few weeks ago."

"Wow. Well, do you know anything about him?" Claire whispered to her Grandmother.

The waiter came to take their orders, both decided to indulge in soups, bread and cheese. Claire got a warm brie spread over apples with a cream of crab soup. Adelaide picked out a small cheese tray and a bowl of their chicken noodle.

"He's thirty-seven. Never been married, is some sort of computer something or another. Cathy's words, not mine," Adelaide continued, as the ladies discreetly stared at the man who was happily chatting with his two lunch dates.

"Is it serious?"

"Cathy seems to think that Marcy is just getting it out of her system. The husband strayed, with a younger model. I think she needs to feel young and beautiful," Adelaide said between spoonsful of soup.

"That's certainly going to do it," Claire confirmed.

"Speaking of hot sex…" Adelaide returned her attention to her granddaughter.

Claire nearly snorted her soup out of her nose. She had planned on telling Adelaide about Max while they dined, but Claire hadn't anticipated the conversation starting out in such a way.

"How's that neighbor friend of yours, is he still just a friend?"

Do I have it written on me, Claire wondered.

"He's…" Claire couldn't come up with any words. Her smile could not be helped and she blushed at remembering the hours that she had spent in bed with Max, discovering him.

"I see." Adelaide laid her spoon down and sat back in her chair to let Claire have her minute.

"He doesn't dream," Claire said.

"And that comforts you?"

"I know nothing about him, and it's the most wonderful thing in the whole world," Claire proclaimed.

"Do you know enough to know him to be a good man?" Adelaide asked.

"Yes," Claire didn't even hesitate with her answer.

"Then you know enough."

She supposed she did know enough. It had been a few days since their evening together, and it seemed they were both treading very carefully. She still had her reservations about pushing the limits of the gift she had gotten with him, and he seemed to never push her. He hadn't asked her what this meant for them, he hadn't pushed for more time with her. However, he had made it a point to call or stop by every day, for a least a little bit. As they stood at the park with the dogs, they stood together, his hand eventually finding its way around her, and always a soft, sweet kiss goodbye.

"Can I ask you a question?" Claire asked.

"Are you thinking about telling him the truth?"

"I'm thinking of what it will be like to tell someone the truth," Claire admitted.

"You never thought of telling Christopher," Adelaide reminded her.

"No, I didn't. Five years, and all I ever did was think of how I could continue to hide it from him."

"This boy is different?"

"I'm different, I think." Claire contemplated. "I'm just Claire. The man doesn't dream. Everything I feel for him is real, it's mine. When I'm with him, I'm free. I don't worry about if the connection we feel for each other is ours or if it comes from me being in his mind."

"Claire, as nice as that is, don't confuse your feelings. Are you falling for him, or are you falling for the freedom that you find in him?"

Wise. Old. Gran.

"At first, I think I fell for the freedom," she conceded. "But he's a good man. He makes me smile. He makes me laugh."

"Oh, the ones that make you laugh. Now that's something." Gran winked. "Just be careful dear. When you find the right man, it will all fall into place."

"He stayed over a few days ago," Claire said, not adding that they had spent half the night making love. "I had a nightmare, one where I was a monster to a child."

"Oh, Claire. Those are the worst." Adelaide knew, from her own experiences.

"He woke me up, he brought me out of it. He held me."

"And it can be like that, Claire. You just have to let it."

"I don't let people in like that," Claire admitted.

"Don't you think it's time you did?"

They enjoyed the rest of their lunch and Claire drove Adelaide back to her small house in the retirement village. Charlie was sitting in a rocking chair on the front porch with a cup of tea.

"Hi, Pop!" Claire said as she got out of the car and helped Adelaide to the porch.

"You girls have a nice lunch?" he asked, as he invited Adelaide to sit next to him in her chair.

"We did. You know, you can come anytime you like," Claire offered.

"Are you kidding me? I look forward to my man time!" He smiled at her.

The man was in a rocking chair with a blanket over his lap and a cup of tea in his hand. Man time, he really was making the best of it.

"Have you taken to people watching?" Claire asked.

"You would not believe some of the stuff that we see."

Claire thought about the daughter, and the very young new boyfriend. She could only imagine the data that one could collect sitting in a rocking chair on the porch, watching the world go by.

"Well, I will leave you to it then." Claire kissed both of them, and waved. "See you next week."

As she pulled away, and headed down the road, Adelaide smiled at her husband of more than sixty-five years.

"She's got a fella," Adelaide offered her juicy gossip.

"The neighbor?" Charlie asked.

"Yup."

"Saw that one coming a mile away," Charlie said as he sipped his tea and continued to rock.

"She didn't. Apparently, he's a mystery to her." She waved her hand in the air like a young romantic.

Adelaide kept her words careful. The way she had for all those years. She didn't know how to tell him the truth those first few years, and then after, there just simply was no need. Day after day passed, and the importance of it faded.

"Oh? Those mind tricks you passed down to her don't work on him?" Charlie asked after a few silent seconds. He kept his eyes steady on the street in front of their house, rocking in his chair as if he had not said anything at all.

Adelaide turned to her husband, a man whose every wrinkle she knew. She looked utterly shocked. The smile broke across his face, but he never looked at her as he softly cooled his tea. Did she really think he didn't know?

"Does she know it goes away?" He shook his head and looked at his wife, reaching for her hand.

You've known all this time, and loved me still. Amazing.

"What makes you think it goes away?" Her mind might be old, but it was reeling.

"Adelaide, you were the smartest girl I knew. Always two steps ahead of everyone. It's a very intimidating thing, knowing you were always going to know what was going on," he said as he pointed his fingers to his head. "But, you loved me anyway."

"I could say the same thing," she said, as she fought back the tears that were threatening her eyes.

"I noticed after Alan was born, there were things that happened. You seemed different."

"Not two steps ahead?" she asked, completely fascinated by the new information.

"No, just settled. You used to have such terrible nightmares sometimes, and talk in your sleep. You'd say things that just didn't make any sense, talk about people we never met. Your brain must have worked all night long to put together what you knew about people."

Sixty-five years he had been keeping these things to himself, she had been keeping them to herself. And here they sat on a Sunday afternoon, sitting in their rocking chairs, chatting as if it was just something that had always been. It did go away, the dreams had stopped. She knew they would, and when. It was the one fact that she held from Claire, for her own sake. Adelaide had damn near altered the course of her own life. Thank God Charlie had come along to save her from her self-destruction.

"I honestly thought I made the whole damn thing up until the year I retired."

"Oh?"

"Yeah. I had been thinking about getting a boat, you remember. Every night at dinner I sat across the table and think as loudly as I could about a boat. I did it so often I even started dreaming about it! I would say it in my mind; Adelaide, say boat! I wanted to see what you would do."

"What did I do?" she asked.

"Nothing! So I thought maybe I made it up. I went on with my life."

"Is that so," she teased.

"Yeah. And for my birthday, Claire got me that little wooden boat. Said she knew I wanted it."

"I remember."

Adelaide also remembered the conversation she had with Claire when Linda told them that Claire was so insistent that Charlie wanted a boat. A blue boat with a silver stripe, she dreamed of him in one. She remembered slipping her hand into Claire's, taking her for a walk, asking her about the dreams.

Don't tell anyone, Claire. Don't tell people about your dreams. Just Gran, okay?

"She knew. Somehow you didn't have your voodoo magic anymore, but she did."

Adelaide had no idea what to say to any of this. She nearly snickered at the fact that this was the most ridiculous conversation she had ever had with anyone, except it was all truth.

"Well, her journey is not the same as mine was. I don't want her to rush into anything for the wrong reasons."

"Did you? Rush into things?" Charlie asked.

Yes, but you saved me from myself.

"I just wanted to be with you, that was my only agenda. I didn't care about anything else." She reached over and grabbed his hand. "Why did you never tell me?"

"That my wife could read minds? It wasn't my secret to tell, it was only mine to keep safe."

He thought she could read minds. She could see how that would be a natural assumption. People dream things, and sometimes they are goofy and have no meaning, but most of the time if you really knew what you were looking for, you could see where those dreams were coming from. She spent years analyzing the dreams that she had been a part of, in a way, she supposed it was very much like being able to read minds.

"And you kept it safe, all these years." They stood together, on the porch and Charlie wrapped his arm around his wife's waist. He kissed her softly on the cheek and opened the front porch door for her, for them to go inside.

"For you, my love, anything."

Chapter 14

The pencil wildly rocked back and forth between Max's fingers. His leg was bouncing at rapid speed under the table, he just couldn't seem to sit still, or concentrate. All of the pans for Mrs. Harrison's three-bedroom, three-bath home had been going uncharacteristically smooth for the last few weeks. He only needed to look over the final drafts to make sure every little grid was correct, every wall in place, and every corner turn-able. She really had done a good bit of the work for them, and was agreeable when they pitched ways to make her ideas better.

Why was it then, that he had made no progress over the last hour? The untouched coffee sitting at his desk had grown cold, and the soft and silent buzz of his phone had gone unanswered. Max threw down the pencil, pushed his legs to the floor, wheeling his chair back from his desk. He stood, took a deep breath, and walked over to the large window of their retail office overlooking the sidewalk. The weather was brisk.

Late November had a firm grip on the city. He watched as people walked past the storefront in their variety of outerwear. Being in Maryland, one could be wearing anything from a long sleeve shirt, to a sweater, to a light jacket, to a coat, and back to shorts again all in the course of a single week. As he noticed more and more light jackets and coats, he realized how late in the month it had gotten. Thanksgiving was right around the corner. The life he'd left behind was fading.

He and Claire hadn't made anything official, but they had been spending solid and steady time together. There had been sleepovers at her place, and even a couple at his. He moved Pilot's little bed out of his bedroom, and last time he was over to her place, he noticed Tilney's bed in a new spot with a few bright and happy new toys to play with. Dogs could be bribed after all.

He hadn't asked her for any sort of commitment, and she hadn't given any indication that she wanted one. It seemed, in fact, that she was just fine with seeing where the nights led them. If he were a normal person, he'd be contemplating if he should casually ask her what her plans are to feel out if she wanted to officially introduce him to her family, or if she had thoughts of being introduced to his. If he had been a normal person, he would have asked her already if she made a habit of sleeping with her friends, or if it was just him that she was sleeping with at the moment. If he had been a normal person, he wouldn't be sick over the idea of one day telling her the truth. Wondering if it would take away everything that he was building.

Oh, by the way, about the wife…

"Everything okay?" Aidan's voice broke the thoughts in Max's mind up.

Max took another deep breath and shook his head, returning to his desk to pick up and dump out the untouched coffee.

"Yeah man, just got a lot on my mind. I'm good."

"Are you sleeping okay? I know you were having troubles."

"That all seems to be straight, I think. I was taking sleeping pills for a bit, but I haven't really needed them for the last few weeks. It was one of those things where you don't take them because you're busy and then you just don't need them."

He also had not been getting a whole lot of sleep over the last few weeks, which he really couldn't complain about.

"Good. Anything you want to talk about?" Aidan asked.

"Yeah, how was the doctor's appointment?" Max sat at his desk and picked his pencil back up, determined to complete the last few finishing touches on the blueprints.

The smile on Aidan's face was hard to miss.

"It's all good. Heartbeat is strong and steady, everything is on track. Charlotte is getting a little routine down with the morning sickness. She's a little bit further along than we thought. I guess she really didn't want to take that pregnancy test for a few weeks."

"But healthy baby?"

"Yeah, healthy baby." Aidan smiled.

"That's wonderful." Max really was happy for them. No two people deserved to be parents more.

"She came home the other day," Aidan leaned over his desk to whisper his findings, "and she smelled like a McDonald's cheeseburger."

"What do you mean?" Max asked.

"She ate a cheeseburger." Aidan shook his head in discovery. "She didn't tell me, but I could smell it. And, she was looking terribly guilty."

Max could not help but laugh at the look of satisfaction on Aidan's face.

"Why would she do that?"

"My guess is that my boy is not a vegetarian like his mother."

"It's a boy?" Max asked surprised.

"It is. I'm going to have a son."

"Congrats, Man." Max threw his arms around Aidan and gave him a big bear hug.

"Thanks. We're telling everyone at Thanksgiving. Now, do you have anything pending on this?" Aidan pointed to the plans on the desk. "I really want to wrap this up before we shut things down."

"Nope, I think we're good. You can eat your turkey and hide from your in-laws for the entire long weekend."

"They got a dog. A little yippy, skippy, dippy dog."

"Hey, man," Max scrunched his face at Aidan, "don't be hating on the dogs."

"Pilot is not a yippy, skippy, dippy dog. He's also not so little anymore."

"True, he has grown so much. It's just so hard to compare with Claire's beast of a dog."

"Oh, that's right, she's got a Great Dane. How's that going by the way? You haven't really mentioned her lately."

It was true, he hadn't. It seemed when they began their friendship, all he found himself doing was talking about Claire. It wasn't a conscious thing, it just happened to be that she was part of, if not the reason for, the highlights of his day. Once things changed between them and they began getting to know each other on a more intimate level, Max stopped talking about her. He felt weird about it. Aidan was forever linked to his past, and the only direction he wanted to be headed in when it came to Claire was forward.

"It's going. It's still an adjustment. She's wonderful, and beautiful, and is hands down one of the most intuitive people I have ever met," Max began.

"But?" Aidan asked.

"But, I don't know. We haven't actually talked about what we're doing. We're just doing it. She seems fine with that, and for now, I think it might be all that I can handle."

"It's time you move on, Max."

"I know."

"Does she know?"

"No, and I don't want her to. I like who I am with her, and the minute she knows, all that goes away."

"Max, you can't run forever," Aidan warned.

You'd be surprised at the things that don't come up if you don't bring them up.

"Not forever, just for now."

* * * *

Claire found herself in her parents' neck of the woods. She packed Tilney up for the day, and dropped him off with them while she went for a regularly scheduled onsite quarterly meeting with a small party planning business that hired her to help organize all their scheduling, marketing, and packages. They felt her coming in from time to time would help her get a better understanding of the day-to-day things they dealt with, and help her connect with their staff. She agreed, it did help. Plus, free food, and it was delicious. She wrapped up her meeting, but not before boxing up two turkey sandwiches with apples on cranberry walnut bread.

"How was the meeting, sweetheart?" her mom asked, when she heard Claire let herself into the house.

"Good. Everything's running smoothly. They've got a few big projects coming up but it's nothing they can't handle," Claire said as she located her mother sitting in the dining room with a binder on the table and coupons spread out all over the table.

"Nothing you can't handle, you mean." Linda looked up and smiled at her daughter who joined her at the table.

"That too." Claire smiled and waved her hand in the air to showcase the couponing skills, "You know, watching you do this never gets old."

"I got four loaves of bread for free last week." Linda smiled.

"Oh, you can't spread the love and get me free bread?" Claire asked.

"You can have two," Linda squinted her eyes, "smartass."

"Thanks, mom." Claire said in a lovingly mocking tone.

"So what else is new?" Linda asked, slipping into her mom tone of voice.

"I don't know," Claire mused, "what juicy gossip did you hear?"

"Just wanted to see how it was going with Max," Linda smiled innocently. "Has he still not committed to anything."

"Mom," Claire was quick to defend Max's lack of commitment, as it had only been her own that she felt might have been stopping them. "We do enjoy spending time together, yes. But I'm not looking for anything."

"You never are, dear. Why is that? Don't you want a family? Kids? You were headed that way with Christopher and it's like the man ruined you for the happily ever after. I want grandkids before I am too old to remember them."

"Because this is all about you," Claire confirmed.

"Of course it is," Linda said, without missing a beat or taking her eyes off the coupons she was carefully clipping out and slipping into sections organized by category of her binder.

"It's good, Mom." Claire twirled her hair in her fingers as she sat at the table flipping through one of the coupon flyers. Linda noticed the nervous habit her daughter had in one way or another for as long as she was alive. She always kept her hands busy, as if to direct all of her nervous energy into one spot.

"You really like him, don't you?" Linda stopped what she was doing and looked at her daughter.

"He's different, and I just, I really like the different." Claire smiled.

"It's been, what, a few months. You haven't talked about where you two stand in each other's lives?"

"It's been a few months since we met, Mom. It's really only been this last month that things have changed. He's doesn't seem to be in a rush, and he's not in my face all the time, so that's good."

"You know, it's been forty years with your father, and I still don't mind him being in my face all the time."

"How'd you do it? So young? I couldn't imagine being a twenty-five-year-old bride."

"It was a different time, as was the generation before me. They got married at twenty years old, like your Gran. My generation got married after college. Yours seems to be waiting until careers are on track. And you, I don't know what the hell you're waiting for."

She was waiting to be normal, which would never happen. She looked at Linda and wanted to hug her, to tell her that she was sorry. Linda was a wonderful mother and deserved to have son-in-law to love and grandbabies to spoil. Claire was unsure if she would ever get married, but she was pretty sure she'd never be a mother. How could she bring a child into the world knowing she was going to pass down her problems to them?

She thought about kids, usually after a night of dreaming the dreams only a child could dream. Her clock was ticking, loud and clear. She just chose to ignore it for the greater good of the children she'd never have. Of course, Adelaide did just fine. The women before her seemed to do just fine. So what did she know?

"I guess I'm just waiting for the right guy, Mom. Not everybody meets their husband on the first day of college."

Linda smiled, thinking of Alan. She had gotten a job at the campus book store and he had come in a few times to collect books for all of his various classes. He was tall and had Claire's shade of chestnut hair, and she learned over the next several months that he was one of the smartest people she had ever met. He was one of those people who didn't know a lot about a little, he knew a little about a lot. It always impressed her when some small fact would be mentioned and he could build on it, history, religion, sports, science. He just paid attention to the whole world.

"Do you think Max could be the one?" Linda asked. "I know it's only been a handful of weeks, but you've known him longer. I feel like, sometimes, you just know."

"Maybe. He's wonderful." It was a truth, no matter how many internal feelings Claire was battling. "How did you know Dad was the one? Wasn't there ever anyone else?"

You know, the guy you dream about from time to time. The young teenage boy with the jet black hair. The one that makes you feel like you're fifteen.

Linda looked out the window of the dining room, her mind traveling back to that exact young man that she didn't know Claire knew anything about. She had loved him with everything that she was, and though she adored Alan and never would wish away the life that she had spent with him, she wondered from time to time what her life would have been like if he had not moved away.

"There was a guy, when I was just a girl. Too young to be in such a serious relationship."

Claire smiled, thinking that perhaps she would finally learn about this mystery boy in her mother's life.

"What happened?"

"Life, it got in the way. He was the boy next door, and I think I loved him from the very first second our paths crossed. I was so young, just barely started high school and I was done."

"Ooooh." Leaning her elbow on the table and resting her head in her hand, Claire listened to her mother's story.

"He was so handsome. I wound up working on the same project with him, and for some reason, I caught his attention." Linda's smile was sweet as she relived the memories playing out in her mind.

"How long did you date?"

"Two years."

"What happened?" Claire asked as she saw the edges of the smile on her mother's face begin to fade.

"Like I said, life. We just weren't on the same path and he left town. Took a piece of me with him."

"Oh, Mom." Claire grabbed her mother's hand. "I'm sorry. Men are pigs."

"No. We just weren't meant to be. It was good while it was mine, and I hold on to that. Besides," her attention refocused on her daughter and the life she built in the days since, "It's always good to have that one really good love. The one that you never get over. Gives you character."

"Do you know whatever happened to him?" Claire wondered.

"I don't want to know," Linda said honestly. "I thought about looking him up, but really, what's the point? I hope he has a good life, with children and grandchildren. But I'd rather just hold on to the piece of time that belonged to me. Sometimes, when you see things that you dream about in the light of day, they disappoint you."

Oh. Yes. They. Do.

"That's so romantic, Mom."

"Yeah, well. You never marry that guy anyway. I cannot tell you how good a life your father has given me. And I love him just as much."

"Oh, I know. It's just sweet to picture you as a teenage girl in love," she saw her mother's dreams so clearly in her mind.

The lines, the wrinkles. The softer figure, and the sensible shoes. All things that stared back at Linda in the mirror these days were gone in a dream. Every once in a while, she'd remember the girl she felt she was on the inside.

"Claire, taking risks for love is always worth it. I gave my heart to a guy that was sitting on a one-way ticket out of town. That love, brief as it may have been, was extraordinary to me. I also dared to take what could be mine by asking a boy at the book store if he was ever going to actually ask me out. I regret nothing. Don't be so quick to shield yourself from something that may be an extraordinary experience."

An extraordinary experience. The advice her mother gave her rolled over and over in Claire's mind as she drove back to her apartment in the city. If only her mother knew that just plain ordinary was all Claire ever wished for.

She walked into the living room and turned on the TV. Tilney hopped up on the couch and contorted his gigantic body to fit next to hers. A half of a dozen shows on her DVR, now separated into two categories in her mind. Shows she could watch alone, and shows she had gotten into the habit of saving to watch with Max. A smile played across her face as she skipped over the ones she knew they would watch together. A simple, ordinary thing they had gotten into the habit of doing.

Pretty extraordinary, Claire thought.

"God, I am such a girl." She moaned.

She didn't know if it was a medical mystery or a miracle and she didn't care. Maybe she was being given a gift—the extraordinary chance at an ordinary life.

"Nothing looks good tonight, buddy," she said to Tilney. "What can we get into?"

Tilney didn't even budge; it seemed as if he was giving her the message for the night; he was done. He'd had a full and fun-packed day with his grandparents. She smiled at the idea that at least she could give her grandchild-less parents a puppy to distract them.

She found herself looking over to her purse wondering what Max was up to. She stood up, and went over to it, but stopped just short of digging through it for her phone. Was she really sitting at home by the phone, waiting for a boy to call?

"I think I overshot the normal," she said aloud, mostly to herself.

She stood straight and marched back over to the couch and plunked herself down with grand animation. She would not be a girl sitting at home by the phone waiting for a boy to call.

"You're thirty-one," she scolded herself.

As her hand went to grab the remote so that she could select one of the TV shows she specifically wasn't watching without Max, the muffled chime of her phone rang through her bag. Her smile was uncontrollable, and she wanted to smack herself for it.

"I guess I'll try to be more thirty-one tomorrow." She forced herself to walk slowly over to her bag for the phone, all the while her heart beating with excitement.

I've got a movie, want to come up?

Claire smiled, and shook her head before she replied.

What do you think? I am just sitting around doing nothing, waiting for a boy to call?

Giggling to herself, she walked into her bedroom and pulled open a dresser drawer.

Okay, I've got a movie. Do you think Tilney wants to come up? I know he's terribly busy and I should have put this on his calendar weeks ago.

She pulled out a white cotton nightgown that sweetly swept her thighs, and swooped low on her chest, innocently covering her, yet not totally. She picked it up just last week, with Max in mind.

Bring your toothbrush ;)

"Already ahead of you," she said to her phone but never replied.

Tonight, she would be ordinary, and it was an extraordinary gift.

Chapter 15

Her dreams settled into a good pattern of familiar and unfamiliar. Five nights out of seven, she would dream of a person she had never come across before. Then, just as the pattern could not be more random, she found herself with people she was personally familiar with. The residents of her building popped up with a fiercely irregular regularity.

Mrs. Doogan was the one she was with the most, often breaking Claire's heart. All of the dreams were of the woman's glory days that felt so good, but so very long ago. She struggled with living so long, and losing things along the way.

Jack, she figured, was just lonely. He may claim the bachelor life was for him, but at the end of the day, she knew he searched for the person he could call his one and only. She'd even taken to not rushing by him in the halls, and not cramming her laundry into a basket for quick escape if he happened to be using the laundry room at the same time. He was polite, he was funny, and he was kind. He was just....lonely. She found over time, when she did dream of him, they were more pleasant experiences.

The other neighbors popped up from time to time with amusing adventures, confusing conundrums, and nefarious nightmares. She continued to enjoy the mysteriously missing Max. And then there was the one she kept tucked in the back of her mind, the girl in the box. The girl in the basement. The girl from Main Street.

It had been weeks since their last encounter; she nearly filed the woman away in her book of dreamers past. The private investigator's automated reply to her request indicated his office was closed for the Thanksgiving Holiday. There was a number left for emergency situations, but Claire did not feel identifying a woman in a photograph, a woman she didn't actually know, was grounds for emergency. She made a quick phone call to the farm to see if either of the Spring+++field's remembered anything about the woman; they did not. Business had been good, and though they could identify it was a school group, they had no idea which one.

There needed to be balance here, so she didn't push it. Her grandmother's warning continued to press into her. It wasn't what she said, it was how she said it. Clear, sharp, focus. However, Adelaide's other words of wisdom could come into play, too. Each traveler is slightly different than the generation before her. Each journey is unique. Perhaps knowing would be exactly what Claire needed. So, it was going to be up to fate. If the PI found something about her mystery redhead, then so be it. If Claire ran into the woman at the grocery store, then so be it. She would write it off as fate, and until that moment, she would treat the woman as she had all other dreamers.

It was just so hard, there was something about her that made her stand out. Claire tried to convince herself it was just the game, the desire to solve the puzzle at this point. She knew it wasn't true; she felt the connection run so deep, there were times where she couldn't tell where the woman ended and she started.

* * * *

Everything around her was blue, with silver flecks floating in the air. Their dance around her face made her wish she could capture them. They were floating. Were they floating? No, she was.

I'm floating.

Investigating her curious space, Claire's thoughts raced at a mile a minute. She felt she might be upside down, or inside out, or possibly both. Her blue world was endless, with only the silver flecks to break up its solidity.

"And the world turns blue," she said to the dreamer who could not hear her.

A single beam of light pierced through the monochromatic scene, shining bright as if it were a beacon of hope. The beam did not move, but it illuminated the idyllically peaceful setting.

Wait! This is water. I'm under water! Pieces of the puzzle were coming together for her latest dream.

The dreamer looked around, exploring the underwater world they had created for themselves. Claire couldn't see her body, so she didn't know if she was a man or a woman, or a person at all for that matter. She might be a fish. There was no sea floor, or pool floor. There was no up, or down, only the water with the slivery flecks dancing around and a beacon of hope off into the distance. The light began to spread and the dreamer could clearly see a surface being formed above them.

"If you think it, it will be," Claire reminded her dreamer. "I'm all for going toward the light."

There was no panic, or fear. The physical buzz Claire got from the dreamer's emotions remained still. She couldn't tell if this was a run of the mill dream or a nightmare yet. The dreamer was not committed to how they felt about it. She felt weightless; it was her only indication. That normally meant happiness, but it was mixed with something. The hairs on the back of her neck tickled and she felt as if somebody was hurrying her along in a certain direction, as if they were right on her heels.

"Curiosity killed the cat," she reminded her dreamer.

She didn't have too many references in her dream journal where curiosity was a factor. Most people don't feel exploratory when it comes to their dreams. They oddly know their own fates, even when they think they don't. She would have to see if she properly identified the feeling after the dreamer gave her a bit more to work with.

Another element crept into Claire's mind. It wasn't as strong, but it was there—lilacs.

Oooooooh, it's been a while. Could it be?

In answer to her own question, the dreamer began to swim toward the surface. As she did, Claire could see soft creamy hands swimming through the water. Strands of red hair floating all around with the movement confirmed the identity.

It is you! Oh, what are you getting into now? I'm looking for you, you know. Want to meet at the grocery store tomorrow? Say around eleven a.m.?

Claire shook her own chatty thoughts away. It was time to really dig in and see what she could learn. With this dreamer, she was willing to open up and let it all flood in. Maybe something would be useful.

As her dreamer continued to swim toward the surface, Claire thought about what she knew of the woman.

Girl, young, but that may be just how you feel. Pretty, soft skin, and red hair. Tortured, such mixed emotions when it comes to you. I always feel guilty the whole damn day after I dream of you. As if I caused your sadness and heartbreak. Damn you, just once could you find yourself at the coffee shop or something so I can see you in real life?

Bubbles floated up and around her, Claire felt the rush through her body as her dreamer imagined the feeling of the bubbles tickling her skin.

The closer she got to the surface, the stranger Claire felt. The hurried feeling dissipated, opening the door for anxious jitters.

Panic? Why are we panicking? No, we're floating around this silvery water. It's nice.

Not for long. The water began to churn, pushing into her, forcing her to rock back and forth with the motion. Her mouth began to water as the slick metallic taste took over. Panic ran right past curiosity, and fear was coming out of nowhere to take the lead. The rush to get to the surface became a frenzy. Her arms rocketed up above her head, coming down in a circular motion to her hips. Her feet kicked hard to propel her faster. Just as Claire thought surely the dreamer would wake up gasping for air, a voice shouted at her from the other side of the water. It was the same sound she heard in all her other dreams with this woman; a man's voice. Perhaps it was her husband, waking the woman up each time. Only this time it was different. It was faint, but for the first time, it was clear. As if the word was being whispered directly into her ear.

"Rebecca."

I'm Rebecca, ok. You're Rebecca. Hi, Rebecca.

When a hand broke through the surface, Rebecca reached for it with desperation pumping through her veins.

I won't save her.

The thought hit Claire like a swift punch: unexpected and out of nowhere. What was she being saved from? As the jitters reached a boiling point, it hit her.

Oh, God. She's drowning.

With anxiety, fear and desperation pumping through her as if they were her own, Claire became wrapped in the moment. This was no longer a dream where she lay safe in her bed, this was no longer just a show. This was real, it was happening and it was happening to her. She felt the overwhelming urge to help this woman, as if Claire herself could pull her from the dangerous waters.

Let's get you out of this water! Come on love, we can do it. Work together.

The dreamer's emotions, Rebecca's emotions pushed back.

Don't want this. I don't want this. I hate this. I hate this. I hate this. Leave me alone!

The words were floating all around her. Rebecca wasn't saying them, but it was almost if she was. As if she was telling Claire to leave her alone, let her be. Claire felt the oddest tug of wanting to be here, but really…wanting to be anywhere else but here. Rebecca was a tortured soul if there ever was one.

No longer seeing where Rebecca ended and Claire began, she reached for the hand to save her. He would be saving them both.

Be. Our. Hero. Claire's own thoughts demanded.

Just as the panic was reaching the point where Claire wanted to scream, she broke the surface. Light poured over her face and she sucked in a hungry gulp of fresh air. A shadowy figure kneeled down in the boat, leaning over the edge as his warm hand gripped around her thin, cold, wet arm. His muscles were firm as he pulled her toward him. His black hair fell into the light brown eyes that she knew so well.

The emotions of Rebecca immediately faded from Claire. The connection between them lost as Claire's own mind reeled at the sight of her lover in this woman's dream.

No, no, no, no… heat flooded her, rage and confusion pumping through her veins.

Why are you here? You can't be here, I don't want you here. It can't be you, no! Help, help. I want out of here…

A sick feeling balled in her stomach, it was not Rebecca's. Claire was pulling from her, separating from her. Fighting to gain control, Claire was no longer interested in Rebecca's state of being or frame of mind. She was no longer interested in bringing her to safety. She fought furiously to escape but it was all too much. Seeing him there was too much. Control slipped from her, and Rebecca's emotions regained the lead.

Guilt. He was looking into her eyes, Rebecca's eyes, Claire reminded herself. He was looking into Rebecca's eyes and all she saw was guilt.

"Rebecca," Max's voice rang into the air. "Rebecca!"

It was his voice she heard each time in the dreams of Rebecca's past. The muffled sound behind the wall, the yelling behind the door in the basement. It was Max. Her Max. *No, Rebecca's Max,* she corrected herself.

What does this mean? Oh God, not again. No.

She was in Hell. And worse, she was trapped in a body that was not her own. She helplessly watched as Max reached around her hand to save her.

Her hand, not mine, Claire reminded herself. *He's rescuing her, not me.*

The water stilled as if Claire's own clarity broke the rage of the storm. She was calmly floating on the surface.

Not me. Rebecca.

He did not pull her any further but he did not bring her into the safety of his arms as she expected him to do. His hand reached down, caressing her face. Claire could not help but feel her own betrayed emotions. She spent a lifetime being invisible, but it wasn't until this moment that she felt invisible. This was a moment between Max and Rebecca. Claire wasn't even there.

"Rebecca," his soft plea rang into the air. "I can't...I can't...I'm sorry."

His hand slowly let go of hers, and Claire found herself slipping back under the water. She watched the emotions on his face as the water covered hers, until she couldn't see him anymore. Everything faded into darkness. He let her go. He let her drown. Claire curiously faded back into Rebecca's world. Who was this girl?

Guilt.

It slammed into her. Rebecca placed guilt with him. It invaded every molecule of the water around her.

As she floated to the bottom, with her feet sinking into the sand of the ocean floor which she finally dreamed up, she felt hollow. Hollow was the only true physical feeling which matched its emotional counterpart. Hollow equaled Hollow. Claire had no idea if the feeling was coming from herself or Rebecca. Did it matter? In the light of day, Max was hiding something. The shoe finally dropped. In Rebecca's dream world, he was guilty. She created a watery world where she literally swam in that guilt. Claire once again let go of herself, and opened herself to whatever it was her dreamer had in mind.

You left me. You weren't there when I needed you. Your lies broke me.

Chapter 16

Her body startled as she woke and gasped for the breath of air she was so desperate to take. The ceiling fan above Max's bed swirled silently, bringing her back to the real world. In his apartment. In his bed. The room was covered in soft early morning light. She shook her head, trying to clear her mind of the dream. Dawn was just on the tips of the horizon outside his bedroom window.

She quietly turned to her side where she could see him sleeping next to her. He lay still on his back, naked and spent from the hours of making love. A tear slipped down from Claire's cheek as her extraordinary man became a little too ordinary for her. She found him in a dream world after all.

"Rebecca." The word came in a whisper out of his lips.

The air was gone. Claire blinked at the sting of hearing him call her dreamer's name. Her chest caved in, and an icy chill ran down her spine. She slowly lifted her head and stared at the man who became a stranger within that blink of her eye.

"Lies. Not there. Sorry," his words were mumbled, but she could place them. The nightmare she just slipped from had followed her into the real world. Walls were crashing down around her as she watched his body twitch ever so slightly, fighting the dream he was still in.

"Your dream," she whispered to him as she choked back tears. "I was in your dream?"

It hurt so bad, she couldn't breathe. She threw the sheets off her body, and found her legs too shaky to make an escape. Instead, she sought shelter away from him. Reality had no place here, confusion was all she had, as her brain worked backward to place him in all the dreams that came before. She stumbled into the walk-in closet. Throwing her hand out, she flipped the light on and closed the door behind her. She crumbled to the floor as her legs would not hold her. *They were his dreams, they were all his dreams. How? Why? Who in the hell is Rebecca?* She didn't realize until that moment how much she had become invested in the idea that he was somehow exempt from her prying powers. He wasn't. He never had been.

"I'm such a fool," she said to herself.

Images of dreams past flashed through her mind at rapid speed with harsh light. If she could have, she would have shielded her eyes from it. Dreams that came in the months before she found out Christopher had been having an affair. Dreams he was having, dreams his lover was having…colliding in Claire's mind, enough to urge her to examine the little things a little closer until she saw patterns and lies in the real world. Here she was, on the floor of a closet in the middle of the night. She would once again be going back, picking apart and examining dreams to find the lies within.

She sat up straight, furious with herself for allowing the fairy tale, and wiped the hot tears from her cheeks. "What the fuck, universe?" she asked to whoever was out there who listened to such questions. "Do I have a sign on me?"

She got to her feet and stood like a soldier with rage boiling through her. Christopher had an affair. This mystery redhead was in Max's life. He was having an affair too, she knew it. Her hand gripped the doorknob of the closet, ready to explode. He would be held accountable for his actions. The memory of Christopher asking Claire for proof of his lies stilled her hand.

"Proof," she said, "I need proof."

Frustrated and confused, she started combing through the clothes hanging up in front of her. She had no idea what she was looking for, but she was determined to find something. As she harshly slid the hangers from one side to the next, she examined the clothes. He was a thirty-five-year-old grown man.

"This closet should be full of crap," she said aloud.

It wasn't. There were only a couple of pairs of shoes and there was more space than there were clothes. One by one, she started looking at everything closer. Slower. Objectionably. It was all new, or in newer condition. There was not one thing here that was a ratty, tatty, torn memory of days past. She pictured in her mind the rest of the apartment. There were no photos of anyone, no trinkets or doodads cluttering the space, just the basics. This was not the apartment of a divorced man starting over. This was the apartment of a man who was hiding something, and living somewhere else.

"Oh, Jesus Christ, they're married." The feeling of defeat and betrayal sunk deep in her as she thought about the wedding ring Rebecca was always wearing. He dreamed of her; his wife, Rebecca. "I'm the other woman?"

Shirts, shoes, pants. Ties, belts, all normal things. Not too many things, she thought as she turned her attention to the shelf at the top of the closet. Winter things, gloves and hats. All seemingly normal. He was married, and this must be a small collection of things so he wouldn't have anything missing from home. She flashed back in her mind to pulling Christopher's clothes from the dirty laundry hamper, examining them, bringing them to her nose and smelling the subtle hint of another woman's perfume. It was the proof she finally confronted him with. Max had been one step ahead of Christopher the whole time. This was an apartment in the city, where he kept a few things…like the scent of Claire on his clothes.

"Mother Fuh—"

A box. There was a box in the corner of the top shelf in the closet. It was an old shoe box, tattered and worn. It was the only thing in the closet that didn't look brand new.

She reached for it, and silently slid it off the shelf. She sat on the floor with the box in her lap, exactly where she was standing and stared at the lid. Her hands shook, a fresh batch of tears clouded her vision. As she blinked, she let them fall freely to the floor. One caught the edge of the box and splattered a wet starburst pattern on the corner. She took a deep breath and removed the lid. She didn't know why, but she knew this box would give her proof.

The scent of lilac filled the air, and Claire's heart broke. She pulled the small, round sash of potpourri from the gathering of tissue paper. Her fingers traced around its round shape, this must be what Rebecca keeps in their dresser drawers to keep laundry smelling fresh. It was in his dreams. The nights he wasn't with Claire, the nights he was with Rebecca. It was in his mind and it was in the room. He most likely kept it places in this apartment to match the life he led with his wife.

"Stupid. Lying. Cheating. Bastard." Each word came out with its own bite.

She placed the sash back in the box and dug into the tissue paper for the other objects she could feel the weight of, she found two smaller boxes.

She opened the small leather box first and the last hope that all of this might just be a nightmare vanished. Proof. The men's wedding band shined back up at her, unassuming. She willed her hands to be steady as she pulled it from the box and studied the pattern that lay on the inner side of the plain silver band.

"Cherry blossoms." The exact pattern she saw on her own hand when she was Rebecca. Her band featured the pattern on the outside, his matched with the pattern featured on the inside. This is where he kept it in hiding, able to slip it back on when he needed to slip out of Claire's life and into Rebecca's.

Stupid, lying, cheating bastard. It was easy to see how Christopher's name now came with a tagline. She knew she would never again think of Max without the same as she put the ring back in the box and closed it. She traded it for the other box in the tissue paper. Or, it was a cloth, wrapping something tight.

Her hand ran smoothly over the soft cotton cloth before she turned it over to unfold it. It was a moment she didn't want to be a part of. The truth did not set her free, it imprisoned her. This would impression her further. She slowly, quietly unwrapped it, and as she did, her heart simply stopped. The metallic taste of realization and fear slid down her throat. This was not the emotions of a dreamer, this was a nightmare come true. The silver was turned and tarnished, the edges rounded and worn. She forced herself to push the little lever, and her world turned upside down as the bike bell in her hand chimed against the silence of the early dawn.

The panic, the heartbreak, the guilt–such guilt.

All. Your. Fault.

Your lies broke me.

You left me here.

All the emotions Max gave her, he was imagining how Rebecca saw it. How she felt. Why would he do that? She pushed the bike bell a second time as she tried to fit the pieces of the dream world together. She noticed a black smudge transferred to her finger. A new thought came to her mind with crystal clarity. The bike bell was real. The bike in the basement was real.

"Was the fire real?" she whispered.

I won't save her.

Max's dream. Max's thoughts. Max's feelings.

"Oh, God, Max, what did you do?"

Chapter 17

"Alright, alright, alright." Max opened one eye in defiance of the morning's job coming so soon. "Damn these dogs, huh?"

The room responded with silence. He opened both eyes, and turned his head to find the other side of his bed empty.

"Claire?"

Again, silence ruled in the room. Max pulled his naked body from the bed he had spent half the night making love to Claire in, and stood in the empty room. He sleepily looked around and noticed her clothes missing. He wondered where she had gone. The scratching at the door followed by a bark got his attention again and he walked over to open it. Pilot was on the other side, dancing around to alert Max that he really needed to go outside.

"Probably took Tilney out this morning, wonder why she didn't take you, buddy." Max lowered his hand to scratch behind Pilot's ears as he looked around the apartment for signs of Claire.

"Claire?" He called out a little louder, in case she was in the bathroom down the hall or in the kitchen. Pilot was the only other life in the apartment, everything around him remained still and silent.

Throwing on a pair of sweat pants and a new Penn State shirt, he grabbed Pilot's leash and the two headed out the door for their morning walk.

"Weird," he said to himself, as he took one last look back at his empty apartment.

He stopped at hers on the way down and knocked, but she didn't answer nor did he hear Tilney trotting to the door. Pilot became rather insistent they go outside, so he hoped he would see her there.

They crossed the street to the park and once inside, he let Pilot off his leash to play and go to the bathroom. No Tilney, no Claire. He looked further into the other areas of the park as Claire liked to let Tilney explore all areas while they walked. Strange thoughts overturned in his mind, but he had to remind himself they had been seeing each other for weeks now, months actually, if you really thought about the evolution of their time from friendship to lovers. He didn't know much about her love life before he came along, but they had spent enough nights together for him to know it was unusual for her not to be there when he woke up. He pulled out his phone and sent her a text. He thought about what he could write to not sound weird. But it was weird, where was she?

Good morning! You got an early start, there was no rush, I hope.

There. Friendly, breezy, no big deal.

"Just, you know, checking because I woke up alone in my bed," he said to the phone.

He held the phone in his hand as Pilot happily ran in circles chasing an imaginary bunny, or fox, or whatever it was he imagined he was chasing when he did these sorts of things. He found with her business being nearly a twenty-four hour a day job sometimes, she was pretty good about having her phone with her. His phone sat in his hand with the same eerie silence he awoke to in his apartment. A small bit of hurt started to tug at him. He wanted to know where she was. He enjoyed his time with her, and though they had not discussed exclusivity, he thought himself more than just a body to spend the evening with.

"Shit," he said to himself as he shoved the phone back into his pocket, "God, I never thought I would be here again. It was never my plan, I hope you know that."

Pilot barked at him, snapping him from the conversation he was starting to have with the woman who wasn't there. The dream he had, the nightmare really, crept back into the front of his mind. He watched his beautiful wife surface in the water, her face pale and frightened. He just let go, and did nothing as he watched her fall back under the water's surface. Deep down, he knew he could have saved her, but didn't. He could have stopped it, but didn't. He looked down at his hands, and imagined hers in them as they had been in the dream. He didn't want to let go, but he did. He watched her as the water sucked her down. He watched the surface then go still, showing no trace as if she had never really been there at all.

He walked Pilot back into the building and stopped once more at Claire's door. He pulled his phone back out of his pocket to check if she had gotten back to him. She had not. Returning to his apartment, he could do nothing but sit and wait, and wonder.

"Fuck," he said as he sat back on his brown leather sofa, leaning his head back and closing his eyes. "Ready or not, you're in love, you idiot. You weren't supposed to fall in love."

Love was supposed to be a good thing, but right now it was the one thing that Max wanted the least. This blank void he'd created worked so well, it became a comfort zone—only the here, only the now. There was nothing of his other life in his apartment. At first, he felt its impossible emptiness. But as the days ticked away, he started to believe in his own reinvention.

It was what he enjoyed most about Claire. She never questioned him. She never asked about his past. When she looked at him, all she saw was the man he created for her. Max, the single architect with a cute dog. Max, the guy who jogged and went to Penn State. She didn't see the things that haunted him. She didn't see the things that followed him. He loved that about her, and he had come to crave it. As he lay in the bed with her wrapped in his arms on the nights they were together, he looked to the window. The clear glass stood silent and strong, protecting them from the outside world.

It's all out there, and will never be here. He told himself so many times, it became truth. He fell in love with the idea as much as he had fallen in love with the girl.

"Fuck," he repeated to himself.

He forced himself to run some errands. All throughout the afternoon he checked his phone again and again. Nothing. He resorted to calling her, but left no message when her voice mail picked up. As he laid his head on the pillow to go to sleep that night, everything still felt so unresolved. The bed still smelled like her, she was just here.

"Where did you disappear to, Claire?"

When he woke the next morning and checked his phone for any communication from Claire, he sighed when he saw that his message had not even been read.

Not read. Maybe something was wrong. The all too familiar feeling crept into his stomach.

Too busy battling your own demons when she needs you.

He threw on a t-shirt over the sweatpants he slept in, and walked down to her apartment. When there was no answer, yet again, he paced back and forth in the hall before he slipped in the spare key to her apartment she provided him when he wanted to grab Tilney to join Pilot for a walk. He never used it once without letting her know first, as she came to do with the key she kept to his apartment. An exception would be made here, it was going on 24 hours of her vanishing.

"Claire?" He called out. "I'm only here because I want to make sure you're not stuck under something heavy."

The apartment did not offer him any response. He walked slowly down the hallway and looked around the living room. The lights were on. The lights were on in nearly every room, which was odd for her because he noticed she was one of those people who was conscious of how much her electric bill would be. He looked into the kitchen which greeted him fresh and ready to go for the morning show. No dishes in the sink, nothing out on the counters to indicate she had eaten breakfast. He walked into her bedroom, and saw her bed was made. He stopped cold when he saw the drawers of her dresser. They were all open, and there were clothes hanging out of them, some strewn on the floor.

He went over to her closet, yanking the door open to see what the state of it may be. Large chunk of empty space indicated she had taken some things out. He had seen her closet once before when she offered him a tour of her apartment one night when he was over. As he stood in this newly emptied space, he remembered the evening from a couple weeks past. They raided her kitchen for snacks and water, and had gotten into a silly conversation about her collection of tea mugs. She was naked, and he kissed every inch of her as she explained some of her belongings in each room. She had too many books, so many it made his brain hurt. In her office, the cabinets were lined with management books, success books, finance books, marketing, organization, and even an everyday guide to being a proper homemaker book. She said she used it for party planning, and prepping for out of town guests. Etiquette books and a slew of computer programming books crammed together. He was sure that if she didn't already know the answer to something, she could just look it up in one of these books.

She had classic books, maybe all of them–Austen, Bronte, Plath, and Hemmingway. She had current books that ranged from psychotic thrillers to trashy romance. He could see the phases she went through within in them. Vampires, Witches, and Demons, and, even the sexy Texas stories about lonely cowboys. There were a lot of dream interpretation books, and though she said she hadn't thumbed through them in quite some time, it had only been a phase when she was a teenager, these were the books that were most worn. They ended the tour standing in this very closet, thumbing through her vast and extensive collection of clothing. The vast extensive collection which had been thinned out quite a bit from the looks of it.

He turned off the light in her closet and walked back through the apartment to her office. Her chair was rolled out of the way and random papers and files were scattered on the floor.

"What the hell?" he whispered to himself.

He quickly walked to her bathroom, where the light was already on and opened up some of her cabinet drawers. No hair brush, very little make up left, no hair dryer. He started back out of the bathroom and stopped when he noticed something he should have noticed when he walked into the apartment. Tilney's giant dog bed was gone. He looked around the living room to the spots where Tilney's things were always gathered. The basket of dog toys by the couch was gone, as was his leash. Claire was *gone* gone, and she'd left in a hurry.

He pulled his phone out of his pocket once more and then shoved it right back in, playing with a new approach. He went over to the cordless phone that was sitting on its charger on the desk in her office and dialed her cell phone number. She picked up on the last ring before it went to voicemail again.

"Who is this?" she asked rather than greeting her caller.

"Hey, it's Max." He didn't know what else to say at this point.

"You're in my apartment?"

"You disappeared on me, Claire. Are you okay?"

There was a silence, where he could hear her breathe in and out before she answered.

"I have some business to attend to," she began. "I don't know when I will get back. I'm sorry. Tilney is with me, there is no need to check on him."

"Did you get my text? I've called you. I'm sorry that I resorted to letting myself in, but I was worried about you."

"I appreciate your concern," effectively cutting him off. "I have to go now. Thank you for calling."

The line went dead and Max had no idea what happened to warrant such distance from her. Something was very off, something was wrong. He played out in his mind the lovely evening they spent at his place the night before last and came up empty handed. He had no idea what was going on, and worse, he had no idea where she was or when she would get back. The unresolved hurt lay like a weight on his chest. He looked around her quiet apartment, and felt its emptiness.

"Where did you go, Claire?"

He huffed, and backtracked through her apartment to turn off lights. He closed her dresser drawers and picked up the clothes off the floor and deposited them into her hamper. *What in the world is happening,* he wondered. Had he done something? Said something?

He continued to pick up her scattered things as he went. As he gathered and stacked sheets of paper that had fallen to the floor in her office, a manila envelope with a singular name sprawled out on it caught his attention. Sweat immediately pooled, and the feeling of dread and doom sank deep within him.

Rebecca Duncan.

"Oh, God, she knows."

Chapter 18

"Do you want some tea, sweetheart?"

Claire didn't move her attention from the computer. She had shown up on her parents' doorstep in the wee hours of the morning the day before, and hadn't offered them much of an explanation as to why she was there. Linda found her typing away on her laptop, hunched over the small desk in her childhood room. Thus far, all they knew was she was looking for a "space to think".

"I'm okay, thank you, though."

"So, are you staying for a few days?" Her mother quietly probed as she looked around the room to find something to do. She needed something to clean up, to keep her hands busy, but Claire had already made the bed. Throwing her hands up in retreat, she sat down.

"That okay?" Claire asked, finally breaking focus from her work and offering her mother a half-hearted smile.

"Honey, this is your home. You can stay as long as you like. I just want to make sure everything is okay. Everything is okay, right? Something going on with you and Max?"

Claire felt a sharp stab in her heart at the mention of his name. No, everything was not okay. It was far from okay. Nothing would ever be okay again.

"I just need a few days, that's all. I'm fine." Claire didn't want to lie to her mother. She just didn't know what to tell her.

"You know where I am when you're ready to talk, hon." Linda kissed her on the back of her head and left as Claire turned her attention back to the computer.

Whatever she was working on, she had been at it all morning. Without knowing what was wrong, Linda prepared for a potential war in only a way a mother could. She went to the grocery store and bought enough food to feed everyone for a week. She fussed over freshening up Claire's childhood bedroom and washed every linen in the house. She wasn't sure if Claire was suffering from a broken heart, a broken spirit, or a broken anything else. Something was on her daughter's mind, but her daughter wasn't ready to talk about it.

The girl had been this way her whole life. She'd go to bed fine, and wake up looking as if she spent half the night battling demons. Linda always asked, but never pushed. Claire's grades were good, she never did drugs or drank. They never worried about where she was because she was never out all night. Claire was just private. Of all the problems a parent could have with a child, Linda was grateful that this was hers. Claire may not want to talk about it, but she did at least, turn to her parents for that fortress of solitude. So that's exactly what she would get, with no questions asked. Even so, it broke Linda's heart to watch her daughter suffer in silence.

Claire pulled the minimized screens back up when her mother left the room. The same screens she had now been avoiding for nearly twenty-four hours. The screens she had hoped she would spend a lifetime avoiding. Knowing nothing about Max had been such a gift, and now it seems, it might have been her downfall. She thought of how free she felt in the moments where she pulled the soft white nightgown from the dresser and the toothbrush from the holder in her apartment, taking them to Max's. She thought about how they made love all night, and how wonderful his slightly rough fingers felt on her soft skin. She mourned for the loss of that brief moment of pure unadulterated normalcy.

Normalcy slipped from her fingers, literally and figuratively the moment she opened her mail. The private investigator had pulled through. She wondered where she would be at this moment had she not opened that envelope. Where she would be if she had not hired the PI in the first place. Where she would be if she hadn't been with Max in the moment his wife's name escaped his lips. She wondered if there was any scenario where she could have gone the rest of her life with the mysterious redhead living only in her dreams.

Ms. Martin,

Not sure who your guy is looking for, but it can't be this girl. She died in a fire two years ago. Let me know if he comes up with a more positive ID and we will see what we can do. No charge, I owed Jane a favor.

Brad.

Why did she open that envelope? Because she knew what was going to be in it. Thanks to her Spidey senses she was a step ahead of Brad Rich of Loch Investigations. Still, she could not wrap her head around how much changed between the moments of freedom with her nightgown and toothbrush in hand and nine hours later returning to her impossibly lonely world with that same nightgown and toothbrush in hand. If only she had not opened that envelope and Max remained just a stupid, lying, cheating bastard. He wasn't a stupid, lying, cheating bastard. He was a murderer. A large white envelope addressed to her, thoughtfully brought up from the lobby with some other delivery boxes, and placed by her door told her so.

The dreams were his. The emotions were his. The guilt was his.

Claire just played the part. She felt sick as she thought of the details of each dream.

Rebecca had been trapped. Rebecca had been locked in the basement. The fire had consumed her. Rebecca faded away. He let her go. The moment he did, guilt overtook Claire's emotions—his guilt—the guilt he assigned to himself, the parts of him hiding from the world, the parts Claire had always been able to find in people.

As she sat at her childhood desk, she looked at the article clipping Brad Rich left for her. It was a picture of Rebecca, happy and smiling. The press had taken to using her teacher yearbook photo, no doubt the one the Elementary School she worked for immortalized her in after her death. The article gave Claire the missing pieces of the puzzle. Rebecca Duncan, age thirty, Kindergarten teacher, dies in tragic house fire. Community comes together while husband is called under investigation.

Now she knew one thing about him; he had no alibi. The article did not give much detail, as at the time it was a new investigation. Sitting at her childhood desk in her childhood home, Claire was able to pull up a few different articles as the case progressed against Max.

Forcing herself to keep looking, Claire followed the trails of research and found herself looking at pictures of a house that burned down to the ground. An older Victorian in the suburbs, not far from where Max had taken her for the Halloween party. The fire was real and it was what took Rebecca's life. As she continued to click on link after link, she finally came to what she had hoped she wouldn't—an article on the guilt or innocence of Max Duncan.

Authorities were investigating him as his whereabouts at the time of the fire were unknown. Alcohol had been a factor. Insurance money had been a factor. A haunting image of a sullen faced man she hardly recognized filled her screen. He was wearing a Penn State Baseball hat hanging low to shade himself from the prying photographers. Ultimately, charges were never officially filed because there was not enough evidence against the widower. As she stared at the image of Max, mid-stride with his hands in his pockets and his face tucked away from photographers, her stomach turned. At the suggestion he may have burned the house down for insurance money, the wheels in Claire's mind turned. He ran a nice business. He had his own office. They had top of the line equipment. He wasn't even forty. As a business owner herself, she knew how much she had to sacrifice just to even graduate from a china cabinet to a home office. Max had an empire compared to her. Had it all been built on Rebecca's money?

Her phone shrilled as it had done every couple of hours in one way or another. Max left several texts and a few voice mails. He was now resorting to calling and just letting it ring before he hung up, eventually he would stop calling. It was a high school tactic, but a high school tactic that worked. She glanced over to the phone in case it was anyone else and a bolt of fear shot through her when she saw her own name and number pop up. Somebody was in her apartment.

"Please be the Super," she said to the phone, even though she knew it was Max. Her hands continued to twitch in back and forth argument. No, he was in her apartment, she had to pick up. Once their brief conversation was over, she thought she maintained her composure well. In reality she knew she did not, as soon as she was off the phone, she ran to the bathroom and let go of the very little food she had in her system.

Chapter 19

"Was that our phone?" Linda asked as she hurried into Claire's room. "I was downstairs, couldn't find the damn phone, your father and those cordless phones. I find them all over the house, everywhere except where they are supposed to be."

"No, it was mine."

"Max?"

"Yeah. He was checking on me, I guess." She damned herself for ever giving him a spare key to her apartment.

She'd have to get the locks changed. Of course, that's to say if she stayed in the building. How would that work? They ran into each other all the time even before they wanted to run into each other all the time. Claire let out a guttural grunt of frustration at the idea she might have to move. No, this was getting too complicated. She would just get the locks changed—today—and avoid him. Things aren't working out. It was fun while it lasted, etc. etc. *Pick something, Claire. He doesn't know you know the truth.* And that was it, how could he know? Claire found herself stuck where she always seemed to be, somewhere between the real and the unreal. Between the surface of the truth, and all of the complicated mess that can lay beneath it. She had looked at the articles; she had read the reports. Ultimately, Max's guilt could not be proven enough for an arrest. She had nothing to offer the authorities beyond her own feelings.

"Everything okay with you two? I know it's none of my business, but you look like you've seen a ghost in that mirror."

I have, she thought.

Claire finished washing her hands in the bathroom and checked her appearance in the mirror. She was a little flushed, but felt the relief in her stomach. The image of herself in the mirror reminded her of when she returned to her parents once before after Christopher's betrayal. She shook her head at the cakewalk he would turn out to be compared to Max. As she left the bathroom, she wrapped her arms around her mother who was standing in the hallway waiting for an answer.

"I love you, Mom," she said as Linda welcomed Claire's hug.

"I'll kill him."

"No, no," Claire said as she braved a smile. "He was just checking on me. I don't want you involved. Everything is fine. I'm going to run some errands today and then go home and decide on a few things."

"This is not fine. This is an asshole who has done something to my baby."

"He didn't do anything to me." That was absolute truth. To her, he was a dream come true. It was to Rebecca he was the nightmare.

"I'm just taking a break."

"From what, Claire? He's the first man that's even made a blip on your map since Christopher. It's only been a couple of months. Did he do something to you, or are you just scared because it's starting to get serious?"

Both, she thought. *Maybe.*

"I need to think, Mom. It's why I'm here. I need to work out all the details."

"Sometimes love doesn't line up in pretty little rows, you know, no man is perfect," Linda warned her. "But they can be perfect to you, if they're good men."

"I know that, Mom, I just need some time."

"Oh, baby. I'll break his neck if he's hurting you."

Claire smiled. She had no doubt in her mother. Linda was a small, but very strong force. Claire inherited her no nonsense way of handling the world at large, and it paid off well within her business. If her mother tackled something, she did it without mercy. Lord help any man who ever stood in Linda Martin's way.

"I said I was fine, and I am. I promise. I'm going home in a bit. It's all going to be fine."

"Okay, you just say the word and your father will take me over there."

Claire pictured Linda marching to their car and Alan casually sliding into the driver's seat. He would be in no hurry, working out a diplomatic way for his wife to express her demands. He felt like if you let things be, they would always have a way of working out. And that was true, things always did work out, but Claire had no doubt that some of it was in no small part of Linda making it so. They were quite the pair.

For now, break things off with Max, and then avoid him at all costs. She had already gotten the ball rolling with unread texts, and unreturned voice mails. She'd now graduate to a few awkward exchanges in the hall eventually leading to offering that, though it had been nice, she needed some space. Couple that with a few quick hellos here and there, and voilà! Break-up achieved. She could do this, yes, she could. She could successfully break up with the best guy that had ever come into her life, and quietly live with the fact that the police would never know what he did. Hell, if she played her cards right, maybe *he* would move!

She went over her plan, working out more details as she talked to Tilney in the car on the way to her apartment. By the time she got there, she had convinced herself that she had a very solid plan. She even called her landlord on the way home, requesting to have the locks changed, at her own expense, immediately. He would be there that very afternoon, it would all be okay. These were the words she repeatedly whispered to herself as she hurried Tilney as quietly as she could up to her apartment and waited for the locksmith to arrive.

The knock on her door came a half hour after she got home. She forced herself not to run and open it for the locksmith before checking to see who it may be. When she looked out to view her guest, she saw Max in front of her door. His head was lowered and it looked like he was leaning forward gripping both sides of the frame on her door.

"Claire, I know you don't want to see me, but I really need to talk to you. Open the door, please."

She thought about letting him knock, but obviously, he knew she had come home, and thanks to her he had a key. Time to face the music, she thought.

"If he tries to hurt me, you're going to eat him," Claire informed Tilney before she opened the door with as much indifference as she could muster.

"Hello, Max,"

"Hi. I, um…may I come in?"

"I'm sorry, Max. I know this is all sudden." Wedging herself in the opening of the door so that he could neither see in, nor expect to be welcomed in, her heart began to race. "Max, I, um…you've been great. I have really needed a friend, and this has been so much fun."

"But?" He could see it on her face, the same look an entire town of people gave him day after day in the weeks after his wife's passing. A polite but firm unwelcome sign.

"My business is suffering. It's just me and I am running nearly twenty-four hours here. I'm in the process of thinking about taking some help on, but I just can't afford it yet. I really need to focus and I haven't been able to do that lately."

And there it was. She checked out, just like all the others. They had all turned their backs, deciding his fate for him. It didn't matter what his side of the story was, he'd never get a chance to tell it. He shook his head, he'd be damned if it was going to happen with Claire.

"Claire, Damnit, don't lie to me. I know why you took off."

"You do?" her voice a little less confident than she wanted it to be.

"Yes, and I don't want to talk about it with you in the hallway."

She straightened her body up, he sure as shit wasn't going to come in now.

"I want you to leave me be, please."

"So that's it. You're not going to ask me. You're just going to believe what you read in the papers. You don't know what happened. Can we please talk about this—inside?"

Yes, I do know what happened, you asshole.

She didn't immediately answer. She found herself too busy waging a war against the human side of her body. She had been falling in love with him, and it was becoming clear that her head and her heart were not on the same side. Love, how could she be in love? She let go of the idea of ever allowing herself to fall in love again a long time ago. It just wasn't in the cards for her. No man could ever be expected to be a saint, but she seemed to ever only find the deepest of sinners.

As she stood with her body blocking the wedge of opening of her door, he watched the emotions rage within her. She bit her bottom lip as it started to quiver, tears shimmered on the edges of her eyes. Her hand was firmly gripped on the door handle on the inside of her apartment, he was unaware of the grip so tight on the knob it made her fingers ache, but he could see her foot. Bending her right leg at her knee, she was furiously tap/kicking the floor behind her left leg. He didn't know if she was going to slam the door in his face, or jump into his arms.

Forever had been the last thing on his mind the night they last spent together. The way they watched TV, brushed their teeth and changed into pajamas. The way she felt in her sweet cotton nightgown, cradled in his arms against his bare chest. The way he whispered sweet dreams in her ear and the way she smiled up at him in the dark, as if it was the most ridiculously cute thing he had ever said. The way he found her in the middle of the night, soft and warm and how insanely hard it made him. The way it felt to find her ready, and welcoming him. The way his name came out in a whisper and tickled his skin as she explored his body.

Forever, he wanted it to be like this forever. It was the ease of it, the warmth of it. Somewhere along the line he stood at the edge of a place he never thought he'd again be.

Bring your toothbrush ;)

Those weren't the traditional three words, but that's exactly what they were. *I. Love. You.* They were the words swimming around in his mind now, knowing that everything between them was going to end before it even got a chance to really begin.

"Claire, I love you." His words were quiet, and kind.

She looked stunned. Of all the things she thought he might say that was not one of them. It lit a fire under her that even she wasn't ready for. She let go of the door, and rammed her hands into his chest pushing him back against the wall.

"You don't get to say that to me." Her words were slow, deep, and came through gritted teeth.

"I love you," he repeated as his hands came up around hers on his chest. "I feel a connection with you I didn't think I'd ever have again."

"Let me guess." She flushed with fresh rage. "You've never known anyone like me. It's like you connect with me on a level that you don't understand. When you're around me, you just feel, at home, at peace. I read people Max, I'm good at it. What you see as a connection is nothing more than a learned skill I use in my business."

No, no, no. No! Nothing was safe.

She had fooled herself into thinking he was different. He wasn't a dreamer. She wasn't going to find the things that he tells no one. The connection she had been feeling toward him was something born of her heart, and not a by-product of the dream world. She spent a lifetime hearing those words from other people. She was easy to talk to. She just had a way to make somebody feel safe. She felt it too, the connection. It was the most unnerving feeling as her mind defied logic and she felt unnatural links to people who were otherwise strangers.

He was supposed to be different. She got her wish, he was different. In the *Did I not mention I murdered my wife?* kind of way.

"Yes! I do," he defended himself as he took a step toward her "is that so bad. Claire, I—"

"Don't touch me!" she shouted as she let go of him and circled around in front of her apartment door.

The growl came hard and fast from the doorway. Max stood still, looking at Tilney as Claire went back the door and soothed him. She held tight to his collar as he barked his loud warning.

"I think you need to go," Claire warned him.

Max made no movement.

"I'm sorry I kept this from you, but this is why. I moved out of my home town because of things like this."

"You ran away," Claire corrected.

"Do you blame me? I'm standing here, aren't I? Did you read the fact that charges were never filed? It was an accident. Claire, I lost the love of my life that day."

"The love…" her words came out in fits of ragged breath "You let her go."

"What?"

"You heard me, you let her go! You think you can just let her fade away as if she was never here? You can't run from this, Max. You can't tuck a wedding ring and her bike bell in a box in your closet and pretend they weren't things that mattered."

He was speechless. Stunned.

"That's right. I saw those things tucked in your closet. I saw her bike bell, wrapped up. Saved from the fire. I know about it, Max. I know about everything. All the things that you hide so deep down inside yourself. You can't just let your secrets slip under the water and keep living your life as if they never were. Just because you pretend something never happened, doesn't mean it didn't happen."

Her words sliced through him like a knife. The perfect little world he created, the walls he built around them all came crashing down at once. She saw what haunted him, she saw what followed him. She dragged it all out in the light of day.

"Claire, I didn't tell you about Rebecca because I didn't want it to change the way you look at me. When people see…"

"The monster?" she interjected. "That's what I see. I see the demons that you run from, that you hide from. I see you for exactly who you are,"

"A monster," he concluded as he shoved his hands in his pockets and took a few steps backward. "You see me as a monster?"

"No, you see a monster when you look in the mirror."

She was right. It was something he worried about for as long as he could remember. She laid the ugly truth at his feet and dared him to deny it. He couldn't.

"Goodbye, Claire." It was all he could say.

She said nothing as she watched him retreat down the hall.

He returned to his apartment, and sat silently on the couch. He looked around at the impersonal world he'd created for himself over the last year and a half. Unsure of what was causing the emotional buzz in the air, Pilot climbed on the sofa and nudged his body into Max's arms.

"Demons, buddy. Oh, I've got some demons."

He gave Pilot a quick rub and walked into his bedroom. He stood where Claire stood, and looked up at the box that sat on the shelf. He didn't even know she had been in there. These were the only things he had kept of his wife, the things that were more than things. The good and the bad lay tangled in that box, and Max rested somewhere in between them. He turned the lights out as he walked, grabbed the leash and hooked it to Pilot's collar.

As he left the building with just the box and dog, he wasn't sure if he'd ever return. He wasn't sure of anything anymore.

Chapter 20

"You've been walking around this house for days like a zombie," Charlotte casually said as she bit into a slice of apple that had been topped with a layer of peanut butter and sprinkled with raisins.

"Uh…out of celery?" he picked up a slice off her plate and popped it into his mouth when she joined him on the couch he had been sitting on for the last hour mindlessly flipping through the four hundred channels they seemed to have.

He lifted the blanket that was over him and she scooted in next to him.

"Nope, baby does not like celery today." She smiled.

Her pregnancy was going well, and she and Aidan finally allowed themselves to be expectant parents. Charlotte had been in such denial about being pregnant again that when they went in for their first ultrasound to see how things were, her due date was moved up a full month. Next week would mark twenty-five weeks, and though she never said anything, she had been counting the days to a baby who would have a viable chance if her body failed her again.

He leaned his head down on her shoulder and laid his hand on her growing baby bump.

"Well, then apples, it is."

"You sweet-talking my wife?" Aidan walked into the living room to see the two of them sitting there, now both under the same blanket and sharing a snack.

"We're watching…what are we watching?" she turned to Max, unsure of what he was on the TV.

"I don't even know," he admitted, and handed the remote to her.

"See zombie. What the hell, Max?"

She had become more firm in her motherhood. Charlotte always took the indirect, direct road to her destinations. Sweetly smiling as her minions gathered the information that she desired. It seemed with the passing of time in her pregnancy, she was cutting the middleman act out and getting down to business directly.

"I…" it was all he ever said as the last conversation with Claire played out in his mind. He'd start to say something and then he'd just trail off into nothing and change the subject.

He hadn't called her, or seen her. He had been back to his apartment once to get some clothes, and though he had no idea if she was home or not, the building just felt empty to him as he walked through the halls. Her spirit was absent, if that was even a thing. She found out about Rebecca. She obviously found out about the fire, and his role in it. She was now counted among those who decided on his guilt or innocence. No trial, no jury, just judgment. It was what drove him to move into the city in the first place a year and a half ago.

"She knows about Rebecca," he finally settled on.

"Did you think you were going to be able to hide that forever?" she listened intently as she nibbled on the snack.

Yes.

"No. I just…people look at me differently when they know. I'm not even talking about the glares and the whispers of those who have condemned me. I'm talking about the widower people. The people who make sad faces every time they run into me, and turn their heads like they're talking to a child who has had a bad day. The *how you doing today, buddy,* look. I somehow escaped that with her, and I didn't realize how much I needed somebody to look at me and not see what I carry with me."

Charlotte nodded her head, she knew that look well. She had stupidly told people of her first pregnancy too soon and when she lost the baby, it was if she was instantly set aside as a special needs case for the rest of her life. *Hang a sign on me—broken.*

"I'm sorry, Max."

"She never looked at me that way. She didn't know about the fire, she's not big on watching the news. When I realized that it had somehow escaped her, I wanted it to last as long as it possibly could, so I did everything I could to avoid it."

"So what if she knows, what does that change?"

"That's the thing, I'm worried about what she knows."

"Like what?" Charlotte asked.

"I kept the bell from Rebecca's bike. The bike was one of the few recognizable things in that sea of ash. I picked it up, and it was like I found a piece of her. I needed to keep it."

"So? I'm sure her knowing that you had a wife who died won't be the deal breaker you think it is."

"It is when she thinks I killed her." He threw his hands up in the air in frustration.

"Oh, shit," Aidan added from the doorway.

"Did she accuse you?" Charlotte needled.

"You know how when you know someone's insecurities, and they anger you, then you sometimes use that as a weapon in your words?"

"The low blows?"

"Yeah, hers were very specific. So much so, I wonder if she got her hands on more than just articles. She knew exactly where to hit."

"What would she get her hands on, Max? You walked away from that fire with nothing left."

"I don't know. I have an appointment later today. Hopefully that will clear some things up."

"You can stay here as long as you need to," Charlotte said seriously.

"I know."

"I love you," she said as they traded support roles. He lifted his head and she placed hers on his shoulder.

"I know." He kissed the top of her head and returned his attention to the mindless TV watching in front of them. "It's what holds me steady."

Steady is what he tried to remain all morning. Steady is what he tried to remain as he drove through town and parked in the parking lot of the therapist's office. Steady is what he reminded himself to be as his leg bounced up and down waiting for his name to be called back for his appointment.

When the doctor welcomed him in, he said nothing and kept his gaze straight ahead of him. He walked by her into her office, and sat on the couch waiting for her to close the door. She noted his brash behavior.

"What's going on, Max?" She skipped the pleasantries as she sat and opened her file with pencil waiting.

"You tell me," he nearly snarled it at her.

"Uh, tell you what?" she asked, confused.

"So, Claire, the girl I was seeing, broke up with me."

"Sorry to hear that." She kept her voice professional, but knew the anger was still being directed at her.

"Have you met with her?" he asked.

"Excuse me?"

"Have. You. Met. With. Her?" The control was slipping already.

She sat the file down on the table, laid her pencil on top.

"Max, what is this about?"

He stood, and began pacing around her small office. He felt like a caged tiger.

"She mentioned a few things. Things she shouldn't know."

"Like what?"

"Like things I've only told you." The arrow of his accusation finally aimed and shot.

"What things?" She kept her voice calm and her demeanor professional. "Max, sit down."

He complied, but she could see his whole body was fighting anger. His muscles were tight and his fists were twisting in his hands.

"Did you meet with her?" he asked, more calm.

"No, I don't know her, only what you've told me of her."

"She found the box in my closet. I don't know why she was in there to start with, but she was. She stayed over at my place and everything was fine. I woke up alone and she was nowhere to be found. When I did finally find her, she made it very clear that she fell into the Max is guilty camp."

"You've dealt with that before," the doctor reminded him. "It was a big local story, it was just a matter of time before she found out about it. I told you that being honest with her about that would be the best way."

"Do you know what it feels like to have somebody have an opinion already formed of you before they've even met you? I've had so much of that in my life, it made me sick. It was a good thing when we moved to Baltimore and my past didn't follow me. And it was a good thing for me to get away from all of this," he said motioning his arms up in the air.

"And everyone here," she finished his thought.

"Yes. It was a good thing. And when I realized she didn't know anything about Rebecca, I just wanted to keep it that way. I needed somebody to see me. It was nice."

"Max, do you love her?"

"Yes."

"Were you going to go your whole life without telling her about Rebecca?"

"I don't know."

"Were you going to make the same mistake you claim to have made with Rebecca and not tell her about your father?"

He stood again and paced with frustration. He had thought about how and when he would tell her about Rebecca. He had not given any thought to telling her about his father. The reminder made him feel the pressing weight on his shoulders. "I was never planning on getting married again, so I think I buried the idea of my father. I was never planning on falling in love. It doesn't matter. Turns out I didn't have to tell her. She knows things, things that I haven't told anyone—except you."

"Max, I promise you, I have not met with her. I couldn't tell you how she knows what she knows. What I can tell you is that the truth always finds a way. Your father is part of who you are. Rebecca is part of who you are. I understand completely why you enjoyed having your relationship with Claire be protected from all of that somehow. But it's not the truth, and if you are ever going to have a real relationship with her, you have to let her in."

"But, she said stuff. She mentioned me wanting Rebecca to fade away, like I told you about in my dreams. The dream where she was walking down the road and I was trying to find her, but before I did, she disappeared."

"Sometimes when we are worried that the truth will be discovered, we read everything the wrong way. You think she knows about your dream, but she means something different. It's just what you're hearing." She picked her file back up and began making notes.

"The box, like I said she found the box. My wedding ring, the bike bell. She knew it was Rebecca's, she knew I took it from the fire."

"So? It's a bike bell."

"Yeah, but it was never mentioned in any article. It has no significance to anyone except me. She knew I kept it, she knew it was something."

"Okay. Do you think you may have mentioned something along the way?"

"No, I know I didn't. When we moved to Baltimore, it took effort not to mention those little things that make you–you. But then, time went by and my past became less and less important. Hardly ever mentioned, and when it was, I could easily edit out the bad parts. By the time I was seventeen my father didn't even exist. I got good at it. Half the town thinks I killed my wife. I needed not to talk about it. I know I didn't mention it to her, accidentally or on purpose."

Dr. Morgan sighed and sat her file down again. She stood, closed the small space between them and sat on the couch with him.

"Max, your past does not define you," she said softly. "She's not going to see you for the monster that you think you might become, if she knows about your father."

"Interesting choice of words, that's exactly what she said. She sees the monster that I see myself as."

"Well, she's found out something about you that you maybe should have told her. She's hurt and reacting that way. It's petty, but it is human nature to hit below the belt when we feel betrayed."

"I just wanted to protect what I have," he said.

"If only for a little while," Dr. Morgan added. "I know."

Chapter 21

He found himself sitting in a bar not far from the office building the therapist was in. He wasn't yet ready to go back to Aidan's house, and didn't feel like driving into the city. It was happy hour, traffic would be insane any which way he went, so he'd just take advantage and have himself a beer to cool off a bit. He really did not need Charlotte pestering him with questions he wasn't sure how to answer.

"Well, hello there." A voice came from behind him and he turned to see two men pull up to the bar seats next to his.

"What brings you out to these parts?"

"Uh, hi." Max had no idea what to say, a little stunned. He stood to allow them room, and aid if need be.

"Getting a little liquid courage before you come to see my daughter?" Alan asked as he ordered two beers for him and his father.

"Umm…"

"Look, I know she's been moping around our house and it's got something to do with you," Alan offered and as he took his first sip of the cold frothy beverage the barkeeper put in front of him. "I'm just here for the beer, I didn't know you'd be here."

"It's complicated, I'm sorry," Max awkwardly remarked.

"Women!" Charlie offered, "When is it not complicated?"

"I don't want to get you guys involved, Mr. Martin. I'm sorry, I can go." Max began to stand and Alan grabbed his arm.

"Sit down, boy. And Alan, call me Alan. Mr. Martin is reserved for the grumpy old man to my right," Alan teased his father.

"I can still kick your ass, boy." Charlie smacked the counter.

"I know you can, Dad, I know you can." He returned his attention to Max.

"Look, Claire has had nothing but good things to say about you. Whether or not you two work out whatever this is about, we're all adults here. It's okay. Have your beer."

"Thank you." Max sat back down. "I wasn't by the way. I wasn't coming to see Claire. I had a meeting not far from here. I want to talk to her, I really do. I just don't know what to say."

"The truth," Alan offered. "It's a simple little thing that we tend to over complicate."

"I love her," the words came out without control as he focused on the wording on the label of his beer. "I just have some things I need to work out first, that's all."

"Well, don't let opportunity pass you by. I damn near missed my chance with her mother."

"Oh? How's that?" Max inquired.

"She worked at the book store on campus at the college we went to. I thought she was cute. I kept going in and buying little things as an excuse talk to her. The more I talked to her, the more I liked her."

"It wasn't mutual?" Max asked. Claire once told him how her parents had met, and to hear her tell it, it was love at first sight.

"It was, but I was too chicken-shit to realize it. I asked around about her, and there were talks about a guy who really did a number on her. Some guy in her past, she was waiting for him to come back. I didn't even know the guy, and I already had it in my head that he was a better man for her than I was. I thought there would be no way she'd pick me over him."

"And she did?"

"He was a part of her past, a ghost. The only person that put him between her and me was me. I made him a thing that I had to get past. I convinced myself she was waiting for him, when the truth was, she was waiting for me."

"What if he came back?"

"Well, I can't tell you the answer to that. All I can tell you is that one afternoon, she got tired of me coming into the bookstore and making excuses. She cornered me, and asked me if I was ever going to ask her out. I did like her and I did want to ask her out. I just over complicated everything around it. I would have never asked her out, I would have missed out on the best thing that ever happened to me if she had not demanded the truth. The simple, honest, truth."

"What happens when the truth is not so simple?" Max asked.

"The truth is always simple. It's what's around it that gets complicated. Claire's a smart girl, give her some credit."

Max took a deep breath in and returned his attention to his beer. *She was a smart girl, who saw too much.*

"Alan, do you have my bag?" Charlie interrupted.

"What bag?"

"My black bag, with all my pills."

"Do you need it?" Alan asked, not wanting to know the answer.

"I do," the old man confirmed.

"Why didn't you bring it with us?"

"Your mother does these things. I'm just a grumpy old man, remember?"

"I'll be right back. It's in the car," Alan explained to Max. "The car that's parked two blocks down."

Alan rolled his eyes, but slid off the bar stool without question and excused himself to retrieve his father's bag from their car. He noted the bag when he picked his father up for the cardiologist appointment, but his mother had not said anything to him about making sure Charlie had his pills. She was usually very good about that.

"What things do you need to work out?" Charlie asked as soon as Alan was out of ear shot.

"Um, just things." Max smiled.

"Weird things? Things that you think you might be imagining?"

There was a long pause before Max said anything. Perhaps Dr. Morgan was right. Perhaps he put a link that wasn't there between what Claire said to his dream, and he shouldn't have. But she knew about the bike bell; that couldn't be imagined. At least, he didn't think it could be.

"Look, boy, I don't have much time before he comes back. Now spill it."

"Excuse me?" Max looked around for help from someone, anyone.

"Does she know things that you can't figure out how she knows?"

Max neither confirmed anything, nor did he deny it.

"Weird, huh?"

"You could say that," Max studied the old man as he took a slow sip from his beer.

"Let me tell you something about when I met Adelaide; she wasn't like anybody else I ever knew."

"You two seem very happy."

"We are, but we had a lot of weird years. She's a weird lady," Charlie admitted.

"Define this weird that you keep saying."

"She just knew things and I'd have no idea how she knew them. Not only about me, but the people around us. She knew things about them too. Some days it was so freaking strange, I would swear she had voodoo magic."

Max's brows came together, his mouth opened to speak but in his confusion, he found himself at a loss for words. Where was the old man going with this?

"Alright."

"I've noticed on occasion that Claire is a lot like Adelaide, if you know what I'm saying."

"What are you saying?" Max was not connecting any dots, the old man wasn't making any sense.

"I'm saying, when you love a girl, you love every part. The good, the bad, the ugly, and the weird. If she had voodoo magic and could read my mind, I was just going to have to love the shit out of that voodoo magic."

Max nearly spit out the sip of beer.

"Is that what you think it is?" *Reading minds? Oh, lord.*

"I don't know what it was. All I know is that I loved that woman, and she made me believe in the unbelievable."

"Did she...show you?" Max was fascinated where their conversation had turned.

"No. I never asked. I believed in her, so I just believed. She didn't have to prove it."

"You're telling me you think your wife can read minds and it never bothered you enough to bring it up?"

"No! Why would it? She knew the parts of me I didn't share with anyone. She loved me anyway. If she wasn't going to judge me, I wasn't going to judge her."

"Well, there might be the problem. Claire doesn't love the parts of me that she sees." Max looked hopelessly into his beer bottle.

"You hiding something, boy?" Charlie bellowed.

"I didn't tell her something, maybe I should have. I don't know."

"Go talk to her. If she's fixing to figure you out, maybe you ought to be there to defend yourself."

"Did you ever have something, that wasn't so great, that Adelaide found out?"

"A few things." He winked.

Before they could finish the strangest conversation Max had ever had in his life, Alan returned to them, none the wiser.

"Here's your stuff, Dad."

"Thank you," Charlie said as he pulled the zipper to the Dopp kit open. His aging, shaky hands pulled a prescription bottle out, eyed the label, and poured out two pills. He made the motion of popping them into his mouth before returning them to the bottle. He didn't need any pills until after dinner, but he needed those minutes with Max.

"Dad, you ok with that beer and those pills?"

"Oh yeah, it's fine." Charlie assured him. He was fine, because he hadn't taken anything.

"Claire's at home. Her home. She left early this morning," Alan offered Max, just for the sake of having information he might see handy. "Your prescription is ready, Dad. We'll finish these beers and go."

"Yeah, yeah."

"Well, it's been…" Max struggled for the right words. "…nice running into you. I have to go."

"See ya round, kid," Alan offered.

Max was driving back toward Aidan and Charlotte's house as he played out the conversation he'd had with Charlie. The man thought his wife was a mind reader. Crazy. As he drove, the words Claire last spoke to him rang out in his mind.

You think you can just let her fade away as if she was never here? You can't run from this, Max. You can't tuck a wedding ring and her bike bell in a box in your closet and pretend they weren't things that mattered.

The images from the dream he had the night Claire left flashed through his mind. Rebecca's face, scared and pale. Reaching for him from the water, and he let her slip under. She sank to the bottom, her feet dug into the sand. He wanted to go back for her, but when he looked at the water again, she was gone. It was calm and peaceful, as if she had never been there. He thought about the dream he had where she was walking down Main Street and as she did, she was fading. She blamed him, and eventually in both dreams it was as if she was never there.

"I am not really entertaining the idea that she can read minds," he told himself. "Just, no."

He picked apart every conversation they ever had. He turned over the words she screamed at him about feeling connected to her in a way he couldn't explain. How she mentioned her learned skill.

"No. Jesus Christ." He tried to convince himself he wasn't entertaining her grandfather's claim.

The feeling washed over him in a wave. *You love her, try.* Before he could stop himself, he made the turn off the exit to get into the city. With every mile that passed, the desire to talk to her grew.

"Believe in the unbelievable," he said to himself. "This is nuts. You've lost your mind, Max."

As he pulled into the apartment parking lot and got out of the car, he heard Claire shouting from across the street.

"Tilney, no!"

He jogged up to the edge of the parking lot and saw Tilney barreling across the park green toward the apartment building. He then noticed the little boy bouncing a red ball, much like Tilney's in front of the steps to the building. Tilney was not on his leash, he slipped out of the dog park gate before Claire got it on him. He took off in pursuit of the red ball.

Max started a brisk paced walk toward the boy to grab Tilney if he got across the street, knowing Claire would not catch up in time. The boy's mother was chatting on her phone and unaware of the huge dog racing toward her child. Max knew he wouldn't hurt the boy, but he might knock into him while after the ball. Just as he reached closer to the boy, he saw the delivery van. The van that could not see Claire around the blind corner. The van that would not see the dog that clearly didn't have the sense to stop.

"Oh, God," he whispered and began running. "Claire!"

The shout got the attention of the little boy's mother who finally became aware of the situation. She scooped the chubby toddler up, leaving the ball while she hurried up the staircase to the front entrance to put space between the dog and her child.

The world slowed down to a near crawl, and everything happened in a timeless blur all at once. Claire saw Max running toward them from down the sidewalk and turned to see the van. He would never get to Tilney on time, and the van wouldn't stop.

"No!" she shouted as she reached the sidewalk, keeping her running pace, and stepped off the curb.

Tilney cleared the van, but Claire did not. She watched Max running towards her and felt the impact as their bodies collided. She heard the screeching tires, and everything went sideways and upside down and then it was still and silent again.

The street was hard, and cold against the back of her head. She slowly turned, and corrected herself. The sidewalk was hard and cold, she was on the sidewalk, not the road. Her vision was spotty, darkness creeping in from every edge.

"Max…" her voice barely a whispering as she looked out onto the street and saw him lying in front of the van. His gaze on her, blinking heavily.

The darkness closed in, and the cold took over.

Chapter 22

It felt like hours. Claire struggled to hold onto reality as she faded in and out of consciousness. She wasn't sure which way was up, she wasn't sure if she was awake or dreaming. Flashes of light passed her line of vision, and muffled sounds were coming from every direction. Bits of conversations from voices unknown swam uncontrollably in her mind. *Didn't see them…came out of nowhere…dog….together, I've seen them.*

Eventually, the world began to make sense again, and there was a face coming into focus.

"Ma'am, can you hear me?"

Purple. It was all purple.

The EMT closed the distance between them and looked closely as he lifted her left eyelid with his purple-gloved hand. He noted the reaction of her pupil dilating to the light and moved to check her right eye.

"Are you upside down?" her voice came out sleepy, slow and cracked.

"No, darlin', you are. Just hold still, I got ya." His smooth southern accent wrapped around her mind warmly. "Do you know where you are?"

"In a freezer?"

The EMT smiled a sweet crooked smile as he removed the flashlight from her eyes and continued to assist his partner who was securing her head, neck and back for transportation.

"It is cold out here, a warm blanket is coming, I promise."

"The van. My dog. Max!" Images of what just transpired flashed, and the muscles in her body twitched as she struggled to get up.

"No, no darlin', you have to stay put. You took quite the fall." There wasn't much of a struggle as Claire was too discombobulated and weak to be able to garner anything more than a slight wiggle on the ambulance stretcher she was being attached to.

"But…" her body had already given up the fight.

"The big dog, he yours?"

"Tilney."

"Tilney," the EMT repeated. "See, Tilney, she's gonna be fine."

At the sound of his name, Tilney struggled and fought with the leash that had been tied to the iron fence on the edge of the property. He was about a foot from Claire, laying on the ground and whimpering. With his big size, and Claire being hurt, passersby had given up trying to contain him with manpower. Her neighbor Jack came to their rescue. He heard the commotion of the accident from his living room and spotted Claire and Max each laying on the ground from his window. He quickly hurried down the several flights of steps to the ground floor and was able to pull Tilney back enough to get Claire some space. He tied the dog to the fence next to her so he could check on Max. He remained with Max as he could see the man was in far worse condition until the paramedics arrived four minutes later. It was Jack who was able to fill in the gaps of information for the paramedics.

"I'm fine, baby," she whispered as she attempted to wave her hand for the dog.

He barked loudly and once again tried to close the distance between them.

"He'll be fine, darlin'. Your neighbor's going to take good care of him."

"Max." Her voice began to gain strength as they lifted her off the ground and began wheeling her toward the awaiting ambulance.

The EMT looked over to the man being put into the second ambulance. His face careful and kind for the fragile woman he was caring for. He wasn't sure which way it was going to go, or if Max was even still alive. He knew the man had taken the full force of the impact from the van. Eyewitnesses on the scene were eagerly and nervously shouting out the details. The driver of the van sustained minor injuries and no doubt would be able to recount his steps, if he chose to be honest. He was driving too fast around a corner known to be a blind spot to both traffic and pedestrians, and didn't see them. The dog ran out into the road, and its owner went after him. The man from across the street saw the van and ran out into the road to stop the woman. He pushed her out of the way, and he was hit instead.

"Your husband is in the other ambulance. He saved your life," he finally settled on.

"My husband," her confused tone was unable to articulate fact from question.

"We will see him there, okay? You just rest. My name is Christopher."

"Christopher? Who's dream is this? I don't want you to be Christopher," she babbled.

"You can call me CJ if you want," he shook his head. He worried about the extent of her head injury. She was babbling. "What's your name?"

"Claire. My name is Claire."

"Good," as he wrapped a warm blanket over her, she lifted her hand and wrapped it around his fingers.

"CJ, CJ is good."

He smiled and slid her hand in his, and talked to her about everything except Max until they arrived at the hospital.

"One last thing, any chance you could be pregnant?" he asked her as he checked off the boxes on the paper clipped to the plastic clipboard in his lap.

"No," she began, but then started to hesitate. She didn't even know what day it was at the moment, her attempt to count backwards twenty-eight days would be useless. "Uh…yeah, no."

"Alright, just sit back. We'll be there soon enough," he assured her, as he checked off that she could be pregnant.

She was rolled in and out of rooms. Blood was drawn, tests were taken, and notes were made. Finally, she was settled into a quiet room, and a doctor was able to sit down with her and fill her in on the last few hours of her life. She was able to match the details of the story with how she remembered them, details coming back to her slowly as the minutes passed.

"Okay, so you're fine, and lucky. Very lucky," the doctor told her.

"Thank you, Dr. Benton. Max—" she started.

"There's just one thing," he interrupted her.

"What's that?"

"You indicated that you didn't think you were pregnant."

"I did." She said the words slowly, not wanting to be challenged.

"Well, you are," he smiled awkwardly, "congratulations?"

She said nothing. The sound went out of the room. Surely she was stuck in a dream, maybe her mother's. Dreaming up a romantic rescue from the handsome neighbor and throwing in a surprise baby. She felt like her mind was going in a million different directions, but as she looked into the doctors eyes for any kind of response on the state of her pregnancy, she only cared about one.

"Is the baby okay?" she asked quietly.

"You're fine. So is your baby."

"I didn't know…how far along am I?"

"Um…looks like about six weeks. Very early. You will want to follow up with an OB once you are home. We're going to monitor everything closely, but right now everything looks perfectly fine."

Before she knew it, she was crying. She fought it, waving her hands in front of her face. The relief she felt over the baby, her baby, being okay was overwhelming.

"I'm sorry," she said.

"It's okay," he patted her knee. "You've got a lot going on."

"Max! How is he? Where is he?"

"He's got a lot going on, too," the doctor's voice took a more serious tone. "He's stable, but he took the brunt of that accident."

"He saved my life," Claire whispered.

"He did. He's got a broken arm and hip. He's in surgery., I will let you know the minute he gets out."

"Thank you."

"He's not your husband, is he?"

"No. My neighbor was there. He must have told the EMTs that. But I…" she didn't know what to say, she laid her hand on her flat stomach.

He was the father of her child, the doctor could see it. "It's okay. I'll let you know as soon as there is something to know."

"Claire!" Linda burst into the room, unfazed by the conversation being had between doctor and patient. Alan quickly walking in behind her, carrying her purse.

"Hi, Mom." Claire sweetly smiled as she pushed herself a bit to sit up straight in the hospital bed.

"Oh, sweetie, don't move. Are you okay?" her hands gently but frantically searched over her daughter's face. "Is she okay? I'm her mother, Linda."

The doctor took a step back and let Linda do her mom thing. He himself had two teenage boys, so he could always sympathize with parents coming in after a phone call from the hospital.

"Hi, Mom. This is Dr. Benton."

"I've been taking care of your girl here. She's tough."

"Of course she is." Claire's father added as he rounded to the other side of the bed and sat in a chair next to his daughter, grabbing her hand and kissing it gently.

"Claire is going to be fine. She took a hard knock to the head, but we've checked her all over. Inside and out just to be sure. She's very lucky."

"Oh, my love. What happened?" Linda asked, choosing to position herself on the side of the bed with Claire rather than sit in the chair offered to her.

"Tilney. He took off after something before I could get his leash on him. A van was on the road, didn't see him."

"Oh, God, was he hit, baby?" Linda was already sure that the dog had been killed.

"No. Max was across the street and saw the van. He started yelling and we both ran for Tilney."

"Tilney cleared the van and is with her neighbor, according to the EMT who brought her in," the doctor began. "Looks like Max pushed Claire out of the way of the van. He took the bulk of the hit."

"Is he here? Is he okay?" Alan asked.

"He's here for a while yet. He has some broken bones; he's in surgery. Claire needs to stay the night for observation, but she should be good to go home tomorrow. She just needs some rest. I'll let you guys visit."

"Thank you, Doctor," Linda said as she continued to fuss over Claire, straightening out the bed sheets laying on top of her. "What happened? They just told me that you were hit by a car."

"Tilney got loose and took off. I saw the van. I saw it. I just…Tilney."

"He's your baby, and that's exactly how a mother would react," Linda assured her.

"Max was on the other side of the street. I don't even know why he was there, he just appeared out of nowhere. He pushed me back and the van hit him."

"I just saw him a few hours ago," Alan admitted. "When I took your grandfather to his doctor's appointment. We had some time to kill before his medicine was ready so we went and had a beer. Max was there."

"Did you talk to him?" Claire asked.

"We did. He was a mess, Claire. He said he loves you, and wants to talk to you but he doesn't know how."

Her heart ached, and tears welled up in her eyes. None of this made any sense. How could he cry in his beer over her? She accuses him of murder and in turn, he saves her life. She still had no idea what happened on the night Rebecca Duncan died, or the extent of his guilt, but at the moment it did not matter. She desperately wanted to see him.

"Will you please take me to go sit with him when he gets out of surgery? I don't want him to wake up alone."

"I'm sure they called his family, sweetheart, but of course we will, as long as the doctor says it's okay."

His family. Claire closed her eyes. She didn't even know if he had a family. She thought of the child they created together.

"Mom, right now, I am his family. I have to go be with him."

"And you will, when it's okay."

It was morning before Claire was taken to see Max. Dr. Benton sat with her after Max's surgery and explained they discovered swelling in his brain. He told her that Max suffered brain trauma in the front from the initial impact of the accident and then in the back of his head from the fall to the ground. They put him into a medically induced coma in hopes of getting the swelling to go down. He was honest with her when he told her Max's condition was not where they wanted it to be.

"We will check you out, and then you can go see him. Darla, here, can wheel you down to the ICU. Do you have somebody who can stay with you for a few days?"

"My parents. They've already called. I told them I would call them when I'm ready to go, I wanted to visit with Max today."

"Good. I'll let the nurses down there know to keep an eye on you today."

"Thank you, Dr. Benton," Claire said to him.

"No problem," he winked. "Take it real easy for the next week. Listen to your body. Baby is in charge, okay?"

"Yes, sir," she said, as the nurse wheeled her down the hall to Max's room.

There had been no dreams for Claire the night before as she lay in the hospital. No dreams from not sleeping. She thought of Max, and waited to hear anything different from the updates she'd been given. She thought about the baby she didn't even know existed twenty- four hours ago. Pregnant. She waited for the tears to come, for the anger and frustration. She didn't want kids, for good reason. She waited for the rage and the why's she would shout to the God who listened. She waited for all of it, but it never came. Instead, she lay all night, rubbing her flat stomach. Hoping and praying the baby would stay safe. Stay warm. There were no shouts asking why. There were only prayers to watch over the little life that had been created.

Max lay very still in the bed, with machines beeping and tubes strapped to his chest and arms. Claire squeezed the nurse's arm as fresh tears sprung into her eyes.

"It just looks bad, but all this is him healing, hon." The nurse patted her arm as she steadied Claire on her feet in the doorway of Max's room.

A small woman wearing a gray sweater and jeans turned from the chair sitting next to Max's bed. She looked worn, as if she had been up all night. She stood slowly, her body protesting moving from the chair she sat in all night long.

"Hello," Claire offered, though she had no idea who the woman was.

"Just let us know if you need anything, hon," the nurse said in her thick Baltimore accent and she disappeared out the door.

"Hello," the woman offered back and quietly returned to watching the man in the bed sleep.

"How is he?" Claire asked as she found a chair to sit down.

"It's been a long night, but he's resting now," the woman said as she pointed to the machine that was beeping and recording the steady rhythmic beat of his heart.

"I'm, um," Claire all of the sudden felt like she was intruding in on this woman's world and hated the feeling. "I'm Claire."

"Marjorie."

"Are you Max's mom?"

Claire hated the fact she didn't know. She didn't even know if Max's parents were living or dead. Living in the area or out of the country. She didn't know if he had siblings, or children. The idea of him having children without her knowing was preposterous, but she would have said the same thing about a wife a week before.

"I am," the woman confirmed, as she continued to rub the edge of the blanket by Max's hand.

"He…" The words felt so heavy, so hard to say. "He saved my life."

Marjorie smiled now, yet did not turn to Claire. She kept her eyes on her boy.

"They told me what happened. Your dog okay?" Marjorie asked.

"Yes, he's with our neighbor, Jack."

Claire watched Marjorie for any sort of recognition. She didn't seem to know Claire, and it ached just a little bit, that Max might not have told anyone about her. He certainly didn't tell her about anyone. At the mention of Jack's name, a small sign of recognition came over Marjorie's face and then faded back to the intent stare toward the screen displaying all of Max's vital statistics. It was if she was studying them, making sure each pulse of his heart came exactly when it should and exactly how it should.

"When they called me, they told me my son and his wife had been in an accident."

A phone call she had actually received once before.

The heat of embarrassment shot up the back of Claire's neck and her face felt hot. It wasn't a lie that she told, but it was one she had perpetuated since arriving to the hospital.

"I'm sorry about that. Jack told the paramedics that we were married. I think so that we could be kept together. Maybe, I don't know. We are friends, I live downstairs from him."

"I know who you are, dear," Marjorie informed her.

A combination of relief and fear mixed in Claire's stomach. It was momentarily exciting to think Max had told his mother of Claire, but it was the way his mother had offered the words. They were quiet and kind, but there was a very brisk tone.

"My doctor knows we aren't married, but he didn't mention it to anyone else. He knew I wanted to be…" she couldn't finish the thought. She felt ashamed at thinking Max didn't have people in his life. As she sat across from this woman who was clearly only half aware that Claire was even there, she felt guilty for accusing Max of anything. Not because she thought he was innocent; that had yet to be proven. But because of the look on Marjorie's face. This was her baby, and he was broken.

"It's okay," Marjorie finally said after a few moments of silence, "I appreciate you wanting to be here for him."

The women sat in their chairs, on either side of his bed. His mother's fingers never wavered playing with the edge of the blanket by his hand, perhaps it was her nerves. Claire twisted her own hands in circles in her lap and then finally settled on sitting on them to keep herself still.

"He didn't tell me about you," Marjorie broke the silence of the room, "I just knew that there was a you."

The ache in Claire's heart stabbed at her again, but she gave Marjorie her full attention. She got the feeling it wasn't time to ask questions, it was just time to listen. She studied the woman, who looked like she would be a fun person to be around on any other day of the year. Her hair was a lighter shade of blonde with strands of white breaking up the solid color. Touches of aging, but it blended so well into her hair you'd almost miss it. It was thick and pulled back into a long braid that ran down her back. She was tan, wore no makeup, but her face defied any signs of age. She was thin, but did not look fragile. She fit nicely in the sweater she was wearing and her jeans were snug. She had silver earrings on, and a silver necklace that had a singular oval shaped black gem resting just above the vee of her sweater. Claire wondered if the woman was even sixty, she looked on the edge of being too young to be Max's mother.

"I've watched this boy fall into the pits of hell," Marjorie offered, "and I thought he was gone. He's been so lost. He needed to fight, but he was just giving up."

She wasn't referring to the accident. She wasn't referring to the fire either. She was referring to the months that came after. The nights she slept wondering where it was that her son went off to as he sat like a spiritless lump on Aidan and Charlotte's couch.

"Then a couple of months ago, something changed. Life, his life, it was finding its way back to him. Love, maybe."

"I don't know about that," Claire blushed.

"He never mentioned you by name, but he mentioned a new neighbor and your dog."

"Tilney," Claire offered. "I was chasing Tilney when this all happened. I am so sorry."

"It's not your fault. Max is a good man. I am glad he was able to be there for you."

Claire didn't know what to say. She wanted to believe Max was a good person, but all of her experience with dreamers told her otherwise. She realized the things Max dreamed about Rebecca were not actual things that happened, but they represented truth. He dreamed she had been trapped in a box. It could have represented feeling lost and confused about something. It would be a feeling of being trapped in real life, perhaps trapped in the web of lies that he told. There was the dream where he played out the fire, which Claire thought was more of a memory than a representation. Maybe he had imagined what it must have been like for Rebecca to be locked inside the house as it burned down. Fires can represent other things, but it was the one dream that had physical evidence. She had held that bike bell in her hand, and she had touched the delicate swirl of patterns on the inside lip of the wedding ring he no longer wore. He had thought out what it had been like for her behind that locked door often enough, that he dreamed about it.

The disappearing act was just that. When one disappears in a dream, the person responsible is either worried that someone will disappear, or they are trying to make them disappear. The drowning was emotional. You can't deal, it's too much, you don't know what end is up and you just want it all to go away.

Claire looked at Max's mother and wondered exactly what sort of hell she thought her son might have been in. Was it one that he fell into, or was it one that he created?

"I owe him my life." A simple fact she turned over and over in her head. He saved her life, yet took another. Why? And now, as it turned out, she owed him two lives.

The knock at the door had them both turning. Marjorie stood and went over to the couple standing in the door. Claire recognized them from the world Max shared with her, at least, these were people who she knew.

"Hi, baby." Marjorie hugged Charlotte, with as much love as she would give her own child.

"Hi." She welcomed the woman's arms and looked as though she wanted to scoop her up and take all of the pain away.

The man Claire recognized as Aidan also offered Max's mom a hug. She noticed that Marjorie laid her hand on Charlotte's stomach, making Claire aware of the baby bump. Max had a family. Claire immediately felt like the intruder she had always seen herself to be, only now in the waking world.

"Hi, Claire." Charlotte smiled and wrapped her arms around Claire gently. "How are you feeling?"

She was left only with a trail of bruises on the side of her forehead and a small set of six stitches where her head had hit the ground, which was unnoticeably tucked in on her scalp under her hair.

"Fine. I'm fine. Just bumps and bruises."

"Glad to hear it, we checked in on you when they brought the both of you in, but with everything happening so quickly with Max, we didn't get to check back."

"Understandable, but thank you for thinking to check in on me." It was an extremely kind thing to do, especially since she didn't know if Aidan and Charlotte knew she and Max had broken up.

His mother gave no indication of knowing, but then again, she gave no indication of being aware they were even dating. Maybe Aidan and Charlotte were in the same boat.

"How's our boy today?" Aiden asked.

"Beeping away. I guess that's a good thing."

"Go home, Mrs. D, get some rest. You've been here all night. We came to sit for a while with him."

Marjorie instantly looked torn. A hot shower, and a cool bed were heaven-sent, but not at the cost of leaving her child laying in a hospital bed.

"I agree, go home. Get some rest. I promise you I will call you if that so much makes a blip," Max's doctor chimed in from the door. "There are too many people in here."

"I'll go," Claire offered, and began to collect the things she realized weren't there. Her purse, her coat, her keys. All of these things back at her apartment, as she hadn't taken them with her to the park with Tilney. They were only going to be a few minutes after all.

"No, you stay. I think he'd want you here. I will go," Marjorie said.

"I am going to go make sure this lady has something to eat before she does," Aidan announced. "You ladies stay here."

Claire sat back down, and Charlotte took the seat Max's mother had been sitting in. She rubbed the bump, and patted it gently.

"Congratulations," Claire offered.

"Thank you."

"I didn't realize you were pregnant. Were you pregnant at Halloween?"

"Yes. Further along than we thought, but we weren't telling people at that time. I've had a bit of a tough road when it comes to pregnancy."

"Sorry to hear that." Claire smiled sadly. Fear crept in for the child she carried.

"It's fine, but thank you. So far, so good with this little guy."

"It's a boy?"

"Yes. We confirmed it at our last appointment." Charlotte smiled with the pride she was just now allowing herself to have. "Now it's just a matter of a name. Well, his first name. His middle name will be Max's name."

"Oh, that's lovely, Charlotte."

"Max has been such a good friend to us over the years. He's my family," she straightened up and spoke loudly at the man lying in the bed. "You hear me? You're family and this baby is going to want to play with you so get a move on the healing, okay?"

Claire could see the tears welling up, and hear the emotion in Charlotte's voice, both of which she quickly tried to wave away.

"Sorry, pregnancy hormones."

"You be however you need to be," Claire assured her. "Can I ask you a question?"

"Sure."

"You've known Max for a long time?"

"Since I was fifteen. He was the new kid that just moved to town and we connected. I'd be lying if I told you that there was never a time that I wasn't half in love with this man, but he has always been a brother to me."

"So," Claire took a big breath in. Once she asked, she couldn't un-ask. "You knew Rebecca?"

Charlotte grew still. She closed her eyes, and a fresh tear slipped down her cheek. She turned to Claire, and smiled.

"I did. She was one of my favorite people in the world."

Claire noticed Charlotte gathering her hand on top of Max's lifeless hand. Her fingers were rubbing the small space that wasn't occupied by tape or a tube. She was moving into mom-mode, making Claire aware that she would protect Max against anyone who came against him.

"Did he tell you about her?" Charlotte asked. Her eyes were focused and her face stoic.

"Can you tell me about the fire?" Claire asked. She was afraid to answer Charlotte's question. She was afraid she would be called out as an imposter, and thrown from the room and Max's life.

Charlotte gently squeezed Max's hand and stood. She walked to the widow that overlooked the city of Baltimore on a chilly early winter day and remembered. She remembered the night when everything changed forever.

Chapter 23

"Oh my gosh, did you die?"

Rebecca rolled with laughter and put her soapy wet hand over the apron on her stomach to catch her breath. She quieted down to a giggle and cradled the phone between her shoulder and ear to continue washing the dinner dishes in the sink.

"It was so hard to keep a straight face, they are so stinking cute at this age," she said.

Charlotte could only imagine how cute it must have been to discover sweet little Josie cornering Luke at independent reading time, sliding a little love letter with hearts colored out in bright pink marker into his hand. Rebecca had told Charlotte about these two before, and the love affair that Josie seemed to be having. Notes, kissy pictures, and inevitably making her way through the playground to ask him to swing with her. Luke was oblivious to it all of course, which Rebecca believed, made him even more tantalizing to Josie.

"Did you tell their parents?" Charlottes inquired on the other end of the line.

"I mentioned it to his mom because it's been so cute. So far, there is nothing to fuss over so I don't think I will mention it to hers."

"You don't think she'd like to know?"

"Maybe, but in my experience, no. Some women kind of freak out at the idea of their daughter chasing a boy at the ripe old age of six years old," Rebecca accounted.

"Yeah, it's so much more socially acceptable at seven," Charlotte teased.

"Just wait until you're a mom, you'll see."

"Hope so!"

"How's that going by the way? And it's fine to tell me it's none of my business." Rebecca wanted to know if Charlotte was pregnant yet. They had been friends for a good while now, but still she would understand if Charlotte didn't want talk about it.

"I think I've got him talked into the idea," Charlotte smiled and looked into the living room from the kitchen where she could see her husband sitting on the couch, watching TV.

"Still just thinking about it, huh?"

"He's not saying things, or making jokes when I bring the idea up, so I think he's thinking about it. I am not going to rock the boat."

"Good call," Rebecca agreed as she stacked and put away the few washed dishes she had made herself dinner with.

"How about you?" Charlotte whispered into the phone.

"I don't know," Rebecca said with a heaving sigh.

She wanted to be a mother, she was ready. She loved kids, and though she had little experience with babies, she possessed the exact right combination of patience and persistence that one needs when handling the young school-aged child. She and Max never discussed children, she never thought she would need to. He was a good man and they enjoyed all of the stages of their relationship. They met in a coffee shop, dated for a while, but not too long, and wasted little time on an engagement period. They wanted to be married, and she dreamed of all the bells and whistles marriage afforded.

It was a bit of a surprise when she dropped even the slightest of hints that it might be time to start thinking about a family, his defenses went up. He was never mean, he used the art of distraction more than anything else. She'd bring up painting a room in their fixer upper of a house a nice pale neutral color so it could be easily converted to a bedroom when need be and he'd start talking about needing to get to foundational work first. She'd slow down when they walked by baby boutiques, and he'd all of the sudden be the hungriest man in the world insisting they change direction and grab lunch before it got too late.

She would get lost in the magical sight-line of a baby at a store or social gathering, and he would gather her up and kiss her wildly, telling her he just couldn't take one more minute of not holding her. There was definitely something he wasn't saying; she just didn't know what it was.

"He'll come around. Thankfully we all have plenty of time."

"The clock begins to tick loudly, my friend." Rebecca admitted. "Thirty is so much different than twenty-nine."

"Yeah, I know," Charlotte agreed. "So what are you guys up to tonight?"

"Well, since the boys are working late, I thought I would sink myself into a bath and finish up this book I've been reading."

Charlotte looked into the living room where Aidan had been parked on the couch for over an hour and wondered what Rebecca was talking about.

"Uh…did Max say how late they would be?"

Choose your words carefully, Charlotte, she thought. She felt as close to Rebecca as she would any sister but her loyalties would stay with Max. He kept her secrets without question, when there were secrets to keep. Charlotte hoped that there wasn't a secret that she needed to keep.

"Oh, you know that Ellis house that they're working on. The whole month has been weird. Late nights, and bad reception areas so I can never get a hold of him."

"Yeah," Charlotte smugly agreed, as she gripped the handle of spatula that she was using to dish out pie with animated force. She smacked the slices down on the cheery little reindeer dessert plates that neither she nor Aidan ever remembered to pack away with the Christmas decorations and wound up throwing into the kitchen cabinet year after year.

Aidan caught the sound of the smack to the plate, turning his attention to his wife standing in the kitchen. Her eyes met his and he could read it all over her face, somebody was in t-r-o-u-b-l-e. He prayed it wasn't him.

"What are you going to do?" Rebecca innocently asked.

Grill my husband.

"Um, I don't know. Catch up on some TV. I really know how to live on the edge."

"Good night, wild child." Rebecca smiled and hung up the phone.

Charlotte grabbed the two plates with homemade Boston cream pie, and casually strolled into the living room and sat next to Aidan on the couch.

"So," she said pleasantly.

"Uh-oh," Aidan said as his attention never left the television while he accepted the plate and fork she handed him. Somebody was definitely in trouble. "Whatever it is, I wasn't involved."

"The Ellis house."

"What about it?" he asked, surprised and confused that his wife was bringing up work. She didn't know the clients personally, so it wasn't as if Mrs. Ellis would go running to Charlotte with problems.

"I thought you guys finished that."

"We did." He looked even more confused. "We wrapped up about two weeks ago, why?"

"Everything go okay with it? Did you have any issues? Has Max?"

It was possible Max would have issues with the house. They were equal partners in their business but they each offered different strengths. Max liked working under pressure, with deadlines looming. He had always been that way, choosing to party for a month and then study all night long for a test. Aidan liked to keep things in order, and plan out his panic attacks well in advance.

"Nope. It all went rather well. It was a big project so we will have a little bit of wiggle room."

"But you had to put in extra time? Did you go in early? Did Max stay late sometimes?"

Please say yes, Charlotte begged in her mind.

"No, why? Charlotte, what are you getting at?" Aidan turned his full attention to his wife.

She could clearly see that he was confused. Nothing was calculating in his mind, which she supposed was good.

"Rebecca just mentioned Max had been working late, that's all. She seemed to be under the impression that you both were working late tonight."

"Huh," he said as he dipped his fork into the pie and enjoyed a big bite. Man, his woman could bake.

"She also said you two have been working late for a few weeks now, and going into areas with shoddy reception. Got any ideas about why he might have told her such a thing?" she scooted closer to him, watching him for any sort of reaction at all.

His reaction was to back up and look at her as if she had lost her mind.

"Trouble in paradise?" he wondered.

"You tell me!" she retorted.

"I don't know, babe. Maybe he is at work. We've had some paperwork pile up and we've both been meaning to get to it. Maybe he just wanted to catch up."

"Well, find out," she insisted. "Find out in your Aidan way, or I will find out in my Charlotte way and nobody wants that."

"He's your friend, technically. Don't you think he'd tell you if there was something going on? You two have always had that secret little club of yours."

"Rebecca is my friend, he knows that. You'd be the next best thing to me. Best friend by proxy. Just find out."

"Okay, crazy lady, can I eat my pie in peace now?"

* * * *

Rebecca sank deep into the hot water of the claw foot tub with the intention of full relaxation. She had a few candles lit, indulging in devoting her time to the book that had been sitting on her bedside table for over a month. As she emptied her wine glass sip by sip, her mind cleared out the busy classroom, the noisy children and the looming deadlines of the upcoming parent teacher conferences. She was reluctant to get out of the tub, but she looked forward to getting into a nice clean bed.

Silently, in the basement, the ingredients to her death were beginning to mix. The furnace that hadn't been kept well over the years leaked gas between cracks in the metal. Max mentioned it needed replacing, he didn't think the years of paper clips and rubber bands the previous owner had rigged up would hold safely. It was on the list of things to do. When the furnace kicked on, the small spark of fire followed the expelled gas, creating a rolling wave out into the air.

The fire caught boxes that were stacked near the furnace. Her junk from her old apartment, his junk from his. She insisted they not throw any of it out until the house was remodeled because you never know where their former fun and quirky things could be used. The fire spread to their other belongings, catching anything and everything that would burn. It climbed the wooden staircase, step by step up to the main floor where flames raged up to the ceiling, spreading its outreach to over the entire kitchen. As embers fell, the items of their home began to catch and spread.

Rebecca was awakened by the burning smell, and the smoke filling the air. She ran into the hallway, and down the steps to the main floor.

"Oh, no!" she screamed as she discovered the flames.

There was a small opening not yet burning leading to the kitchen, and the back door. She ran through the living room, with the flames dancing around her. The front door was already blocked. Just as she turned the corner to get to the back door, a wall of fire blocked her way. She turned to retrace her steps back, but the path narrowed with every passing second. She dropped down to the floor, trying to keep away from the smoke and make her way back. If she got to the stairs, she could go back up and open a window. She never made it. The smoke was too much for her lungs, the fire too much for her eyes.

It was only fifteen minutes before the neighbors could see the fire from the outside of the house. With no means of getting in, they were only able to let the fire department know a young couple lived there. Max's car was gone, and Rebecca's was tucked in the garage so they weren't immediately sure if they were home. The fire department was able to control the fire from spreading from beyond the house, but the house itself was a total loss. With nothing but rubble left, the search for Max and Rebecca Duncan began with phone calls to their next of kin.

Both Max and Rebecca's parents called any contacts they had, hoping to find the pair unharmed. It was Aidan who was tasked to check the office and found Max sleeping on the couch in their reception area. It was Charlotte who was tasked with confirming to everyone she had just spoken to Rebecca and knew she was home. When Aidan and Max arrived at the site, Charlotte was waiting for them, standing in the shadows of Rebecca's fiery grave. It was Aidan who held him back from climbing through the rubble to find his wife, and it was Charlotte who held him as he shook and screamed out her name as it finally sunk in that there would be nothing to find. She was gone.

* * * *

"It was a house fire," Charlotte began, "we found out much later the furnace in the basement started it."

"Rebecca was home?"

"She was. We spoke on the phone earlier that evening. She'd had a long day; she was a kindergarten teacher. She'd called to see what I was up to, and mentioned since the boys were working late, she was going to take a bath, read a book and go to bed."

"When did the fire start?"

"I guess around 11 p.m.? Maybe 10? She wasn't in her bed like I thought she would be. When they finally found her, she was in the kitchen by the basement door. I don't know if she was trying to get out or maybe even put the fire out. The details are sketchy, there wasn't much left."

Claire could see the tears welling up in Charlotte's eyes as she relived those chilling memories. Charlotte returned to the chair beside Max's bed and slipped her hand into his.

"Aidan had to tell him about the fire. He insisted on going back to the house, even though there was nothing left. I knew he would go. I don't blame him, I even needed to see it for myself. When he got there, he just fell to his knees. It was a full six months before he was even remotely human again."

The rise of sorrow gripped around Claire's heart. The strands of truth were being pulled from a dream.

He was dreaming of her trapped because that's what he thought she was. He was dreaming he couldn't reach her in the water because he couldn't get to her in the aftermath of the fire when he was standing not five hundred feet from her body. The fire still raged for him, it still took her from him. Watching Charlotte's face as she retold the story, and how she kept looking over to him with the concerning look on her face, there was no guilt here. There was only heartbreak. But why did he have such guilt over it? Why did the authorities circle, and re-circle around him? There were still so many more questions.

"Where was he?"

"Max?" Charlotte hesitated. "He was at the office, he had a late night and decided to sleep on the couch there."

"Why did he tell Rebecca he was working late when he wasn't?"

"Who said he wasn't?" Charlotte asked.

"Aidan had to tell him, which means they weren't together in the office like he told her. You said she told you since the boys were working late she was going to take a bath, but they weren't. Aidan was home."

Hmm, clever girl, Charlotte thought. The police had pointed out the same discrepancy.

"He was at the office, but no, he wasn't working late. He just needed some space." Charlotte's hand squeezed Max's.

"Were they having problems? Is that why he was pulled in for questioning?"

Charlotte struggled with what she should tell Claire. Max obviously cared about her, but Charlotte wasn't sure what he had already told her. She knew of their fight, and his return to her couch. She knew he mentioned Claire knew more than she should. She huffed and sighed at the man lying in the bed.

Forever keeping secrets, he was forever keeping secrets from the wrong people. He wasn't awake, so he didn't get a vote as to what she would tell Claire.

"They weren't having problems. They were thinking about starting a family," Charlotte admitted. "Has Max told you anything about his father?"

"No," Claire said. *Or anyone else for that matter…*

"There's a reason for that. It's not my story to tell, but the idea of having a family weighed heavily on Max. He wanted to be a good father, he just didn't have a good example to work from. It worried him. He went out for a beer to clear his mind and think things over. He stayed in the city. He blames himself for the fire simply because he wasn't there, and because it was caused by something he knew was going to be a problem and needed to be fixed."

"I get the feeling he blames himself down to his core," Claire twisted the emotions of his dreams into words.

"He's does and it makes me so sad. He did the coulda, shoulda, woulda thing for weeks. Even months afterward. Months. I'm sure he still plays with it in his mind. He's a good man, Claire."

That he does, she thought sadly.

"He saved my life," Claire murmured. *And the life of his child,* she thought.

"Was he looking forward to having kids?"

Claire watched Charlotte closely for any sort of reaction. She had no idea what the future would hold for anyone who sat in that room, but her mind could not help but center around the baby and its future. Charlotte didn't look at Claire. Her eyes remained fixed on Max, and her body rose and fell with a large sigh. Claire could see it, the sadness wash over the woman sitting across from her in the small hospital room.

"He's going to be a wonderful uncle," Charlotte smiled as she rubbed her hand across her stomach "and I hope the experience will show him that he will be an amazing father when the time comes."

It didn't slip by Claire that Charlotte had not answered her question at all. It didn't slip by Charlotte, either.

Chapter 24

Christmas was just around the corner, and cookies were warm in the oven. Claire could smell them so easily; her mouth watered in anticipation of having one. Decorations made the space around her twinkle, and the star on the top of the tree shined bright with a warm, magical glow. This was a sweet place, this was a safe place. The room came into focus and she saw the back of the large man by the tree. The red on his suit was bright, and the white brilliant. He was larger than life, and round, and looked as soft as a teddy bear. Her heart raced with a mixture of fear and anticipation as she watched him empty a large bag of items out in front of the tree.

Please be good, she thought in her mind. *Please be a good dream.*

The reflection of light came out of the bag like a lightning bolt, and Claire knew that this was what her little dreamer was waiting for. She watched as the image of Santa pulled a perfectly put together pink bike out of the bag. The bike had white accents and brightly colored butterflies on a white wicker basket. Her heart leaped as she found herself tiptoeing across the floor.

"Is that for me?" she heard the little voice ask.

"Just for you," the man bellowed in a deep baritone voice, though he never turned around.

Her little hand touched the wicker on the bike basket so gently, and the wings on the butterflies fluttered into life. *Kids dreams are so cool,* Claire once again mused. Just as her hand was letting go of the basket, there was a soft electric buzz in the air. Jagged images of a bike basket that did not belong came into view. Natural wicker in color, burned around the edges. As quick as it came, it went.

Claire shot up out of her bed, gasping for air and shaking. Tilney immediately assumed his position as caretaker and guard dog, putting his giant head down on the bed next to her. She wrapped her arms around him, pulling herself closer to hug him.

"Jesus Christ," she said breathlessly, "that was weird."

It had been just two days since she came home from the hospital. She had insisted on returning to her own apartment, much to her parents' chagrin. She promised them she was fine, and she wanted to be close to the hospital in order to keep apprised of the situation with Max. She agreed with her mother to allow them to hang around her apartment during the day with her until she got a doctor's note saying she was free to be on her own.

The first thing she had to do was take care of Team Metis. It had been days since the accident and there was already a small gathering of phone calls to return and emails to look over. Claire contacted the temp agency she used to work for and asked specifically for Jane. She was confident Jane would be able to keep things afloat for her until she was fully back on her feet. She was also confident Jane would keep Linda from *helping out*, or in other words, completely taking over and running amuck.

As much as it killed her, she would not be with Max today. He had his mother and his friends. She'd already invaded enough in their world, a world where she still wasn't sure where she fit. She had a lot of thinking to do, a lot of processing. There were so many unanswered questions. Who was Max's father? Why did Max lie for weeks to Rebecca about where he was? Why did it take six months for the cops to stop investigating him? And the dreams, what did they all really mean? Only Max would truly know, and he wasn't talking.

She wondered about the connection she felt for him, the connection he felt for her. Once thinking it was coming from an organic place, she now knew he was no different from all the others. Tears rolled down her eyes, already giving into the idea that he literally was under her spell, and not in love with her at all. She worried about what would happen when he woke up and she told him she was pregnant. She worried about what would happen if he didn't wake up and she'd never get the chance to tell him at all.

She had a lot to work out; it was time to call in the expert. She made a few phone calls, and arranged a visit with her grandmother for the day. She didn't want her mother involved, because Linda was already somewhat jealous of the secret bond her daughter and mother-in-law seemed to have. Jane would drive her out to the retirement center and back.

As Claire locked her apartment up for the day, Tilney barked to get the attention of the man down the hall. He diverted his path from going up the stairs to say hello to them.

"Hi, Jack." She smiled.

"Hey there, champ. How ya feeling?" he offered her a warm smile.

"I'm doing better, thank you. And thank you so much for everything you did."

"Oh," he blushed and lowered his head, "no big thing. I'm so glad you're okay. I know Max would have done what he did a thousand times over. I sent flowers over to the hospital, to his family."

She was familiar with the big bouquet of various followers sitting on a table in Max's room with the little Get Well Mylar balloon sticking out of the vase.

"I saw them, a nice bouquet. Thank you for taking care of the dogs."

"That was my pleasure. This one is just a gigantic goof ball," he said as he bent to give Tilney an indulgent rub of the belly.

"He is. And if you need anything with Pilot, you let me know. I know Max will be very thankful to you for keeping him. I can take him, any time, really."

"He keeps me company; it's nice. My apartment is quiet too often, I'm afraid. I might get myself a dog when it's time for him to go home."

Claire smiled, "I think that's a really good idea. You're a great guy, Jack. You're going to make some woman a good husband."

He blushed again. Claire had been standoffish with him at first, but over her few months in the building she seemed to warm to him. He enjoyed the small, budding friendship with her. They stood in the hall for a few minutes, Claire wanted so badly to apologize to him for every nasty thing she ever thought of him when they first met. The man had called the police, he had gathered and calmed Tilney down as she lay on the sidewalk. He took the spare key from the laundry room to Max's apartment, and rescued Pilot from what would have been days in the apartment alone. He didn't need to do any of these those things, but he did.

"May I ask you a question?" After he nodded in agreement, she continued, "Why did you tell them that we were married?"

"Oh, that." Now he looked embarrassed. "I just thought you two needed each other. I know how hospitals work, and I know they wouldn't have told you anything. I've known Max since the day he moved in here, and he's been so different since you arrived. The boy was hiding from his own life. Why, I don't know, but he was. And then you show up, and he was finally beginning to live."

Claire said nothing as the warmth of love spread through her.

"That was very kind of you, I appreciate it."

"Absolutely. You let me know if you ever need anything, okay? I know you're a perfectly capable person, but I just…" He searched for the words he wasn't sure of. "I just feel like I need to make sure you're doing okay."

The connection. Claire's shoulders lifted and fell with a sigh that he couldn't even begin to understand. He felt connected to her, and though it had disgusted her at first, she felt it too. She would welcome his friendship, but she wondered if he would have done any of those things for her if she had not been with him in his dreams. She wondered just how much these connections were responsible for.

"I will, thank you." She smiled as she began to walk down the hall with Tilney. "I'll be checking in on Max, I'll keep you up to date."

* * * *

The hot tea was a heavenly gift to wrap her cold hands around.

"Thanks, Gran." Claire smiled as she smelled the aroma of the black tea she held to her lips to blow on and to cool off.

"You're welcome, sweetheart. What brings you by? Who was the young lady with you?"

"That was Jane. I've sent her on some errands for me and she'll be back to get me. I'm fine, Gran."

"How's Max?"

"I don't know. He's in a medically induced coma. They want him to heal. He had a lot of injuries."

"And what say you?" Adelaide asked as she dumped sugar into her tea by the heaping spoonful.

"I did something terrible, Gran."

"I doubt it," she smiled, "but tell me. What did you do?"

"I chased down a dreamer."

"I told you so," Adelaide shook her head from side to side. "Who did you chase? What did you find out?"

"There was that woman I was dreaming of. Well, I found a lead. I hired a PI to find her."

"Claire!" Adelaide scolded.

Claire threw up her hands. "It didn't matter. I found out who she was before the PI even got back to me."

"Who was she?"

"Max's wife."

"Your mother told me you found out he's a Widower. That's not so bad."

"No, but I did something worse."

"What?" Adelaide asked, her eyes wide with wonder.

"I accused him of murdering his wife."

Adelaide had been surprised by very little in her life, but she nearly spilled her tea as the words came out of Claire's mouth.

"Oh my, I didn't see that one coming." She set her tea down and picked a cookie up. "Do tell."

"He was married. A girl named Rebecca. I don't know how long they were married, but they were talking about kids. She died in a house fire. Now that I've put the pieces together, I remember hearing something about it on the news. Couple of years ago, local school teacher dies in a fire. Under investigation, husband being brought in. I was swamped with an advertisement campaign at the time so it was just background noise on the TV."

"So how did all this come about?"

"Well, I thought I was dreaming with her. But she died three years ago. I was with Max; all the dreams were his."

"Oh," Adelaide said as she grabbed another cookie. "Plot twist!"

"Gran, I swear. Anyway, the dreams were one thing. There was such guilt there, I felt like I was swimming in it every time I woke up. One night, I was at his place and he was talking in his sleep, I realized the dreams were his. I thought maybe he was married, and was feeling guilty over having an affair, but the PI I hired sent me a clipping about the fire."

"That's terrible." Adelaide picked her tea back up and sipped as Claire continued on with her story. "So you thought he started the fire, but now you don't?"

"No, I don't. It was an accident. He wasn't home, which is why he blames himself and why I thought he had done it. His friend told me about the night Rebecca died, and the look on her face was enough. There a still a lot of unanswered questions, but I feel like I owe it to him to figure it all out."

"Does your gut tell you that?"

"Yes. He saved my life when he didn't have to. We could start with that. I accused him of murder to his face, and he still saved my life. If he was guilty, he would have let me get hit by that van."

"I've been telling you for years, Claire, Dreams don't make the man," Adelaide advised.

"I know. It's just that after Christopher…"

"Stupid, lying, cheating bastard," Adelaide corrected.

Claire said nothing, but smiled. Her grandmother was the sweetest little thing, but ballsy as hell.

"I love you, Gran. When I sat down and really picked apart those dreams, I can see they are nightmares for him. I felt fear and panic. Hopelessness and loss. It was all his, not hers. I guess because I had been working on the idea that they were her emotions, I placed that on him. He must have been imagining how trapped she was feeling. He relived her panic as the fire raged, or at least, how he thought it all happened. Nobody knows what exactly happened, unfortunately. I think him moving on and dating again may have triggered anxiety or something. He dreamed that she was fading away once."

"Worried that he would forget her," Adelaide stated as a matter of unquestionable fact.

"I think so, yeah. And in the last one, she drowned. He didn't know how to make it better, or go away. He was just sorry that he let her hands slip through his fingers."

"You've given this a lot of thought," Adelaide said.

"I have. I even pulled out some old dream books. Cross -referenced things in my rule book looking for answers."

"Your rule book?"

"Yeah. I've been writing down all the rules of the dream world as I discover them so I know what's what."

"I wasn't aware there was a set of rules."

"Gran, be serious. There are rules, you must know them. I've just written them all down. You know, for the next generation to know and not have to figure out all on her own. I mean, I know they will be slightly different than the next, but we can at least establish a baseline," Claire quipped.

"Oh, my child. You are the cutest little control freak I ever did know. Do you honestly think that there is a governing secret society who that has passed down rules on you? You have the ability to see people's dreams and you think it comes with a rule book? That's brilliant. Tell me, what rules did you come up with?"

"Okay. Well, for starters when you say the same thing the dreamer says at the same time in the dream. For me the air vibrates, it makes a weird static echo sound. You said you had that too, right?"

Adelaide thought back to her time as a traveler, and remembered the sound well.

"Yes."

"Let's see. Smells are most of the time not smells, but the idea of them. And people are not people, but just the idea of them. Very few are in focus."

"Oh, yes. The faceless blobs."

"See, a baseline! Sometimes you have the perspective of the dreamer. Sometimes you have the perspective of a person in their dream, like I was always Rebecca in Max's dreams."

"Interesting," Adelaide said.

"It was why I had no idea Max's dreams were his, he didn't see himself in dreams. He only saw Rebecca. Except the once."

"His thoughts were only with her, and how she felt. So that's what you saw, that's what you felt. The last dream was about his failures. Or the failures as he saw them."

"I hope so. These are the times I wish you could talk to dreamers."

"What do you mean, you can't talk to them?" Adelaide asked.

Claire looked at her grandmother with curiosity. For a woman who possessed the ability for over eight decades now, she should remember the number one rule.

"The number one rule, Gran, you can't talk to them. You can think, but you can't talk."

"Bullshit."

"What?"

"That's bullshit, Claire. You can, too, talk to them," Adelaide insisted.

"No, you can't, Gran. You can't control it, and you can't talk to them. At least I couldn't."

"Claire, if there ever was a baseline, this would be it. You can do anything you want to; you always have control. If you want to talk to them, you can. You said it yourself, that echo sound. What do you think that is?"

"I told you, a jinx." Clearly this was too much conversation for one afternoon for her grandmother.

"That sound comes from you breaking through, Claire. It's not you both saying it at the same time. It's you actually saying it."

No, you can't. It was a fact that stood as long as time did. Claire had never once been able to communicate in a dream with a dreamer. Adelaide had flipped her lid.

"Gran, I have never had control—"

"Claire, you have. It's a just a matter of want. The control, you have to want it. And you have to want it enough. You said something and you believed it with your whole heart or you wanted to be in the moment so badly that you broke through."

Claire thought of the bright sunny field with the cute little girl clapping her hands in the air and catching lightning bugs. The girl asked her if it was amazing, and she fell in love with her sweet little innocence. She was in the moment, with her whole heart.

"Shit," Claire said to herself as she sat back in her chair taking in this game changing information.

"Pretty cool, huh?" Adelaide smiled.

"Gran, why didn't you tell me? Why do you never tell me anything?"

Adelaide looked at her granddaughter and saw more than frustration. Frustration came so easily to Claire, and Adelaide would be damned if she would tell Claire what she knew when Claire would only use it out of frustration. Today, as the next generation of dream traveler sat across from her, she saw something different. She saw sadness. She saw need. She saw the attempt at acceptance. It was time.

"Alright, child, alright. I haven't been keeping things from you because I want you to suffer. I want to keep you from suffering."

"What do you mean?"

"When I was young, very young, my great grandmother told me about this power that she had passed down to me. She was older than dirt, like I am now, so I guess she figured she was low on time."

"Gran, you're not older than dirt," Claire complimented.

"I am, but that's okay. Anyway, I was fifteen and she called me to her bedside and told me a story. It changed everything for me. I didn't want it to do change everything for you."

"Will you tell me now?"

"I will; it's time."

Chapter 25

The wind tickled her nose. She watched the grass dance, the fields before her long and flat. She could see the herd of buffalo from where she was standing. They looked like little ants. The village was already busy with activity but there was an eerie silence among her people as they prepared for the day. This was a new land for her tribe and they were tired and worn from their journey from the Great Lakes.

As the oldest daughter of her family, Kimimela worked her fingers to the bone to help her mother set up their home. She woke up early to prepare the day's food for her father and his men. She sewed and stitched pants, shirts, and moccasins as they prepared for another round of battle. Each man would have at least two sets of clothing. She was the oldest daughter, but she was the youngest child, so she prepared her two older brothers for their battle.

"What are you doing, child?" her mother's voice broke her concentration.

"I want to go." Her voice was small, but solid.

"You want to go where?" her mother's arms wrapped around her shoulder.

Mina knew exactly where to look when she noticed her daughter no longer sitting on the large fallen log, sewing clothes with the other girls. Her girl was always looking to the lands spread before their village. Watching and waiting for something, but for what, Mina did not know.

"I want to go with them. I want to stand for our people."

"You do, child. You stand here. These men, they cannot do what they do without us doing what we do to prepare them. They cannot battle if they do not have a warm home to return to."

"It's not enough, Mama."

These were the words carrying her through the night that evening. The thought going through her mind while she tiptoed around in the darkness as her family slept, to gather supplies for her journey. Her hand swept gently over her father's coup stick with its many feathers. He saw them as victories; she saw them as acts of selflessness and bravery. She patted the small stick she'd honed herself, which was resting at her side in a small leather belt she finished just that morning. One day, she'd have a feather.

Three days passed before they saw her again. Her mother nearly went mad with worry. Her father and brothers set out to find her. Their only clue being some of her belongings were gone, and her father's finest horse had been taken. They hoped the child and horse were together.

Kimimela's oldest brother, Hotah, was the one to find the child. She slept cradled in the rocks on holy ground on the nearest mountain. She made it up quite far on her own, the horse waited by the water at the foot of the mountain.

"You did not leave her, you are my finest warrior," her father whispered in the horse's ear.

"Father, here," Hotah said, as he carried the twelve year old girl in his arms down to the foot of the mountain.

"My girl," Mahkah said as he joined his oldest son and took the child into his own arms. She was alive, but weak.

"Why, child? Why?" he feverishly checked her over for injuries. Tired, hungry, but not a scratch on her.

"I wanted to prove myself. I wanted a vision. I came here to the holy ground."

"It is not your time yet." He kissed her small, dirty hands.

"But the battle is now."

Mahkah could not help but smile. The girl was just like her mother. Beautiful with skilled hands, keen eye, and fierce determination.

"Did you find one?" her brother Chatan angrily asked. "You could have been killed. We do not have time for your childish games."

"Chatan, silence. Go get water for her," Mahkah boomed. "You have no worth to prove, child. You were born with it. There will be no match when you go for your quest next year."

"I did it, Father. The quest. I saw, Father, I saw."

Mahkah's hand stilled from brushing the dust off her little dry face. He sat her on her feet, but held on in case her legs gave out. She wobbled, but stood her ground. "Is this why you left us?"

"I fasted here. I did not sleep. I saw lightning bolts, and an eagle flying. I saw a white owl. I saw men, reaching camp under the stars and rising up like giants above us."

These were all strong visions. His heart grew with pride, but ached with sadness. She was his last child, his only girl. Why did she have to be as headstrong as her mother? As stupid as he?

"I fear I do not see the woman you are becoming because I want to keep you a child. Your thirteenth year is among us and I should have been preparing you. I will take you back. We will finish this ceremony for you."

"Thank you."

She rode back to her people on her father's horse with him, her brothers and the horse she had taken trailing behind. Her father announced the spirts called her early and she completed her vision quest, and the final ceremonies were prepared. When the Medicine Man examined her, he discovered a marking on her body. She had been marked by the spirits during her journey. A small crescent shaped impression behind her left ear would be the symbol of her power.

"Kimimela, you have had the vision of a warrior. You will prove to be our most valuable weapon." The Medicine Man's voice boomed across the gathered people around the large bonfire.

Kimimela said nothing, but stood tall in her best dress and shell necklace. Her long dark braidslay on each side of her shoulders, cascading down to just above her small waist.

"You have been marked. You have seen the white owl. I believe you will transcend between this world and the spirit world. Your owl is a symbol of clairvoyance. But in our case my child, you have also become our messenger."

"How do you mean?" she kept her voice small, unsure of if she should question him.

"You were given a gift by the spirts while you lay in at the holy place in wait. They marked you with a slice of the moon." His old and wrinkled tan finger pressed to the crescent shaped just behind her ear. "You spoke of seeing giants at our camp, men rising up like giants."

"I did."

"Our men went out last night, into the fields. They found our enemy sleeping under the stars. They were to attack us at dawn but they never got the chance."

"I did not see men, I saw giants."

"It is how they thought of themselves; you saw them as they slept. You saw deep into their souls."

"I did?" Kimimela's dark brown eyes went wide.

"They did not yet reach our land, and they never will. I've seen you watching and waiting in the fields. I've seen you searching, child. You do not always know what you are looking for, but you know it is there. Your reach goes as far as your eye can see."

Mina and Mahkah stood on either side of their daughter. Her brothers stood behind her. Pride ran through them all.

"There is more, child," her father's deep voice said from above her.

He was wearing his nicest clothing. His headdress heavy with eagle feathers, a chain of bear claws around his neck. Her brothers' faces were painted with their warrior symbols and her mother looked like a queen. Her slim figure fit nicely into the tan hide of her dress. Turquoise around her neck, with her long hair usually kept in tight braids flowing freely in the breeze of the spring afternoon. Her father bent down to his knee, and from behind one hand presented her with the very coup stick she had made herself. From behind the other arm, her father presented her with one small feather.

"The men who slept. The men you saw in your dreams. The victory belongs to you."

"Father," her voice shook.

The Medicine Man spoke his final words as her ceremony came to an end. "You are a warrior, child. You are a strong Lakota woman. This legacy will remain with your people, with your daughter and your daughter's daughter. You will see deep within to bring light to what hides in the shadows. The people of your tribe will always see what lies in the fields ahead."

Chapter 26

"So, my great, great whatever went on a vison quest and now we have a super power?" Claire asked, rubbing the small crescent shaped birthmark she knew was behind her left ear.

Adelaide remained quiet. She knew it was time to give Claire the final piece of the puzzle.

"You have it, Claire. I don't. Not anymore."

Claire looked at her grandmother with confusion. She hoped the woman was not beginning to suffer from Dementia.

"What? Gran, are you feeling okay?" She kept her tone light, but was beginning to worry. She nearly laughed off the idea of trying to explain to a doctor something was wrong because her grandmother claimed she could no longer see into the minds of others. Claire would be the one on the examining table.

"It was passed down from Kimimela to her first born daughter. The gift transferred as the baby took her first breath. That was the way. It was the way with my great-grandmother and me. When I was pregnant with your father, it began to fade. At first it was flashes, but then my own dreams started coming. With his first breath, my journey ended."

"Your own," breathless from disbelief Claire thought back to the night where she dreamed of the child at Christmas. Visions of a shiny new bike danced in her mind until the thought of Rebecca's bike came into vision. It was only for a split second. Could it be the child she carried, already preparing to be the next?

"Jesus Christ," it was all Claire could say. "Gran, I love you. But don't you think I could have known all of this? You knew I hated this. There's an end game. There's a fucking end game?"

She didn't know if she should scream at her grandmother or kiss her. She flew out of her chair and began pacing back and forth in the small breakfast nook.

"Claire, I had my reasons," Adelaide said softly.

"What reasons?" Claire shouted, but then corrected herself and asked with a softer tone as she forced herself to sit back in her chair. "What reasons?"

"Well, like I said, my great-grandmother was short on time. So she tells me about the Lakota legend and then she tells me that I have control over it. I can do things I want to do, I can say things I want to say. Over time, our people have discovered the ability to control this gift."

"Is that so bad?"

"It is when you're too young. I began to play on the connections. I began to force people to do what I wanted them to do without them even knowing it. I manipulated, without mercy."

It was the first time Claire had ever seen her grandmother look small. In her mind, Adelaide was always a powerful woman, full of life and energy. Even in her older years, with her body aging and slowing down, she will still full of life. As they sat at the dining room table, Adelaide looked small and ashamed.

"Gran, I'm sure..." she wanted to assure her grandmother that she didn't believe this. Adelaide couldn't have possibly used this ability in the way she thought she did. She was being too hard on herself.

"I did it, Claire. I am guilty, and I know it. When I hit high school and I started floating through every dream of all those kids. My friends. Boys I liked. Well, I may have done a few things."

"Like what?" Claire imagined a slick and sly Adelaide on the prowl.

"There was a boy. I liked him. He didn't even know I was alive. But when I found him in dreams, I used the information I knew about him to get closer to him."

"Gran, that's not so bad. I kind of do the same thing every day with my business."

"Yes, but you help them see what they want to but can't. I broke through his dreams and made him see me. Made him dream of me. Made him want me."

"Oh." *Good Lord.*

"And I haunted the hell out of his girlfriend."

Claire was honestly shocked. "Gran!"

"I found her in dreams, and I would turn them into nightmares, on purpose. I warned her to stay away from him."

"I can't believe you would do something like that, Gran."

"I did. Your grandfather, he saved me from going down a very dark path."

"Was he the guy?" Claire asked.

"No. He was my friend, but he paid attention to me. He knew it when I was acting weird, when I was playing a game. And that's what I was doing, I was playing mind games. Just on the most intrusive level imaginable."

"You were young."

"And that's my point, child. That's my point. I didn't want you to go through that. I got so damn lucky with your grandfather. He kept at me until I paid attention to him, and then when I went to see what I could find out about him, he just wasn't having it. I kept rushing into things, and he kept pulling me back. Insist that I enjoy the journey; he said I was in too much of a rush to get to the finish line. I need to know everything about you, so I can make us a couple. He let me into his world, but he kept me firmly in my place."

"I'm glad you found him," Claire smiled. "Why didn't you tell me about it being passed down? What harm would it have done to know that?"

"Well, you have always hated it. I was afraid you'd go out and get yourself pregnant to get rid of the problem. I didn't want that for you, either."

And I went the furthest way from it, didn't want to get pregnant at all.

"Funny, I never wanted to have kids because of it. I don't want them to suffer the way I have."

"I am so sorry you see it as a curse," Adelaide began. "It really was designed to be able to see people for who they really are. Not all people are bad, Claire. It breaks my heart you can't see what good this has done in your life."

She was right. Most of her dreams were thoughtless. Just every day, run of the mill dreams. Not all people were bad. She was able to soak up the very best of them sometimes, which helped when she soaked in the very worst of them. And she did see, she was able to see when it was time to walk away from things, like her relationship with Christopher.

"Do you regret passing it on, to me?"

"No, child, I would not want to imagine my life without my son. He has brought me such joy. When he had a daughter, I knew she would have this gift. You are an amazing person, Claire; you just don't know it. You have used this ability your whole life to help the people around you."

"How's that?"

"You help them find the connection they are looking for. I've seen you with people. I've seen how you talk to them, how you let them talk to you. I've seen how you've shown people at your work the things they need and think about but can't quite get into words. Your father has shown me some of your projects; he's so proud of you. Sure, there have been a few duds in there, but for the most part, you've been able to see the best in people. You've helped them see the best in themselves."

Claire thought of the little girl, Ava. She showed her where to find lightning bugs. She thought of the skin care rep who dreamed of everyone yelling at her all at once and how Clare used that to create a color-coded schedule for the woman so she had plenty of time for everyone.

"Well, I guess that's a good thing because I found out something in the hospital."

"What's that?"

"You're going to be a great-grandmother yourself."

"Well..." Her smile was a mile wide. "...hot damn!"

"Yeah, so I guess I better enjoy these last moments with my...gift before it goes away. I had something weird happen the other night. I was in a kid's dream, but then I wasn't. Only for a second though."

"It begins already. Are you happy about this?"

"Max is lying in a hospital because of me. The doctors say he's doing well, but has a long road. I might never get the chance to tell him he's going to be a father. I always feared having a child, and now that I know there is one..."

"You can't imagine it any other way." Adelaide smiled.

"No, I guess not," Claire began. "But there is so much going on right now. With Max, so many unanswered questions."

"Claire, do you really think he killed his wife?"

"No," she said honestly. "I don't. Nothing makes total sense yet, but it's like pieces of the puzzle that have yet to come together. Kind of like when you start out in the middle of a dream and you have to work your way back to figure out what's going on."

Adelaide reached over and squeezed her granddaughter's hand. "I remember the first dream I ever had of my own. I was on a pirate ship and we were sailing across the sea. Your grandfather was with me. I knew it was mine because for the first time in my life I had no control. It was just a dream that played in my mind in the moments after I woke up."

"Like no big thing? Do you remember a long time ago I went out and spent the weekend in the woods? I felt like I spent the whole night awake, waiting in the darkness for the dreams to come. It was terrible. It was normal for you?"

"None of us are ever normal, Claire. Being a little weird is normal. But yes, it was gone. Honestly, sometimes when I really think about it, I miss it. It's kind of like my mind got too lonely. It's been gone most of my life, I only had it for a minute. Your minute is almost up."

"I can't imagine that."

"It's true. I don't miss all of it, but some of it. I missed the connection with people so much that I've become friends with just about everybody I meet."

"That I believe." Claire smiled. "You're the most popular girl I know. But it's those connections, Gran. What if they are making me feel things that aren't there?"

"Your heart knows, Claire. Your head might recognize a song and know all the words, but it's your heart that sings it."

"That's sweet, Gran."

"It's true. Whatever you are feeling, beyond knowing that you've seen a person's dream, that's yours to keep."

"I worry what Max feels for me isn't true. He said he felt a connection to me that he can't explain. The kiss of death line."

"Honey, you're a young, sexy girl. He'd be a fool not to be in love with you," Adelaide said.

"Be serious."

"You've spent time with him; you've built something with him over these last months that has nothing to do with his dreams. The rules are only there because you put them there, so don't look at them as law."

Claire thought about the book she had, back in her apartment. A book started when she was a teen, trying to figure out why and how this thing worked. Dream after dream she would write something down, and cross reference it after other dreams. She connected all the pieces, and could step back and see the patterns. It was what calmed her, making sense out of madness. If she wrote it down, if she learned how it worked, then she could control it. Maybe Gran was right. The older she got, the more desperate she became for there to be rules. She needed them there, she depended on them. What would life be without them? She wanted them in place, so they were.

She pulled her phone out and began to type in words.

"What are you doing?"

"Looking up how far is, as far as the eye can see."

"Does it really matter?" Adelaide asked.

"Ha!" Claire shook the phone, "Twenty to thirty miles. That's how far her visions went and that's how far I can find a dreamer."

"Does it really matter, Claire? Adelaide repeated. "Would you have accepted Lakota legend as fact in your little rule book?"

"Yes," she said confidently. Then she began chewing her bottom lip, "Maybe. I don't know."

"Exactly. You like the rules. You weren't ready for me to tell you anything about myths and legends."

"So you're telling me if I want somebody to see me, to hear me, they will?"

"I'm telling you this thing is what you make of it. If you don't want it to stand in your way of living your life, it won't. And pretty soon, it won't be an issue at all. But Claire, if you do anything for yourself, stop trying to make sense of it. Just be free within it. You might find a little bit of happiness before you pass it on to the next generation."

"To my daughter, or maybe a granddaughter?"

"Or a great-granddaughter," Adelaide reminded her.

"That's weird. It might be a long time from now. Or it might be nine months."

* * * *

Claire drove home and sank into a warm bath. Her grandmother's words floated around in her mind. She thought of the last few months with Max, and the friendship they'd forged. The connection she felt with him may have been what opened the door, but it was the friendship that led them to love. There wasn't one side to him that she didn't smile over when she thought about it. She wondered how things would be when he got better, and they talked about Rebecca. Would he talk about her? Would he tell her the truth? Would he love her? Would he love the child she carried?

"Wake up Max, come back to me," she whispered.

Chapter 27

Cold. She couldn't feel it, but she could understand it. *I am cold, I am tired.* She felt as though her bones were aching, and worn from battle. Slender and fragile, when the wind blew she had a hard time keeping her feet in one place. The outskirts of the land where she stood was strong beneath her feet, insolent to the time that was behind her. Claire did not have to turn around to see that it was her past scattered across the earth, the idea surrounded her. *I am at the edge of time.*

She was wearing black combat boots; she could feel the leather and lace tied firmly to her legs. The breeze tickled the fabric of her silk and sheer pale yellow dress as it fluttered over her knees. Brown curls danced around her face. Her gaze never wavered as her eyes shimmered with reflection of the sunset dipping into the horizon. The sun was five times the size it should have been, warm orange swirls mixed into the deep yellow surface. The sky was purple and red, with yellow glowing brightly on the edges of the clouds.

It was the most beautiful thing she had ever seen. Despite the heavy boots her feet were in, she felt weightless. There was such contentment here. She wanted to close her eyes, and soak it all in. She felt the memories of a life lived, this dreamer's life, sweep in. Momentary images of a child riding a bike, with the feeling of the wind whisking by her body. Being lifted high in the air and twirled into huge loving arms. The bellow of a deep laugh captured in her heart. *My father,* she thought.

She felt light, like a princess as moments of dancing filled the air. The people around her, spinning in real time as she and her partner slowed the world down. Rain teased her lips, and hands wrapped around her waist, instantly filling her with love. Passion erupted as the memory of a kiss flooded her senses. *He is the love of my life,* she thought. Serenity filled her as she felt a little hand warm within hers, one then two. Her body felt whole as she leaned into the memory of the grown man wrapping his arms around her. *My babies,* she thought. Claire ached a little. Sadness, there was sadness here. She misses them.

Claire's own emotions gathered a lump in her throat as she experienced and witnessed this woman, standing at the edge of time, remembering a life lived. She came to love these dreams, this woman. Claire counted it a blessing to know this side of her, a side that would have gone unknown under any normal circumstances.

"You are my friend," Claire said to the younger version of her dreamer.

As Claire stood and watched the sunset, she became aware she was no longer wearing the combat boots. Instead, she was standing with the young woman, a friend by her side.

This is better, Claire thought.

She was able to see the young girl's creamy face with her soft curls blowing in the wind. Robust strings, low and steady tip toed around the sound of the wind, playing gliding notes across the air.

I wait.

She is strong, Claire thought as she opened her eyes bringing herself back into the real world. The morning grew late, as the sun was filtering in through the sheer white panels of fabric over her window. The bed felt big and fluffy, she immediately wanted to pull the covers back over her head to cocoon herself until the winter was done.

It would be Christmas soon and there would be much to keep her busy as people often took on too much for the holiday season and sought out an extra pair of hands. It was her busiest time of year, and it always made her laugh at all the emails and phone calls she took. Do you handle office parties? Do you offer personal shopping services? Can you keep my in-laws so busy we barely know they're here? Depending on how busy she was, she would entertain the smaller requests, but over the last year her business had become steadier with full time clients. She referred these requests to business associates she thought could help, or offered standard packets of information and organization to guide people through the holidays on their own. Her 'So…Your In-Laws showed up on your Doorstep: A quick guide to the city guaranteed to keep them busy and your sanity in check' packet was one of her best sellers.

Tilney trotted into the bedroom to greet her hello. He had been very good about letting her sleep as long as possible. He walked slower on their walks, stayed by her side more. He waited, even when the door was open, for her to be ready. It amazed Claire that he could possibly understand he may have lost her.

"I had the best dream, Til. Or my girl did, she just felt happy. Complete." She smiled as she threw the covers off her and stood next to the bed.

The room spun a little and she threw her hands out to steady herself.

"Whoa," she put her hand on her stomach, "Okay, okay. Guess I should get a pregnancy book." The idea was still so foreign. There was going to be a child in her life. She walked through her bedroom, examining the new life she had set up just months ago. Tilney dropped a long torn and ratty stuffed frog that was a favorite of his to play tug of war with. She picked it up, tracing its happy little face with her fingers. Sitting on the couch, she wrapped her hands around Tilney and rubbed her hands through his fur.

"A year ago, I would have never imagined my life with a dog in it. Now, I can't imagine my life without you."

He happily snuggled in, climbing onto the couch that now barely fit his body.

"A year from now, I will say the same thing about a child. But today, I'm just scared. How are we going to do this?"

She walked into her office, still in her PJs and quickly checked her messages. She had farmed out what she could to Jane. The woman had been a Godsend. All of her clients were happy, and there wasn't a peep of question or complaint from Jane. Just *I got this; you rest up.*

The knock at the door had her smiling, right on time. "Good Morning!" Claire smiled as she opened the door.

"You're still in your PJs? It's nearly ten," Jane asked as she walked in with hot coffee and a bag of mid-size containers full of soup. "I brought you some soups for when you get hungry."

"You keep it up and my mother will be out of a job." Claire smiled as she took the bag from her friend, leading them into the kitchen.

"Has Tilney been out?"

"Jack took him out early this morning. I gave him a key since I've been at the hospital so much. I'll take him out a bit later."

"Jack, the upstairs guy, Mister single and ready to mingle?"

"Yes, he's a nice guy," Claire said in his defense before Jane could go a step further.

Claire complained to Jane about Jack early on, for no good reason as it turned out. The man had been so helpful over the last couple of days. In truth, he was always helpful. He helped Claire whenever she asked, no matter what she asked. He was always around to chat with. He listened. She had passed judgement so quickly on him, and should not have. Just like she did with Max. She was so quick to think he was married, and then so quick to believe his guilt. She may not know what the whole truth was, but she knew he deserved the chance to share his side of the story.

"Your apartment looks like a florist shop."

Jane's words broke Claire from the line of thought she was beginning to have.

"What?"

"Flowers, you have lots of flowers."

"Oh, yes. Clients have been so kind. Come sit. We can have coffee and go over some notes."

Not long after they wrapped up business, Claire found herself on the couch with some of Jane's soup warmed up in a small bowl in her hands, and the woman who stayed far enough out of her life to become her best friend. It always made Claire laugh, finally being able to bond with a woman because their friendship was mostly online and Jane didn't live in the city. She commuted forty-two miles from her sleepy, pin-sized little town with four traffic lights and two men who served as the entire police department. It was the sort of town where horses and cows were in equal number to the residents, and she loved every inch of her family's small farm.

Her help meant more to Claire than Jane could ever possibly imagine. As she watched Jane fuss over her, with her dark curly hair, purple framed glasses, black sweater and wild colored leggings, she began crying. This time, Jane got to be the friend in real life, a treat for both women. She listened as Claire had told her that she had formed a friendship with a man in the building. They saw each other regularly with the responsibility of puppy parenting, and often got together for doggy playdates. Jane smiled as Claire described the night of the Halloween party, and how she eventually introduced the man to the world of the Doctor and his beautiful River while cuddled up with him on the sofa. She described how her heart pounded through her chest and her stomach fluttered with anticipation to the point where she couldn't take it anymore and just jumped…literally, on top of him.

"Do you know how much you're grinning right now?" Jane asked.

"I think I'm really falling for him," Claire said.

"Falling? Hon, I think you already fell."

The smile faded as she confessed she found information, and accused him of what her mind filled the blanks with. She automatically assumed the worst of him, when he had never given her reason to. She let her past dictate her future, and all of this was her fault. The accident was her fault.

As she thought about how her actions put all the working parts into motion, the guilt washed over her. If she had only woken him up, and asked him about Rebecca instead of running. If only she had allowed him to explain rather than to close the door in his face. If only she had done everything exactly opposite of what she did, he would have not been standing there when Tilney got away from her. He would have not been racing toward her, the last image of his face imprinted on her mind, the look of absolute fear. Not for himself, but for her. He threw himself in the way, with only fear for her on his mind.

"He didn't do this," she whispered to herself as tears fell.

"Do what?" Jane asked as she wrapped her arm around Claire and rubbed her shoulder.

She finally understood in a way that she could never before. She felt, absolutely certain the accident and his injuries were her fault. This was where Max was trapped, and would never escape. Rebecca was lost to him; he was not able to hold on. It shattered him, and now, it shattered her. Jane held her as she sobbed at the real life nightmare that she could not escape.

"Why did you never tell me about him?" Jane asked.

"I didn't know what to do with it. I found something completely amazing, and I didn't trust it enough."

"You are far too closed off in your little world here. I worry about you."

"I know you do. But, I will be far less closed off, coming up. My life is going to change, big time. How would you feel about bringing the actual team part to Team Metis?"

Claire would certainly need a second pair of hands to help her balance business if she was busy trying to balance motherhood.

"Flipping finally! We are going to be rock stars together." Jane hugged Claire in excitement.

"You be a rock star, I'm just going to work on being a little more human." Claire smiled.

The partnership would take time to set up, but it would be very good when it happened. For the time being, Jane was doing an amazing job keeping the company afloat. She sent daily reports as to what she had done with each client. This part of her life, at least, was on solid ground. She showered and dressed as quickly as she could, feeling as if the hours she spent away from Max were far too long.

As she was walking through the hallway of her building to take Tilney for a walk, something stopped her in front of Mrs. Doogan's door. It was Thursday. She should stop and say hello, she thought. Mrs. Doogan's health had been declining in the last couple of weeks. Her granddaughter, Janice, had let everyone in the building know visits would be appreciated because it seemed like her grandmother was getting ready to finally say goodbye. Claire had taken to stopping in for an hour or two on Thursdays to read to Mrs. Doogan. It was selfish on Claire's part, but it did give Mrs. Doogan a break from her routine, and Janice a break from everything. Claire grew fascinated so quickly with the old woman who always dreamed of herself young and amazing. It made her want to find the young spirit that she got to spend time with in the dream world on occasion within the aging grandmother and great-grandmother.

Mrs. Doogan moved and spoke slowly. Every word had purpose, because every word took effort. As Claire brought her classic books over to read, she would catch glimpses of the girl this woman used to be.

Her name was Lucy; she had been born in Germany but brought to the US as a child. She grew up in the thick of Baltimore, and as her granddaughter told it, was quite the scrappy teenager. There were stories of cutting school to watch the horse race at Pimlico, and dancing their way into smoky clubs with live bands. That's where she met her Edward. He was the guitar player with the smooth voice in a club she frequented. When they met, she told him she was there because he had been waiting for her all his life. He knew better than to disagree. Claire would see flashes of that girl, as she read books. They had been working their way through Gone with the Wind. When she knocked, Janice opened the door.

"Claire! Oh, I didn't think you were coming over today," Janice smiled.

"I wanted to at least stop by and say hello. I can't stay long, I'm afraid," she admitted.

"Oh, I am so glad you're feeling up to it. Will you be going to see Max?"

"Yes."

"Please give him our love. I would go see him, but I've got my hands full here," Janice conceded.

"Understandable."

"Well, want me to take Tilney for a nice little walk, and you can sit with Mom-Mom? Say ten minutes?"

"Perfect. I have fallen in love with your grandmother. She's such a sweet lady. I get glimpses of who I think she was when she was young."

"When I was a kid, she was the spunkiest grandma in town. So fun to be around. It's a good part of why I wanted to come stay here instead of anyone else. She'd tell me stories of her and my grandfather. He passed away about thirty years ago, but she still loves him so much. It's why she came back here."

"What do you mean?"

"This apartment. They didn't always live here. They had a house, raised their kids. Sold it to move into something smaller and more manageable. When he passed she said there were no memories of him there. No memories of them. She asked me to keep an eye on this building, and this apartment. This is where they lived when they got married, this is where their life together started. I called the owners, explained to them what I was looking for and they kept my number. It took three years, but the apartment finally came up for rent and they called me. We moved her in and it was like she immediately became the young girl who once lived here again."

Claire thought of the young girl from her dreams and smiled. "She's the coolest lady ever."

"She is," Janice agreed. "I was commuting back and forth from my place, but when the apartment next door opened up, I took it. It's a great building, I can picture what it must have been like for them all those years ago. She's got pictures, I'll have to show them to you one day."

"Please do, I'd love to see them."

"I'll move on from here, when she moves on. But for now, it's the right place. It's home to her."

"You're a pretty cool lady too," Claire added.

"Thanks. And thank you for coming to sit with her and letting me get out. It's a nice break."

It was one of the few times Janice was able to get out of the house, and she looked forward to it so much. Claire happily handed over Tilney's leash and waited for them to get out of the apartment building and across the street before she went in and sat down at Mrs. Doogan's bedside. The TV was on, blaring so that Mrs. Doogan could hear it. Claire felt for Janice as she knew having something on that loud all day must be jarring to the nerves. Walking to the bedroom, Claire found Mrs. Doogan propped up watching TV. The movement in the doorway caught the old woman's eye.

"Claire, how are you, sweetheart?"

"I'm good, Mrs. Doogan," Claire spoke clearly and loudly as she grabbed the remote and turned the volume down. She sat next to the woman and slipped her hand on top of the small, frail hand of her friend.

"Janice said you would not be coming to read to me today."

"I can stay only for a little bit, but I wanted to at least say hello. I'm sorry I can't stay and read."

"Oh, that's okay. I know how it ends," she smiled and patted Claire's hand.

"Did Janice tell you I'm going to visit Max?" Claire wondered how much Janice told her grandmother of the accident and what had been going on for the last several days.

"She said he was in a car accident. That's a terrible shame. Said you were with him. Glad you're okay."

"Thank you," Claire smiled.

"He is a strong boy, honey. He will be fine."

"I hope so," Claire said quietly, and then spoke up again, "what will you be up to today? Got any fun plans?"

"I've packed my suitcase up, honey; I think I'm just waiting now. It will be nice when I see him again."

Her husband. Claire knew she was speaking of Edward. The woman had only loved one man her whole life, and she carried him with her still.

"Oh, hush now," Claire insisted.

"It's okay, child. I've had my life. My heart is full. My children are grown and happy. My grandchildren are grown and happy. I dream only of what waits for me."

"Sounds like a nice dream."

"You saw the sunset. It's a happy place, sweetheart."

Claire's heart skipped a beat when Mrs. Doogan mentioned the sunset. She wondered if she was speaking of the dream that Claire had the night before. She knew the dream belonged to Mrs. Doogan; the combat boots always gave her away.

"What sunset, it's morning, silly."

Mrs. Doogan turned to her, and focused on the young face that had years and years of life ahead.

"You were there, weren't you?" her eyes wondered, thinking hard to remember, "You came to visit. You didn't have a book then, either."

Claire's hand quietly slipped out of Mrs. Doogan's and she sat back in her chair and turned over the words in her mind. It was quite possible that the old woman was nothing more than confused as she merged dreams with reality. There was just a small tickle in her stomach though, telling her that there was no confusion.

"Mrs. Doogan," Claire scooted closer to the old woman and spoke slowly as she asked, "did you see me?"

"Of course I did. We talked about life; about my life, my parents, my husband, my kids. Claire, you remember, don't you? When was that?"

They had not talked, but she did remember the moments. Flashes of a life lived, seeing them as if they were playing out in real time, how Mrs. Doogan felt in her heart, standing on the edge of time. She must think it actually happened, they actually watched a sunset together. She was confused about the where and then when, but she had all the details correct.

"I do remember. They were lovely stories." A tear had slipped down Claire's cheek.

She had wanted to be there, she felt as if she would burst if she wasn't. She remembered feeling that way, as Adelaide's voice rang in her ears. *If you want to be there with them, then you are there.*

"I have to go, Mrs. Doogan. I can come by soon, though."

"Go be with your man." Mrs. Doogan patted her hand again. "So much life to live with him yet."

"Can I ask you a question?" Claire paused at the woman's bedroom door.

"Of course."

"Why do you always wear combat boots?"

Claire felt the pages of her neatly kept dreamer rule book being torn at the seams as the words came out of her mouth. Never, in all of her life, had she discussed this side of herself with an outsider.

"My boots? Oh, I don't know where those things are. Haven't seen 'em in ages." Mrs. Doogan spoke as she stared out the window to watch the afternoon blooming outside her window. "The boys, they went to war, and we wives went to work. There was a time, child, when things weren't so easy. We had to be strong, and stand tall. I wasn't by his side, but I stood with him. I fought with him."

"Your husband? Edward?"

"Yes. I'm not by his side, but I still stand with him."

And there it was. She stood in combat boots because she longed to stand with the man who was on the other side of the edge of time. All these years later, she still longed for him. Incredible.

Chapter 28

The beeping of the cardiac monitor became something that calmed her nerves. Every day she came to sit. And every day, as she watched the steady heartbeat flowing across the screen, she convinced herself rest was being had. Healing was at work.

His mother only left his side to sleep and shower. She was staying with Aidan and Charlotte now, and they took turns sitting with him while Marjorie rested. Marjorie had been quiet, but friendly. She had said nothing when doctors spoke to Claire directly about his condition, as if she had any sort of authority over him at all. Claire wanted to say something to this woman she didn't even know existed before the accident.

"I was eighteen when I had him," Marjorie said out of the blue.

"Must have been hard," Claire offered quietly.

"You would think. No eighteen-year old wants to have a baby. I was just a young foolish girl who had fallen for the charms of a snake."

"Sorry to hear that," Claire said and then confessed, "Max has never told me about his father."

"He's done his best to erase the man out of existence. I don't. Every moment that led me to this boy was worth it."

"So it's just you and him?" Claire asked.

"It's always been just me and him, even when it was before we were a just me and him. I was scared to death when I found out he was on his way. I had no idea how to be a mom, and I didn't know if I wanted to bring him into…"

Claire could see Marjorie's eyes welling up, felt for her as she watched the woman rub the edges of Max's blanket in her fingers.

"That's the scary thing, I think, bringing your child into a world that you don't know how to explain. That you don't know how to protect them from."

Marjorie smiled, shook her head, letting out a small laugh.

"He protected me. He was just a boy, but I think if he hadn't come into my world, I'd be long dead."

"How so?" Claire knew it wasn't her place to ask, but she desperately wanted to know everything about the man she spent months not knowing anything at all about. "Never mind, I'm sorry, it's not my place."

Marjorie looked at Claire, and saw the sleeplessness in her eyes. Claire had been by his side every day, traveling back and forth from her apartment. She checked with the doctors, checked in with Jack about his dog. She tried so hard not to be intrusive at the hospital when Marjorie or Aidan and Charlotte were there. But Marjorie could see the love that Claire carried for her son.

"It's okay. I married right out of high school, captain of the football team. Tobias Duncan was going places, all eyes were on him. I think I got pregnant under the bleachers just before the last game of the season, our senior year. The college scouts were out, and he had offers coming from every direction. He picked Texas. Looking back on it now, I'm not sure he would have taken me with him, but by the time it was time to go, we knew Max was on his way. We got married at a court house somewhere between here and there on a hot summer day in August."

"That's a lot on your plate."

"It was, but it was an exciting time. All eyes were on Toby, and his head was in the game. Second game into the season his freshman year, he took a hard hit. Tore his ACL on his way down, and broke his collarbone when he hit the ground."

"Wow, that sucks."

"Yup. We didn't know it at the time, but it ended his career. His arm couldn't throw the way it used to, he couldn't take the hits like he used to, or run."

"That had to be hard."

"It was," Marjorie admitted. "But you deal. You make a plan B. He was a smart guy, he could have done anything. It was just the nature of his beast though; he was mad at the world."

"And he took it out on you?" Claire prompted.

"Pain killers. Pain killers and alcohol turned the worst of him all the way up. Max never really knew him before the accident. There were moments where he was a good man, he was so loving and charming and made me feel like the most beautiful girl in the world."

"I'm sorry, Mrs. Duncan." Claire didn't know what to say.

"Marjorie, please," she insisted. "I kept it under control for a while. I hid his pills, and watered down his whisky bottles. Sometimes he was already so drunk he didn't notice. But other times he did. He would say terrible things to me, push me around."

"Oh, my God!" Claire was already picturing a young Marjorie with a small child, living in fear of the man who was supposed to love her.

"I thought I was good at hiding it from the world, but Max," she rubbed his hand as she spoke, "Max knew. He heard me crying myself to sleep sometimes. He helped me when I moved slow, aching from bruises that Toby put on me."

"Did you leave him?"

"I'm not sure I would have ever been brave enough, not for myself. Toby had his moments where he would be so sweet and I felt unbelievably loved. I held onto those moments more than I should have. But as Max got bigger, Toby took a heavy hand with him."

"Jesus," Claire looked at Max, sleeping peacefully as the machines continued their rhythmic song. "Oh, Max."

"Toby was hard on him all along, and that poor child did his best. I found him trying to wash sheets in the laundry when he was just four once. He wet the bed and was terrified of what his father would do."

"That's awful." Claire felt sick. "He was just a baby."

"When Max was about ten, he was nearly as tall as I am. He left some toys out and Toby came home drunk in the middle of the night and tripped over one. He yanked Max right out of his bed, and nearly broke his arm."

Claire's heart was racing with anger and hurt. She took a deep breath in order to keep from crying.

"I waited until he was asleep, passed out from whatever it was that was in his system and Max and I left with just the clothes on our backs."

"That was very brave of you," Claire smiled. "It was the right thing to do."

"He saved me," Marjorie repeated. "I was brave for him."

"Did you, did Max ever see him again?"

"He came after us a couple days later when he sobered up. I was staying with a friend of mine, who let me stay until I got on my feet. He wanted me to come home; I served him with divorce papers instead. He was smart enough not to argue custody. He faded out of our lives, and Max and I let him."

"Do you know where he is now?" She wondered if the man would care about the son laying in the hospital room fighting for his life.

"Dead," Marjorie said without emotion. "He wrapped his car around a tree one night. Max was about fourteen, just before he started high school. The hospital called, I was still listed as his emergency contact. I went, I claimed responsibility for him."

"That was good of you,"

"He did give me Max, but I think I did it for closure. Max and I buried him. I let him feel however he wanted to feel about it. If he was sad, that was okay. If he was mad, that was okay too. If he was scared, or happy, or anything else, that was okay. We packed up what little we had and moved here."

"Fresh start."

"We both needed it," Marjorie said. "I think that's what he was looking for after Rebecca. He did what he knew, he hit the reset button. I mean, he lost everything—his wife, his home, and the life he'd built. Like once before, he was torn from his life with just the clothes on his back."

That's why nothing in his apartment is old; it was all lost in the fire. A stupid little fact, Claire realized, as she sat and listened to his story.

"I didn't know about Rebecca, but I am sorry he lost her. I'm sure he loved her very much."

A fact she was sure of now, knowing he felt such guilt even two years later. Knowing he dreamed of her and worried about her fading from his memories.

"She was a beautiful girl. It killed him; he feels responsible."

I know the feeling, she thought. She felt just how responsible he felt through his dreams, and now with her own experience and guilt staring her in the face as he lay there in the hospital bed, she could relate.

"I know he does. I feel responsible for him being here. We had a fight and things are very much unresolved between us right now. It's very kind of you to allow me to sit with him."

"He's better when you're here." Marjorie confessed as she pointed to the machine counting the beats of his heart, "The beats aren't as steady when you're not."

The doctor stood at the door, not wanting to interrupt the quiet conversation between the women.

"She's right, you know," he agreed. "His vitals calm down when you're here."

"Can he hear us? Does he know what is going on?"

"Comas are funny like that, people are kind of here and then they aren't. He might be able to hear you and know what you are saying, but he might be processing it differently. It's kind of like when you're dreaming and the phone rings but in your dream its music or a fire alarm or something."

Claire could relate to that; she nearly laughed.

"We took him off medication last night, he needs to wake up," Marjorie added.

Claire looked at the doctor for confirmation.

"We did, he's healing enough. It's time. He should be coming around bit by little bit. It can take a few days. He's got to do a bit of fighting."

"Is he, fighting?" Claire asked, turning her head from the doctor to Max's mother.

"Not as much as we'd like," the doctor admitted. "It's a sad thing when people lose their will. It's amazing how mental health can affect physical wellbeing. Good thing is, looks like he stopped taking sleeping pills a few weeks ago, so that should be out of his system."

"Sleeping pills?" Claire wondered.

"Your husband had been taking sleeping pills," he checked the chart to confirm, "Looks like for a few weeks a while back, but he stopped recently. Did you not know?"

Claire thought back over the last couple of months, and closed her eyes, shaking her head. He had not been a dreamer, and now she knew why. He must have started taking them soon after they met, causing that long pause between her dreams of Rebecca.

"Now that I think about it, he was sleeping pretty sound there for a while. He just never mentioned it to me."

"Well, for now we just wait. But I know having you here will help."

"I think you're giving me too much credit, doc," Claire said honestly.

"I'm going to be honest with you; he does need to fight a little. He's not as stable as I would like him to be. But, love is a strong weapon. He's just better when you're around."

Claire didn't say anything, but her heart ached. She spent three or four days researching him, reading articles written in the paper after the fire. She had seen a handful of reports that had indicated that his whole story seemed odd, and it wouldn't have taken much to rig the furnace in the basement and then conveniently be out late on the night it went haywire. The reports mentioned he was alone at a bar and then claimed he stayed the night in his city office.

This was what the police held most to. The bartender confirmed he was at the bar, and also confirmed Max had been coming in regularly to drink alone. The man went on to tell the police he had been a bartender for thirty years, and he knows a man with a lot on his mind; Max was battling something.

When they followed up with checking his financial records, they found Max had taken out a generous loan to pay for the startup costs of his business. They also found a life insurance policy on Rebecca, recently taken out. Their home was in need of repair, and they were living on a shoestring budget. It was very easy to be swayed into seeing his guilt.

"Why didn't you just tell me about her?" she asked out loud, though she didn't mean to.

"About Rebecca?" Marjorie asked, not sure if Claire was talking to her or to Max.

"Sorry, I didn't mean to say that out loud." Yet she confessed, "Yes, about Rebecca, about anything. I'm in love with a man I don't even know."

"That's my fault, I think," Marjorie said. "When we came here, we both wanted to be rid of everything that weighed so heavy in our life. It was about six months into the school year and I had come for a band concert, got to talking to one of the teachers. He said he admired me, being a single mom all these years. Must have been hard, having lost Max's father in a car accident."

"That's not untrue," Claire mused.

"Exactly. I was a single mom from the moment he was born and I worked my ass off to keep a roof over our heads while Toby was drinking it all away. Max chose his truth, and stuck with it. I think he didn't want his past to haunt him; he didn't want people to know. He found a lot of freedom in starting over. Made a lot of friends, it was a good thing.

Eventually, the story became, it's been just him and me. He became so skilled at the story, he never had to mention his father."

"So you think he wanted to reset? Get so good at the story, Rebecca didn't exist?"

"No, he speaks freely of her to me. To Charlotte. But it was hard for him with the others. Half the town accused him of killing his wife. And the other half never looked at him the same. He needed to be free of that. That's what he wanted to pretend wasn't happening."

"He was very good. I had no idea. The only thing in his apartment from that life, as far as I know, is Rebecca's bike bell and his wedding ring. They're in his closet."

"He wore that ring for a long time. I remember him spinning it around his finger, and I remember thinking he must be wondering when he should take it off. I don't know when he took it off, but I know it wasn't that long ago. I noticed it was just quietly gone, over the summer I think, I never asked. I just hugged him, and told him I love him."

"I can't even imagine."

"He could have personalized that apartment more. I mean, he needed all new things, new furniture, and new clothes. But there were pictures he could have reproduced. This is the digital age; he could have recreated his world, easily. But I had done so well after we moved here, I never mentioned his father, ever. He only saw good things from my pretending our life didn't exist until we moved here."

"You did what you had to do," Claire agreed.

"He keeps a picture of Rebecca in his wallet, I guess his way of never really keeping her far from his heart. He once told me his biggest fear was forgetting what she looked like."

He remembers every inch, Claire thought. Setting her own feelings aside, she was happy he could do that. "Thank you for sharing your story with me."

"Give him time, he will tell you his story. I think it's time for me to go home and get some rest. I've been here all night. Charlotte will be here later, Aidan has taken to throwing himself into work so Max can jump back in when he's better and they won't be swamped." Marjorie gathered her things and offered Claire a hug.

Claire returned her attention to the man in the bed. The bruises on his face were fading, and his cuts and scratches were dulling. If it weren't for the casts and the tubes keeping him healthy, he looked as if he was enjoying an afternoon nap.

"You do know I'm here, right?" she asked him as her hand slipped over his.

The slow and steady beeping of the monitor continued on with its march.

"You need to fight, Max. You need to wake up. I have so much to tell you."

I love you, she thought. *I love you, and I have no idea what to do about it.*

She read him the book she had picked up from the library, the newest heart thumping thriller from G. Everett, an author she knew he liked. They had discussed books one evening as they lay naked in a heap of blankets on the floor of her bedroom. He grabbed a book off the shelf just above his head, thumbing through it and making her laugh with his interpretations of her tastes in fictional men.

"I need to leave a few books here, I think. I don't think I can hang with," he checked the spine of the book he grabbed, "uh…Mr. Musgrove and his friends."

She smiled, as he mentioned the main character of the book in his hands. For somebody who teased her about her reading so much, he slipped here or there as he mentioned themes or characters he wouldn't otherwise know if he hadn't read them himself. He was a closet reader; she knew it. She tickled the confession right out of him, too. *One more thing to re-file*, she thought. He knew them because Rebecca knew them. They were books he once had in the home he'd shared with his wife, books he had no doubt discussed with her.

As she began to read, the words of the doctor played in her mind. He can hear, but it would be a dream. She wondered if he was dreaming. She wondered what he was dreaming of. Out of nowhere, the thought of the conversations she had with Mrs. Doogan popped into her mind.

The old woman was surely slipping from this world, but there was no denying she saw Claire in her dream.

"Would you see me?" she asked Max. "Will you let me find you?"

The monitors beeped with irregular annoyance as if to answer her question. Her attention shot to the screen as she watched the machine light up and beep in ways she had not heard before. Just as she stood to walk over and look more closely at it, a nurse walked in briskly to check on Max.

"Everything okay? I've never seen the machine do this before."

"He did it once last night, but we got him back."

"Back?" she asked alarmed "Where did you get him back from?"

The nurse momentarily stopped and made eye contact with Claire, causing a cold chill to go down her spine. Claire backed up to give the nurse room, and the doctor came in to check on him.

"What's going on?" Claire asked.

"Well, he gets into these little fits where his body stops responding. I told you, willpower is a strong thing. He needs to want to fight."

"Is he going to be okay?" she asked.

"We're doing what we can, dear. But this part, it's all on him. If I could go in and pull him out, I would. Unfortunately, we have to wait for that kind of magic to happen."

Claire's mind spun with possibilities; she did not want to lose him.

As the machines calmed down once more, and the doctor relaxed and assured her with a pat on the shoulder, she took the breath she had been holding since the first beep went sideways.

"I'm sleeping here tonight," she informed him.

"I think that would be good for him," the doctor agreed.

Chapter 29

It was a game of cat and mouse. Hide and seek. *Ghost hunters?* Claire was determined, for the first time in her life, to track down a dreamer in the dream world. She came up with the idea of finding him, hoping she could pull him back with her into the waking world. But it was the silly little matter of finding him, her needle in a haystack.

A sea of dreamers she wanted, and a sea of them she got. Every single time she closed her eyes, she found herself in the strangest of lands. Thanks in no small part to the amount of drugs some of these people were on; they made for very psychedelic dreams. Still, she did everything she could to remain sleepy. She filled her bag with a couple of the most boring thick text books she could find. She drank tea with chamomile and valerian. All safe for baby, who was also playing a vital part in the whole process. Claire found it easy to sleep; she had never been more tired in her whole life. Making a baby was hard work, apparently.

The most surprising dream had been Charlotte's. Or at least, the baby Charlotte carried. Claire found herself in a world of swirled colors, with muted sounds all around. Though it was an environment that didn't make any sense, her dreamer felt completely safe and at home. Then Claire heard a soft voice, singing. She heard a deep voice, sweetly talking. Claire imagined that perhaps it was a patient in the hospital, under the effects of medication, until she heard the same soft voice singing the same soft sound. Charlotte stood in the little bathroom of the hospital room, and as she brushed her hair, she sang of the black bird that was waiting for the moment to rise.

"I like that song," Claire said.

"Oh, sorry," Charlotte sheepishly smiled "I sing to the baby. I sometimes forget that there are people around me that can hear it. I have no idea if he can hear it."

The song was stuck in Charlotte's head, the song she thought belonged to Max. He was her little bird who had so much to overcome. She had been singing it to herself in the days since he arrived on her doorstep, broken once more.

"He can." *He can, and he loves it*, she thought. "Don't ever be sorry for doing your mom thing."

"Makes you wonder what Max can hear, if he knows we are here."

"The doctor said there is noticeable change in him when we are."

Charlotte stood at the door, her hand gently soothing the child that was yet to be, and fought back the tears of an emotional pregnant woman.

"When he wakes up," she struggled to get the words out with the lump in her throat "you two have a lot to talk about. He's a good man. He's worth whatever it is you're working out in your head."

"I know he is," Claire smiled. "I just wish he would have told me about things. Maybe everything would be different."

"Oh, geeze," Charlotte smirked and aimed her attention at Max. "Are you hearing this? Did you hear what she just said?"

"He had his reasons." Claire defended him.

"I know. He's been this way forever. It just drives me mad; he needs to trust people more."

"We all do, sometimes," Claire admitted.

"When I met him, he fed me some sap story about his childhood. It wasn't a lie, but it wasn't…he just…spun it. Enough that my bullshit detector went off."

"Well, that was one thing Max did tell me once. One cannot pull anything over on Charlotte."

"Damn straight," Charlotte agreed. "I got him to tell me the truth, eventually. And then I got him to trust me with the truth. I wish the world could see what I see."

"I see it," Claire offered. "Or I'm starting to."

"Good."

"So he told you about his father?" Claire was curious.

"He did. It's amazing how something that happens to us in childhood can break us."

"Or make us," Claire added.

"Or make us," Charlotte agreed. "I think he's a product of both. His father broke him, but it was before he was strong. What he's made of himself, the man he's become…I don't think he sees it."

Claire knew what it was like to let an idea consume you. Her whole life, she felt her uncontrollable assault on the sleeping world broke her spirit. Yet, because of it, she had been able to help people. She had been able to see through people. She had been able to understand the world on a very organic level. She made something of it, something good. It was hard for her to remember that, but having the time to be reflective about it now, she would. She thought of the child who went on the quest, who was blessed by the spirits, and wondered what she would think of Claire's modern day adaptation.

"The past sometimes has no bearing on the future."

"He certainly had a hard time with that," Charlotte sighed. "You know where he was the night of the fire?"

"No."

"He was at a bar. He ordered himself a beer and just stared at it. He never even touched it. He sat and he wondered if he was anything like his father."

"Why would he be worried about that?"

"Rebecca wanted a family, it scared him," Charlotte said sadly.

Claire felt the heat flush her face, and tried to shake off and hide her emotions.

"He didn't want kids?"

"It was actually why he got those life insurance policies. Max wanted her to have something should anything happen to him. Her and whatever family they had but he was so damn scared of the idea of kids. He confessed to me he had been lying to her for weeks, telling her he was working late because he needed time to work it all out, for her. I suggested a therapist, who he finally saw after Rebecca died. But until then, he spent his time sitting at a bar, drinking, to see if there was any chance he would ever become his father. The monster he thought was buried deep inside."

Oh, Christ. A monster, I called him a monster.

The conversation she had with him, the last conversation she had with him in fact was about that very monster. He asked her if she saw a monster when she looked at him, and she threw back in his face that no, he saw one. It wasn't at all what she meant at the time, but she felt so small now. She was the monster.

"He's got to know that's not true," Claire almost pleaded.

"He was trying to work it out, because he had never told Rebecca about his father. Much like, he never told you. He's an idiot sometimes."

"I'm glad he's had you, to keep him grounded. I feel like that's what you do."

"We keep each other grounded," Charlotte continued. She saw the love in Claire's eyes, but she also saw the confusion. The kind you have when you want to trust in something, but you're not sure if you can. Perhaps showing her the Max Charlotte knew would clear Claire's vision. "I lost two babies before this one."

"Oh, I'm so sorry," Claire said.

"The first one I lost before I even knew there was anything to lose. The second, I was about twelve weeks. It's amazing how you can love something so much, even when you don't have it yet. The road to motherhood has not been easy for me."

"Oh, Charlotte…" Claire reached over and touched Charlotte's hand.

"This guy was amazing. He let Aidan stay with me as long as I wanted him with me. He worked all the hours. He came and sat with me and let me just be the ugliest, most human version of myself. Do you know the gift you have when somebody knows you at your inner most level, the level you barely even let yourself admit you have, and they love you anyway?"

She thought of her grandparents.

"It's the goal," she said honestly.

"He's just being his very most human, right now. We're letting him. It's all going to be fine."

"Did he tell you I accused him of killing her?" Claire felt ashamed saying the words.

"He told me you knew things, and he didn't know how you knew them."

"I looked at him, and I called him a monster."

Charlotte remained stoic, but Claire could see the word hit home for her as much as it did for Max.

"He was talking in his sleep, calling for her." Claire accounted the best version of the story she could for her audience. "It woke me. I was confused, but rather than waking him up and talking to him about it, I chose to take a selfish minute. I wound up running into his closet and staring at his things. It hit me, everything in that closet was new. There were no old do-dads, and trinkets, no ratty clothes."

"The fire. There was plenty of that before the fire. He lost everything but the clothes on his back that night," Charlotte reminded her.

"I know that now, but I jumped to conclusions. I thought maybe he was married and keeping an apartment in the city. Our rent is super cheap, so I could see how he'd be able to swing it."

"He put every spare penny he had into his business."

Claire hadn't thought about that, but it made sense. She did the same thing.

"I started going through his clothes, making this story up in my mind. Married, living in the suburbs, a little apartment on the side. I was engaged once, and there was another woman. I was furious to think I had been made the other woman."

"That's terrible, I'm sorry."

"I feel sorry for the woman he's with now. At least I know he's a stupid, lying, cheating bastard." Claire shook the idea of Christopher out of her head. "I found a box at the top of Max's closet. It had a bike bell and his wedding ring in it."

"It was hers. The bike was a gift from him. It was a strange little thing, but it somehow survived the fire. He couldn't bring himself to part with it. To throw it away. He kept it in a box because it reminded him of the night he lost her, but he kept it. It became the only piece of their life together the fire didn't take. That and his wedding ring."

"I saw the bell, and saw it was damaged. I didn't know what it meant. I went home and I found an article about the fire. I never looked into him, I was enjoying discovering him." Claire continued to be honest in her own strange way, "When you do what I do, you sometimes find yourself with information you don't necessarily need or want. It's hard to be objectionable when all the information is clouding your mind. I find in my personal time, I try not to overanalyze, over research, over plan. Sometimes it's just nice to discover as you go."

"It is," Charlotte agreed.

"When I read he'd been spotted at bars for weeks, drinking, when I read about the insurance money, and can see his business is…"

"Doing well? Nice office, nice things?" Charlotte had been down this road before. It made her angry because the truth was, they had all sacrificed and saved. Rebecca and Max, Charlotte and Aiden. They all gave up luxuries and worked hard to help that business take off.

"Yeah," Claire confessed.

"You know what he did with that money? He built a playground. Actually, he built four. Every elementary school in the county where Rebecca taught got a brand new, top of the line playground. Every single one has a little plaque, which does not have his name on it."

"It has hers," Claire finished.

Charlotte smiled as she wiped away her final tear of the day. "Max didn't benefit one bit from the insurance policy he took on his wife. He did what he thought she would want to do. That money was for her children.

Max found a way to honor that, and gave the money to the place where her children were."

"You're a good friend to him, Charlotte. Go home, get some rest."

The day had been long, and little had changed with Max. Nothing was bad, but nothing was good. It was if he was trying to decide if he wanted to wake up, and couldn't. Clare sat and watched him, wondering if she'd find him before the baby she carried took her ability. Her grandmother told her the gift faded; she'd lost her abilities one at a time over the course of carrying Claire's father.

"Clock's ticking," she whispered to Max as she settled on the sofa next to him to get some sleep herself.

The long day behind her and the rhythmic beeping of all his monitors soothed Claire to sleep. She had spent the day working on her laptop, sitting on a little moveable tray in the hospital room. She took on a few projects for work, needing an actual break from all the determined sleeping she had been doing. The result was her mind had been busier than it had been in a week, and she was genuinely tired. Tonight it would be sleep, just for sleep's sake.

Chapter 30

Swirls of blue, she was floating in swirls of blue. *Drugs,* Claire thought to herself. She had seen a lot of these sorts of dreams in the last few days. Soon the blue broke into yellow and Claire found herself sitting in a field of grass with wild flowers sprouting out around her. Everything was yellow, the sky, the field, the air. As if she was sitting, watching, with bright yellow sunglasses on. The edges of the world, this dream world, faded with a soft white. It reminded her of an old photograph. Faded to a muted yellow with age whitening the edges. She was inside of a photograph.

She heard the voices before she saw the two people sitting on the picnic blanket. Wanting to see who it was, Claire wished she could move forward, and with complete astonishment, she did. She moved forward, free from the idea of what the dreamer had in mind.

Huh, that's different.

Welcoming the change of freedom, she walked up the hill toward the voices. The breeze brushed through her hair, tickling her shoulders. The man and woman sitting on the blanket were having lunch. Their clothes were muted shades of cream and brown, but clear. She could see both of them with no usual limitations of the dream world. They weren't blurry, they weren't faceless—they were people. The man sat, unpacking the contents of an old fashion wicker picnic basket as the woman drank from a long Champaign flute. They were laughing, and looked at such ease with each other.

Very unusual, indeed. I'm free…I can see them clearly. I don't think this is the dreamer's point of view at all. I wonder if they can see me.

As she got closer to the people, it was clear to her they couldn't see her. However, it was what she discovered that stopped her from getting any closer. The man sitting on the blanket, so busily putting together what looked to be a very romantic little meal was Max. The woman that sat across from him would surely be Rebecca.

Oh, thank God, her thoughts said to the sleeping man in the hospital bed. *I found you.*

The woman's hair tossed, and the color finally caught Claire's eye. Though everything was within the strange yellow dream filter Max had going on, Claire could see the chestnut shine. The woman's toned skin looked soft and welcoming, and her eyes shined with flecks of light green and gold.

Oh, that's me, she thought to herself as she hesitated getting any closer. She was flying blind here, having never experienced a dream from her own point of view. Only from where the dreamer sat, and she had certainly never saw herself in a dream. *Baby magic? Maybe.*

"I think maybe Tuscany," Claire said—the Claire sitting on the blanket sipping her Champagne.

"Really? Any particular spot? Leaning Tower of Piazza? Piazzale Michelangelo?" Max asked, smiling at her.

"No. I think I just want to rent a bicycle and get lost." She set the Champagne carefully down and threw her arms in the air. "We can ride into town and have lunch at a little café. We can people watch, and try on silly clothes you only buy when you're on vacation."

"Sounds wonderful."

Claire felt warm, and happy. She had no idea if it was her own emotions, or Max's pumping though her. She studied herself, now solidly believing that Max could not see her. She walked over to the couple and stood behind Max to observe herself, the Claire of his dreams, sitting on the blanket.

She was beautiful. She was wearing slim jeans and a silly black t shirt with white writing on it. She couldn't see the writing, it was all blurry; Max must not have been concentrating too hard on the finer details. She did know the shirt though, one of her favorites. A statement simply written out that books turn Muggles into Wizards. She smiled, this is how he thought of her. This is how he saw her.

Her hair was pulled back in a sweet ponytail, and her shoes were off with her toenails painted blue. This was weekend Claire, which was her favorite kind of Claire. Morning Claire wore yoga pants and sports tops, and week day Claire wore smart blouses and slim pants or skirts. Weekend Claire loved a good pair of worn in jeans and fun comfy t-shirts. When fall hit, she would add a long sweater and boots. It was sweet that this Claire was the one tucked in his mind.

Her skin looked so soft and warm. Her cheeks just a touch rosy and lips shined with a bit of gloss. Her eyes danced with light colors of green, gold and brown. Claire felt herself blush at how pretty the girl sitting in front of her was, Max was far too kind in his dreams.

Happiness swam all around them as they chatted about music, and food, and the plans they had. Claire stood watching them, selfishly not wanting to interrupt. But as quickly as the happiness filled the air around her, the color began to turn gray.

The yellow faded out and everything turned very cold. Though Claire could not physically feel the change in temperature, the idea of it made her shudder.

What's happening, Max? she wondered.

The feelings of happiness were replaced with the saddest feeling she had ever experienced in her life. Her chest ached with hopelessness, and she nearly bent down and put her hand on Max's shoulder.

"It's all gone," the Claire of his dreams said to him as she sat still on the blanket.

"I know, I'm so sorry," Max said as the things around them began to disappear.

"It will never be better," that other Claire continued on, without emotion.

"I can't do this anymore. I've lost them both. I've lost everything," Max said.

She wanted to hug him, make it all better.

Okay Claire, break the rules.

Just before she began to bend down and wrap her arms around Max, images flashed through the air around her. She stood and watched them play out, in slow motion.

One by one, black and white images flooded Max's mind. The image of Claire standing on the edge of the fence by the dog park. Claire's face, turning into panic as she realized the Van was coming around the corner. Claire felt the way Max felt when their bodies collided as he pushed her out of the way.

Then she stood, over a singular image that remained still. It was sideways, she realized it was from the point of view when Max was already on the ground. She looked up, where she saw his dream version Claire laying still on the sidewalk. Black liquid poured out in a massive puddle around her head, and her eyes, once warm with life, stared icily back at him.

She's gone. It was the feeling that consumed him, and it was consuming her. Claire's heart broke as she realized that Max must think she did not survive the accident.

"I hear you, sometimes."

Claire turned to see Max, still sitting on the blanket. Now, alone, and his world black and white.

"I think you're still with me. I hear you."

"I'm here, Max! I'm here!" Claire walked over and sat with him, in the exact spot that the Claire of his dreams had been sitting.

"Your voice is so beautiful," he sadly offered to the nothingness he believed was in front of him.

Claire took a deep breath and remembered Mrs. Doogan. She had wanted to stand with Mrs. Doogan so badly, expressing such respect for the woman who lived such a magnificent life. So she did. She stood with Mrs. Doogan and Mrs. Doogan saw her. She closed her eyes and counted to three, digging as deep into her soul as she could imagine. When she opened her eyes again, she locked at Max.

"Find me, Max," she said to him.

His eyes formed very small recognition, she could feel the curiosity flood his emotions.

"I'm right in front of you, love, right here."

"Claire?" The image of her became clear to him. She sat in front of him, wearing gray sweatpants and one of his Penn State t-shirts. She let herself into his apartment one evening and pulled a few of his t-shirts out of his drawers, sleeping in them, missing him. This was the outfit she was wearing now, as she slept next to him in a reclining chair in his hospital room.

"There you are, I've been looking for you." She smiled, and reached her hand out to touch his leg. He wouldn't feel it, she knew, but he would get the idea of her touching him.

"I miss you," he offered.

"Oh, Max. I miss you too. You have to come back to me now, okay?"

"I lost you."

"No, you didn't. I'm right here. Max, I am going to tell you a story, okay?"

"Okay."

How in the world do I do this? she wondered. Was he even asleep? He was talking to her, he was responding to her. How was that even possible in the dream world? People don't control their dreams. But maybe they did in comas. The doctor said it was a strange place, somewhere between dreams and reality.

"Jesus Christ, Claire, stop trying to make rules!" she scolded herself.

The shout was so loud that the static echo made her want to cover her own ears.

"Claire. I lost Claire," Max said slowly as he continued to try to figure her out.

"Max, you're dreaming." *Start with the truth, see if that works.*

"I'm dreaming?" he repeated as he looked at the world, his black and white world.

"Yes. You're in the hospital, and you're dreaming. Remember the accident?" she carefully prodded.

"Yes. I lost you then. I didn't get there in time. I wasn't where I was supposed to be," he rattled off.

Claire felt the swirl of confusion going through his mind, while flashes of herself and flashes of Rebecca ran through the sky above her.

"Max, stay with me. I am real. I am not a dream, I am in your dream."

"Claire, she can read minds. She told me. I think," he said slowly.

"I can't read minds, Max, I see what's in your dreams. That's how I saw your dreams of Rebecca. But I'm here, Max. I didn't die. I'm not lost. You have to come back to me."

"I will lose her," Max offered in a thick, slow tone.

He didn't have to tell Claire who he was talking about; she knew. She could feel it.

Just as she could feel it, she saw the massive house form behind him and watched it as fire tore through it. Shattering windows, and collapsing into ash.

"Rebecca, you will lose Rebecca?" she asked.

"I will let her go, and never remember." The fear was setting in now.

"Oh, Max. You won't. You won't lose her. Don't think about that, now," she said, pointing to the house that was raging with fire. "Remember her when you loved her most."

Swirls of colors flew by and Rebecca sat on a sofa with fuzzy pajamas on, her hair pulled into a loose bun on the top of her head. She looked up at Max, standing in front of her and smiled at him. She was looking over papers that had scribbles of crayons all over them.

"She's beautiful, Max," Claire admitted.

"I will lose her."

"Max, do you see her? Do you see her red hair? It's long and wavy and it's soft."

"Yes."

"Do you see her skin, how it glows? Do you see the sparkle in her eyes?" Claire continued.

"Yes."

"Do you smell the lilac in the air?" Claire took a deep breath in and smelled the scent of what Rebecca smelled like to Max.

"Yes," he repeated himself again.

"That's because she's in your heart. Max, when people dream, they don't see images this clearly. They see blobs, faceless blobs. You have the idea of a person, but you cannot see them in great detail. You see Rebecca in great detail because your heart has her image in it. You will never forget her. You carry her with you."

"I don't want to lose her."

"You don't have to, Max. It's okay to remember her as much as you'd like. She would want you to be happy. She wants to be carried in your heart; do that for her."

"I want to love Claire," he offered.

Claire felt the warmth of love wash over her, again not sure if it was Max's emotions or her own at play.

"I want you to love me."

He slowly lifted his hand and reached for her. She had no idea if he would feel her or not, the rules of space and time were being broken apart by the second for her. She had never known herself to be an observer of a dream, and was never able to control her movements or speak. She slid from where she was sitting into his lap and wrapped her arms around him, burying her face in his neck.

"I want this forever." His voice was so sad, and soft.

"Max, you understand that this is a dream, right? You have to wake up."

"I don't want to, I want to stay here. With you."

Claire knew what she had to do. She closed her eyes and concentrated.

"Then come back to me, Max. Wake up. I'm waiting."

She set her emotions aside, and knew she had disappeared right before his eyes. She did not think she could be seen by him, so she wasn't. He sat silent, in his black and white world, still on the blanket. His Claire was gone, the basket was gone, only he remained. The wind howled around him and fell into a rhythmic pattern. Beeping, Claire could hear the beeping.

Claire shot up out of the recliner chair with fury. Her mind spun, and she nearly fell back down on her backside trying to get her bearings. The room spun, but she calmed herself down enough to see she was standing alone in the dark hospital room. The rhythmic beeping marched on, and she went to Max who continued to look as if he was sleeping peacefully. She carefully sat down on the bed next to him, and picked up his hand and, sliding it between hers.

"Find me, Max," she whispered to him.

His warm hand inside of hers gave the slightest of wiggles. She looked down, wanting to believe she felt his hand move, pleading he would do it again.

"Max, come back to me," she said again, louder.

The machine began to grow tired of its function and beeped erratically.

"No, no no!" Claire said as she read the numbers going across the screen.

Within a minute, a nurse hastily made her way into the room.

"What's all this ruckus?" she politely asked Max as she checked the monitor. Her friendly demeanor quickly changed when she turned to check Max's vitals herself and called in the doctor in charge.

"What's going on?" Claire asked as she backed into the corner, not wanting to be in the way.

"Not sure, hon. We'll get him straight."

The doctor who Claire had chatted with several times came in, he checked Max over before he said anything. He opened Max's eyes and shined a flash light into each of them.

"Doc?" Claire asked, as her voice cracked and her hands began to shake.

The doctor said nothing, but administered another drug into Max's system.

"Is he okay?"

The monitor began to beep normally again, and Claire felt herself relax just a bit.

"He does this. I don't know why, but I think he's okay, now. I am going to go order a few tests. I'll be back in a few."

They left the room as quickly as they came in and Claire returned to his side.

"Max, just stop it. You're scaring me. You come back to me. You find me," She demanded through fresh hot tears.

Max took a deep breath in, and his eyes slowly opened.

"Max?" she wiped away the tears from her eyes and held his face. "Max, I'm right here. Come back to me."

His hand, slow and shaking, lifted and touched the arm that was holding him.

"Claire?" he whispered.

"Yes!" she kissed him, and tears she had little control over began to flow with abandon "I'm here. I'm right here."

His eyes opened, and began to focus on her face. The room was dark, with only the moonlight coming in from the window.

"I lost you," he said.

"No, love. I'm here. I'm not going anywhere." She smiled.

"I was just..." his mind was so fuzzy. Wasn't he just talking to her? They were at the park, having lunch. He was sure of it.

"It's okay. It doesn't matter. You came back to me."

"What happened?" he asked.

"There was an accident. You saved me. You pushed me out of the way."

Images of the last moments he remembered flashed in his mind.

"The van."

"Yes, the van. That van hit you."

He tried to move, but his body disagreed with the idea.

"No, no. Don't move. You've got some broken bones." She smiled as she tried to show him he was in the hospital.

"Tilney." He whispered as he struggled to stay awake.

"He's fine. He's with my parents. Jack is taking care of Pilot until you are back on your feet."

"Claire," he focused in on her, lifting his shaking hand, pressing it to her cheek.

"What?" she asked softly as she wiped the tears from her eyes.

"I just had the strangest dream."

She smiled. It would be a while yet before his brain would piece together what happened. She wondered if he would be able to remember it all once he was up and moving.

"Tell me about it," she said.

"You were with me. You were there, but you were with me. There was two of you."

Claire said nothing, waiting for judgement from the jury. Her heart pounded, she had no idea how he would react if he was of sound mind and body.

"It's okay, it was only a dream. You're here now, that's what's important."

"Claire."

"Yes?" she asked.

"Stay with me."

"I'm not going anywhere." She kissed him gently.

"You were there," he said as his brain began to wake up from its deep sleep.

"Where?" she asked nervously.

"There. You told me you were there, Claire...you..."

She could see the wheels turning. She could see him trying to make sense of it.

"You found me."

"I did," she admitted, "because I love you."

He said nothing. The world came into focus, the doctors came in and checked him over. They welcomed him back to the waking world, and pulled out tubes he didn't even know he had attached to him. He watched Claire smile through her relieved tears as he thought about all the things that played in his mind. The voices, the conversations...the doctor said he had probably picked up on every word that was said in one way or another by his visitors. His mom's voice floated through his mind, flashes of memories of his father came with it. They had talked about his father. Claire knew about his father, he was sure of it. The doctors left and told him they would call his mother to let her know he was awake.

"Claire," he said as she fussed over him with renewed spirit in the middle of the night. *Was it the middle of the night? Was it today? Tomorrow?* He realized he had no idea.

"Yes?" she asked.

"You saw," he said quietly.

"Max, you don't have to talk about it; I can't control it." She began to babble in her nervousness.

"And you love me?" he raised his weak voice over her.

"I do." She quieted down.

"I love you." He looked at her, grabbing her hand and pulling her to sit on the bed with him. "I should have trusted that more. I'm sorry. Will you let me tell you now?"

"I will."

"I want to spend the rest of my life talking to you about things."

"You do?" she asked.

"I do. I didn't know I was ever going to fall in love again. I wasn't expecting it. But you are the most brilliantly, amazingly, funny girl. You have been the air I forgot I needed."

Claire smiled, and pulled in closer to him on his little hospital bed. She kissed him lightly, wishing she could give all of herself to him.

"I am a very broken man," he said, seeing her hesitancy to touch him.

The giggle came effortlessly. Yes, at the moment, he was a very broken man. Poor guy. He smiled.

"Yes, I am literally a broken man," he repeated but then returned to his original thought "but I have not been honest with you. I have so much to tell you. So many parts of me that I want you to know."

"It's okay Max. You can tell me when you're ready, or you don't have to tell me at all," she said, as she thought of her own secrets and wondered how much of them he would remember.

"Claire, I love you. I love every damn part of you. I love the funny, and the silly, and the romantic. I love how you fall asleep at eight o'clock on the couch, but when I wake you up to go to bed, you can't get back to sleep and talk to me for hours. I love how you can't ever remember where you put your keys. I love how you treat the people around you, and you think of the smallest thing to make their world a better place. I love how you talk to everyone, even though you are one of the shyest people I've ever met. I love how you insist on microwaving ice cream."

"It makes it softer," she argued.

"I love everything about you. I don't understand how you do what you do, but I don't care."

Was he telling her that he knew her secret and didn't care?

"Max, we all have parts that are broken."

"You're not broken, Claire. You're perfect, exactly the way you are."

"I love you." Three words she managed to tell everyone but Max. "I love you. I love you."

"Marry me. Say that tou'll spend this life with me," he said.

"What?" The bolt of un-expectancy and surprise shot through her. His mind was foggy.

"Max, your mind isn't clear."

He took her hand, brought it to his lips and kissed it. "My mind is more clear, now that it's been in a long time. I don't want to wake up every again without you by my side. In this world, or…" he tried to find words to describe the dream he woke from but couldn't, "any other. I want this, forever. Marry me."

Just like that. He was accepting her, all of her, just like that.

"Forever," she agreed.

Epilogue

The room she found herself in was sweet. The walls were gray, with a silhouette of a cherry tree dancing in the background. Rebecca's tree, Claire thought of it as. She can watch over Max, watch over his child. Claire found herself sitting at a small round table, with a little ceramic tea set. She noted the two china cabinets in the room, now painted a friendly bright yellow and bursting with baby books, toys, stacks of soft little blankets and diapers. A new space, a new role. The role they were always meant to have and were just waiting for. A small child, with big brown bouncy curls sat across from her.

"Would you like some tea?" the small child asked.

"I would," Claire said.

"What would you like to do today?" the child asked in her sweet, little voice.

"Oh, I don't know. Anything at all," Claire mused.

"How about some swings?" the child asked.

"Okay," Claire agreed.

The child looked like Ava, the little girl she met in the park over two years ago and bonded with over a silly dog and a field full of lighting bugs. Ava's mother's name was Alice, which Claire eventually learned when the women introduced themselves to each other. Alice and Ava. The time they spent at the park was their walk to and from Ava's school. A special time, just for the two of them. Claire thought she was the cutest little girl, and admittedly, her biological clock would always tick a little louder when Ava was around.

"What's your name?" she asked the little girl.

"You call me Lucy." The child smiled up at her.

Happiness filled the air around her.

"I do?" she asked.

"Yes. You and my daddy."

"Claire," Max's voice rang from the walls as everything shook.

The child faded, and Claire woke in her nice warm bed with her husband snuggled next to her, his eyes still closed and his skin feeling soft and warm to her touch. Three months had passed since they married on that first sunny Saturday in June, and she still woke every morning grateful for where her life had taken her.

"You were talking in your sleep," he whispered.

"I was?" she asked, tears tickling her on their way down her cheeks.

"And you're crying?" he asked as he wiped away her tears.

"Holy shit! I was dreaming." She smiled.

"Did you think you weren't dreaming?" he asked.

"No," she said and sat up, looking half-astonished. "I had no idea. I was just dreaming. Like…a regular dream! Me!"

"Was it a good dream?" He had no idea what she was talking about, but the look on her face was pure joy. Her happiness was infectious, he smiled at her with the cute dimples she hoped their daughter would get.

"It was. I saw her, I met her, Max."

"Met who?"

"Lucy," Claire said.

She knew her daughter would be called Lucy. A sweet gesture to honor the friend she made with the downstairs neighbor who finally passed in the last remaining hours just before the New Year at the age of one-hundred and two. Claire hoped for the child-to-be the name would bring forth someone much like the young girl standing on the edge of time she once knew in a dream.

"How do you know?" he asked.

"Because she was there," Claire said as she rubbed her hand over baby yet to be. "Lucy. I felt it. I felt the connection, she found me in a dream."

Max thought of the night he woke in the hospital to find Claire by his side. His brain was slow to separate dreams from reality, with the doctors telling him he was most likely hearing things going on around him, but processing it in a weird dream state. He didn't think that was it, though, he couldn't shake the feeling that somehow Claire was with him. Somehow she pulled him through, and back to her.

Max sat up and laid his hand on her stomach.

"Lucy, you saw her?"

"I saw Ava. Remember that little girl who lived in the city?"

Max remembered the way Claire looked at the little girl more than he did the girl. She always had a dreamy look whenever she would watch the child play with Tilney at the park.

"Yes, I remember Ava."

"I saw her, because that's what I think of when I think of our little girl. Big brown bouncy curls, a sweet little voice and your eyes." Claire snuggled into her husband's arms.

"What were you doing?"

"We were having tea. It was such a sweet dream, the sweetest dream I've ever had. Max, it's her turn. Our little girl, she's already amazing. And strong. I wasn't with her, she was with me."

Believe in the unbelievable. As he listened to Claire talk, he couldn't help but remember her grandfather's words. Adelaide was the weirdest girl in the world, and Claire was just like her. Lucy would be, too. Warmth spread through his chest; he couldn't love his wife more. He could not love the child they waited for more. He would not change them, he would just believe.

"So does this mean that she can…"

"Yup," Claire answered before he could even finish his question.

"Already? She's just a peanut."

"An eight pound peanut who will be here any day now. She dreams, Max. She thinks. She hears. It's her time."

"How does that make you feel?"

"It's not so bad," Claire smiled as she looked around the quiet room. Her husband was next to her and two silly dogs on the floor at their feet. "When it leads you to the right people."

Claire closed her eyes, settled back in, and rubbed her stomach.

"I thought I would worry. So much I wasn't even sure if I wanted kids. I didn't realize nothing is set in stone. What was doesn't have to be. I can use what I know to guide her. The path I took doesn't have to be hers. My demons, they're nothing in her world."

A lump formed in Max's throat. When Claire told him she was pregnant, he waited for the fear to set in. He worried about the demons within the darkness. But being with his wife, and feeling the joy and happiness of impending fatherhood, he worried a little less with every passing day.

"She's happy, Max," Claire said as she knew what was going through his mind. "She feels safe and loved when you're around. That's never going to change. It's going to be wonderful," she whispered to Max.

"How can you be so sure?" He kissed her stomach before lying back down next to her.

"Because of you, and where I am right now. This new house. Charlotte, Aidan and little Owen Maxwell in their new house down the street. I have a house. I have a business, and real office space."

"You're welcome," he winked. The small retail space next his architecture firm opened up and they were quick to see about renting the space for Team Metis. With the addition of Jane's support and Max's already outstanding relationship with the building owner, they were able to get it.

"Thank you," she kissed him on the cheek. "Seriously, all of it. I have a husband. I have two silly dogs snoring away on the floor. I have a little girl that I cannot wait to meet. It's all taught me something."

"What's that?" he asked as he trailed a line of kisses down her cheek and onto her neck.

"Believe in the unbelievable."

About the Author

Alexa Jacobs is a member of local and national Romance Writers Associations. Her debut novel, *Rising Ridge*, was released in 2015. She resides with her husband and two sons in Maryland, and enjoys both the adventure found in travel and the contentment found at home.

For more information or to kindly leave a review please visit www.alexajacobs.com

Follow Alexa on Social Media:
Facebook, Twitter, Instagram & Pinterest
@booksbyalexa

Like Alexa's Author Page:
Facebook.com/alexajacobsbooks

For your reading pleasure, we invite you to visit our web bookstore

TORRID BOOKS

www.torridbooks.com

35443069R00148

Made in the USA
Middletown, DE
03 October 2016